PENGUIN BOOKS

BETHANY

Anita Mason was born in Bristol and read English at Oxford. She then worked in journalism and publishing, and at being a 'sixties dropout', before starting to write fiction. *Bethany*, which is her first novel, appeared to great critical acclaim in 1981 and was followed two years later by *The Illusionist*, which was short-listed for the 1983 Booker Prize. Her other novels include *The War Against Chaos*, *The Racket* and most recently *Angel*, which is published by Hamish Hamilton and forthcoming in Penguin.

Resident for many years in Cornwall, she now lives in Leeds, a city for which she developed a liking during a two-year Writer's Fellowship there.

ANITA MASON

———————

BETHANY

PENGUIN BOOKS

PENGUIN BOOKS

Published by the Penguin Group
Penguin Books Ltd, 27 Wrights Lane, London W8 5TZ, England
Penguin Books USA Inc., 375 Hudson Street, New York, New York 10014, USA
Penguin Books Australia Ltd, Ringwood, Victoria, Australia
Penguin Books Canada Ltd, 10 Alcorn Avenue, Toronto, Ontario, Canada M4V 3B2
Penguin Books (NZ) Ltd, 182–190 Wairau Road, Auckland 10, New Zealand

Penguin Books Ltd, Registered Offices: Harmondsworth, Middlesex, England

First published by Hamish Hamilton 1981
Published in Penguin Books 1994
1 3 5 7 9 10 8 6 4 2

I

THE BEAN-PATCH

I am right.

There was a time when I believed that rights and wrongs were relative, that there was no ethic based on a truth beyond challenge. Pressed, I would attempt a definition of right in terms of some temporal good, the good of the many. Pressed further, I would admit that this was Utilitarianism and had been seriously discredited by G. E. Moore, but I would ask, with what I thought was disarming honesty, what credible alternative there was. I was taking a course in philosophy at the time. I gave it up soon after I met Simon.

How pointless it all was, how shallow. And yet how hard it was to step out of that shallow pool where the children play, into the sea. How frightened we are that in that thundering immensity we will drown. Why has no one ever told us we are built to swim?

All we have to do is let go.

See, and understand. There is nothing hidden. There never was. All systems of knowledge are irrelevant. All systems of secret knowledge are not merely irrelevant but a fraud. The book of the universe is open. Every creature can read it, because every creature has written it.

An emerald-green insect lands on my knee and anchors itself with long fine legs to an airfield of blue denim. I curve my hand to shelter it from the breeze. It winks its strange eyes at me. Myself looking at myself.

I must not be complacent. Constant vigilance is essential. On either side of the true perception lies the old way of thinking, waiting like a bog to suck one down. One lie, one lie not pursued and purged can blind the eyes for ever. One evasion . . .

She looked at me almost pleadingly as I went into the kitchen. For a moment I felt a twinge at my heart, but I maintained my detachment and gave her a friendly smile.

It is difficult. But it is not too difficult. I have found that I have great strength, now that my mind is clear. After all, there is nearly forty years' evil to be undone. And however difficult it is, it must be done, because now I have started we shall both be destroyed if I do not finish the task.

God help me keep my clarity, and my love.

Love must be the motive, the only motive. All other motives are impure. Impure motive contaminates the deed, perverts its outcome, and damages the doer. Eyes narrow with self-interest cannot see the truth.

This is obvious and very hard to accept.

We chain ourselves with motives. We wriggle and creep to evade the true, the straight response, because that response will not gain us our ends. The words that do something are always preferred to the words that do nothing, the transparent words that purvey truth. The trick of lying becomes a habit, becomes a dreadful necessity, until the mind is stupid with the poisonous junk it cannot stop manufacturing.

But all you have to do is let go.

Then the peace. The bliss. The ease. One is almost weightless: one flies. One is almost immaterial: problems dissolve and

2

one slips through them. Carrying no luggage, one can roam the universe. Defenceless, one is invincible.

These things I discovered as I raked the bean-patch one warm May evening. It was the same patch I had been working on two days earlier, when they came and I refused to talk to them. I was afraid: I knew that if they came to live with us my life would be changed utterly. I thought I would lose everything. I was quite right, of course; what I didn't realise was how glad I would be to see it go.

So when they arrived, Alex being out, I made tea and polite conversation, and avoided Simon's questioning eyes. As soon as Alex returned – after all, it was she who'd invited them – I went off to the field again, and dug until my back and arms ached and my throat was like a sandpit. When I finally went back to the house they'd gone.

I was angry. Angry with them for coming, when they must know that I didn't want them there and should have known that Alex, having invited them, would change her mind, as she changed it about everything. Angry with them for their simplicity and their grave happiness. Angry with Simon, because I had hurt him.

Angry with Alex, who for the seventh summer in seven years was about to fill the house with people who would not understand about gates and animals and the Rayburn, and whose children would chase the poultry and shatter the quiet of the woodlands with their noise. Certainly it was Alex's house; but after seven years had I no rights in it at all?

And, obscurely, I was angry with myself.

Alex was quiet after their visit, but bright-eyed. It was obvious that having regretted inviting them that day – to the point of convincing herself that the invitation had not been accepted and she was free to go out – she had now returned to her original position. It was a familiar manoeuvre but one which for some reason I never foresaw. She had given up smoking, which I took as an ominous sign, and, even more ominously, was not bad-tempered. She was all sweet reason as I rolled a cigarette at coffee-time and fouled the kitchen with smoke. 'You don't have to give it up if you don't want to,' she said. She meant, 'You don't have to save your soul if you don't want to.'

I didn't. I was quite happy, thank you. Dabbling in farming, dabbling in writing, working for the local newspaper a few days every week since neither of the other two activities made anything but a loss; I was involved in the world and I liked it. I liked the company of sinners. I was at ease in that worldliest of places, a pub.

I was not at ease with Simon.

He was tall, lean, bronzed, and handsome in a particularly English way which the traces of his many years abroad – a beard with a hint of the Chinese mandarin, the suspicion of an American accent in the way he pronounced certain words – could not diminish. He wore jeans – much patched, but always clean – and sandals. He spoke softly, and when he spoke you listened. But when you met him all you saw were his eyes. They were bright blue, and they blazed. There was no avoiding them, and once you met them there was no avoiding the shock of recognition. For you had been looking for this man all your life. People look in different places: I had always looked in books. I put away my books, which had never told me anything. This man had the answer to the riddle.

Yet I fought him. He demanded too much. He demanded total honesty. That was painful. He demanded that one be prepared to think again, from scratch, about everything. That was a threat the magnitude of which could scarcely be comprehended. He demanded a level of thought which had not been required of me by one of the most eminent universities in Europe. He demanded an unswerving morality; and if there was one thing I hated it was morality.

Side by side, Alex and I, fascinated and fearful, we fought him. Side by side we ran out of arguments and excuses, and

4

faced our own moral and intellectual bankruptcy. Side by side we laughed and capitulated.

Until the next time.

He came to see us every few months, arriving without warning, but always after we'd been thinking about him. We would be appalled to see his car come up the drive, and exhausted by the time he left. Yet every time he came it seemed he teased out into the open and exploded some problem that had lain like a dull weight at the back of the mind for years. The effect was exhilarating, intoxicating. It was like having one's brain serviced by an expert mechanic.

The price was whichever of your illusions he fancied extracting that day. He dealt swiftly with my pet interest, literature. I shyly showed him my study: it was lined with books. 'Very nice,' he said, 'as long as you realise that they're all the same book.' It was a long time before I saw that room with his eyes.

I expounded to him my pleasure in working the land. He listened courteously and asked whether I did not think an unploughed field, with its diversity of flowers and grasses, insects and wild animals, to be more beautiful than a ploughed one. Reluctantly I agreed, and away went half my joy. People had to eat, I said. There was a banquet all around them, he said. He brought a hazelnut out of his pocket and, watching me, cracked and ate it. I remembered that the drive was strewn with them; they were so much smaller than the imported ones in the shops that we did not even bother to pick them up.

To my image of the farmer at one with the land, Simon opposed another – the farmer at war with the land. I could neither bear the personal implications of this nor unravel its global ones. I retreated to my study and consulted William Blake, a Roland for this Oliver. I came back in triumph.

'The cut worm forgives the plough,' I said. Clearly it had to, or life must stop.

Simon smiled at me. 'Is that what the worm says?' he asked.

No, I could not cope with Simon except in small and infrequent doses. And now Alex had invited him, his family and

5

the couple with whom they were staying, to come and spend the summer with us. They were all living in a small flat in the city twenty miles away. We had a large, almost empty house in the country. It was a fine, civilised idea. It was utterly intolerable. Hearing Alex make the suggestion, and ask them to tea in a few days to talk about it, I was seized first with incredulity and then with despair. She was a little incoherent, and for a moment the insane idea flashed into my mind that Simon had hypnotised her.

Two days after their abortive visit I had worked myself up into a fury of indignation. Really, what did Alex think she was playing at? It threatened to be by far the worst of her indiscretions. She had always been hasty and impulsive, ready with offers of help and hospitality which as often as not she regretted when the time to honour them came round. The first summer of our living together had been blessed with visits from an old friend of hers now teaching in Holland, his Dutch wife, their three scrubbed children and a discontented au pair, and from another friend in London, *his* wife, three children and Alsatian. The first set of children regarded me with cold contempt, knowing well that I disliked and feared the human young; the second set brawled, swung on the gates and dug penknives into the exquisite cherry-laurel tree in front of the house. The Alsatian fought our Airedale, and terrorised callers. Alex promised not to do it again, and did it again every single year.

In an unending stream they came: old friends, new acquaintances, ex-admirers (rarely ex-lovers – Alex had broken many hearts, but mostly by refusing), and lame ducks. The lamest were a family living on the caravan site a mile away. The man was, Alex told me, a most interesting person, and she was sure he had once known another friend of hers from Soho days. He had. Ridiculous coincidences happened to Alex daily.) The woman was Spanish, and there were the statutory three children. They were all living on Social Security in a tiny caravan. Before I could blink they had moved in.

Jacques was, it is true, interesting, but mainly by virtue of a past he could no longer support. Alex's hopeful eyes had detected the visionary in him and missed the alcoholic. He drank the contents of every scent and spirit bottle in the house, and beautiful Manuela shoplifted matter-of-factly for him at the off-licence. Jacques – who was not French, but vaguely Irish – lay in bed all day, covering the margins of a large hardback edition of the *I Ching* with small pencilled notes and periodically bellowing for Manuela. She cooked for all of us, and screamed in Spanish at the children. I hid alternately in the vegetable garden and my study. I cannot remember what Alex did, except that towards the end of their ten-week stay she accepted an invitation from a rich ex-admirer to spend a week in the south of France. While she was away Jacques got out of bed and went to London, where he renewed his acquaintance with heroin and rang Manuela up every night asking for help. I lay in bed listening to her frantic weeping. When Alex returned I issued an ultimatum, and the family left to stay with other friends elsewhere. A year later Jacques died of renal failure in a hospital in the city. Manuela survived, as she had to for her children, and casually introduced us to Simon.

I had forgiven Alex, but the episode had left a scar. I shied away from any suggestion of house-sharing or long-term guests as a horse shies at a corner where it was once frightened. I knew I could not go through that experience again. If anyone had asked me what the experience was, I would have described it as a kind of rape.

Over the years that I'd lived there, my sensibility had extended to penetrate every inch of the house and its surrounding acres. I felt it was the first real home I'd ever had: boarding school, university and a series of depressing bedsits in London had succeeded a childhood home so far distant that it might have belonged to someone else. But this place, this once gracious, now dilapidated house overlooking a tranquil valley, where five magnificent ornamental trees bore witness that the sloping pastures had once been parkland, where a grassy track

7

opposite the kitchen door led unexpectedly into woods, where a barn owl swooped nightly, whitely, along the hedge and buzzards reared their young in the same tree every year . . . oh this was a home not just for the body, but for the soul. Wrest it from me who dared, for my life-blood ran through it.

My passion was rendered fiercer by Alex's neglect. Alex loved Bethany, but in rather the same off-hand fashion as she loved me. She was a bit rough with both of us. She could not rest until she had remade the house. She started by taking the rendering off the front and having the stonework pointed. The appearance was much improved, but that wall, facing south-west, had been rendered for a very good reason – it took the whole brunt of the gales that swept in from the Atlantic – and no amount of pointing could henceforth keep the rain out. Then she had new windows put in the front, where the old frames, intricately patterned with small triangular panes, were rotting. If she had stopped there all might have been well, but she went on to change the pitch of the roof at its two ends to allow room for dormer windows along the east and west walls, knock down half a dozen non-structural walls inside, and eventually apply for planning consent to convert the west side of the house into a separate unit. Unfortunately she got it. Her relations with builders were stormy and in course of time she ran out of money, so that as I worked on my bean-patch that May evening the sun shone down on a black-felted, not a blue-slated roof, and the breeze played through unglazed window-frames and disturbed the sawdust on a half-boarded floor.

In between times Alex embarked on projects outside, the most striking of which was to be a paved patio area outside the kitchen door, with steps leading down to the drive. A vast quantity of concrete was hand-mixed by an unemployed lame duck from the caravan site, and Alex started to pave the thing. Something else caught her interest and she never finished it. Nettles colonised the bare patches, and dustbins and old pieces of cast iron collected on corners. Alex liked cast iron. One day she was going to melt it all down, and make our own knives and forks.

I loved her, and despaired.

I thought I understood the cause of it. Alex and her brother and sister had been brought up in somewhat unusual conditions. They had spent the greater part of their childhood in wooden shacks in a Hampshire forest, helping to hew wood, draw water from a well they had dug themselves, and clear the woodland for what later became a nudist colony run by their parents. The wonder and the insecurity of that half-wild childhood had never quite left Alex, and having worked hard for ten years in London to buy herself a proper house, she then set about reducing it to a wooden shack, since that was home. So at least I reasoned.

And yet none of these was the worst thing. The worst thing was so bad that I did not let myself think about it. It was that Alex, having tired, presumably, of playing such small games with her house, had staked it in a property gamble. That had not been the intention, but that was the result.

She had bought very cheaply, with money borrowed from her father, the freehold of a building in London on which she held a lease. She had intended to do the place up quickly and let it. It was a shrewd idea: the property was in a run-down area which was about to become smart. But a structural flaw requiring work on the foundations was found, and a property boom sent building costs rocketing, and Alex ran short of money. She approached the bank and negotiated a £10,000 loan on very little security. She had a way with bank managers. The money somehow disappeared without very much to show for it, since Alex, in an attempt to get the work done cheaply, had hired some self-employed builders who smoked pot all day and built nothing at all. In the end, having taken the roof off to build an extra storey, Alex found herself without the money to put it back on. Matters were not helped by the fact that the building, listed as being of architectural interest, was such an odd shape that it was unlikely that any design so far produced for the roof would be structurally sound in any case.

A number of things then happened at once. The property market collapsed, and Alex, attempting to sell the property to recoup, found that nobody wanted to buy a building without a roof. The architect resigned from the job when simultaneously his nerve broke and his wife left him. Alex found a new architect who turned out not only to be incompetent but to have an unhealthy interest in the amount of building materials the job involved, and refused to pay him. He sued. Alex counter-sued. The neighbour sued for damage to his harpsichords. A small-time gangster told Alex that he wanted the building for a pornographic bookshop and blue film club and would buy it at his price, failing which he would cut off her toes, and Alex, too incensed to feel fear, drank him under the table and consulted her young Jewish solicitor, who dialled a few numbers and got the gangster moved on by the local Mafia. Alex subsequently regretted this, since the gangster's offer was the best she ever got for the building.

The bank began to press for repayment of the loan, or at least a reduction of the interest, which was mounting alarmingly. Alex had no money, neither did I. The bank asked for Bethany to be offered as security. Alex bluffed, hedged, prevaricated, pretended not to hear, pretended not to understand ... and in the end signed a piece of paper. A ghost moved in to live with us.

As I raked the bean-patch, Alex's debt to the bank stood at £18,000 give or take a hundred or two. The only way of raising this sum was by sale of the London property which nobody wanted to buy, and in any case the debt probably now exceeded the property's value. If the money was not found within about a year, the bank would start pressing Alex to sell Bethany. What could I do? The capital sum was so far beyond my reach that it might as well have been a million, while even the weekly compound interest, multiplying like a cancer, was approximately twice my weekly earnings. The only person who could save the situation was the person who had caused it, but Alex, who could always see a perplexing number of sides to every question, was paralysed by indecision. Make an effort to get a roof on the building? Advertise it yet again as it stood? Apply for a change in planning permission? Make Bethany over to me, in hope that the bank could not take it? Or just skip the country?

'Oh, let's go to the pub': so these debates usually ended. Yet I felt that Alex could solve the problem if she really set her mind to it, and it sickened me to see it drift on, worsening a little every day, while she made plans for damming the stream to create a pool where we could grow water-chestnuts, or designed an improved geodesc dome, or went for drives round the countryside and came back with hundredweights of edible seaweed and irresistible pieces of cast iron. I would not have had her different. I just wished that once in a while she would earn some money. She was a very talented jeweller: she could have earned a lot.

I raked and smoothed, raked and smoothed. A bean-patch. Alex's idea. We would grow field beans, they required little care and would feed both us and the animals. I did not much like field beans and was fairly sure that Alex didn't either, but I supposed they would do for the dogs. I had marked out three large patches separated by grassy strips. They really were large patches – this was only the first one, and already I had spent several days on it. Alex had brought home half a hundred-weight of seed beans: we had to do something with them. It was typical of Alex: get an idea about growing something, buy ten times the amount of seed required, and leave me to sow it.

As I worked, my feelings of anger and hopelessness grew. Was I never to have any peace? Struggling always in the wake of Alex's impetuosity. She never seemed to struggle. She always did exactly what she felt like, and devil take anyone else. And now, having tossed around for twenty years on assorted seas of experience, she had finally sailed straight for the hurricane. She was going to open her house – my home – to a group of tee-total, non-smoking, love-thy-neighbour mystics who once they had moved in might never move out. After all, why should they? All places were the same to them, and the only time was the present. The concept that on such and such a date they would have to go back to the city was not likely to impress them as very meaningful.

I would have to share the solitude of the woods with them. I would have to explain about keeping the dogs in and the cats out and the goats tethered and the ponies calm, and why they must not waste water or use bleach, and why the water sometimes went orange although it was not dangerous, and why the children must not go into the ruined cottage because it was dangerous. I would have to say all these things because Alex never thought of anything, and they would look at me with the gentle incredulity that drove me mad. All this I would have to bear, and I would have to stop eating eggs. It was insufferable; it must be prevented. I slammed the rake down edgeways on a clod of earth with such force that it sprang up again violently and jarred my wrist. Suddenly I started to cry.

I don't quite know what happened. Tears are always the release of a greater sorrow than one knowingly feels, but these tears were for my whole life. They convulsed me. I laid my head on my arms on the low stone wall and disintegrated. Part of me assumed the role of cinema projectionist and exhibited me to myself. I observed my behaviour: cold, selfish and calculating. I noted my complete inability to feel love, compassion or even genuine interest in response to another human being. I saw my pitiful arrogance and the void it was founded on. I looked at my heart and saw that it was a mean and frightened thing. I saw the faces of the people I had hurt. I saw Alex, brave, lost, indomitable, haunted by a spiritual need that drove her to excess after excess, a seeker whose quest I blocked at every turn, while at every failure she grew more desperate and I more sure of my deadening power. And I said that I loved her! Cruellest of all, I had made her believe it.

12

Down that pit I fell, like Alice, slowly and with my eyes wide open. I could not stop the descent: something beyond me was forcing me down through every bitter level of my experience. Down, down, through the lies, betrayals and manipulations. Down through the utter aridity of a life lived only for self. Down to where, I wondered, for surely this despair could find its end only in death.

'Let go.' It was a whisper: Simon's voice in my head.

The descent stopped, then started again with a lurch. For I knew that I would not, and that it was because I would not that I was here weeping out my heart in a Cornish field, and that I had condemned myself most justly to the punishment of those who will not give up their misery. That is, their misery.

'Let go.'

'I can't.'

'Yes you can. These are all ideas. Let them go.'

A breath of hope stirred in me. Suppose I tried letting them go just a little bit, and saw what happened?

I suddenly had a vision of myself. A child standing on the seashore holding a cup of water. A child, its feet lapped by the waves, its ears filled with the roar of surf, fighting and screaming to retain sole possession of its tiny cup of water.

I raised my head and looked around me. I saw a world I had not known I could perceive. It must be the world that very young children see, before they are taught words to nail it down and kill it. But it was not seeing, because sight is of something outside oneself, and this world was not outside me. It enveloped me, it breathed through me. The dancing leaves of a tree fifty yards away brushed my skin. A bird sped into the sky and the ground fell away beneath me. The soft spears of grass tickled my feet through the soles of my boots. Life blazed and throbbed in ceaseless ferment everywhere I turned my gaze; life prodigal, inexhaustible, beyond comprehension, filling and creating the universe and perhaps other universes not to be imagined. This was my birthright. To claim it all I had to do was . . .

Humbly I wiped my face on my shirt and went to find Alex.

Strangely, as soon as I realised how desirable it was that Simon and his friends should come to Bethany, Alex began to exhibit signs of disquiet. She urged me to go and see Simon without delay, but her joy at my conversion was already clouding when I got into the car to drive to the city.

It was an extraordinary evening I spent there. Gently Simon talked me through my purgation; brilliantly he took up first one and then another of the things I had said, analysed them, and explored them with the relentless logic and daring intuition I had come to expect of him but which still left me breathless; finally, when I had followed him for three hours through these foothills without faltering, he took me by the hand and led me over mountain ranges of such height and splendour that at each step I thought I must fall, while at each step I climbed higher. Where I stood, at last, there was no thought, only perception which comprehended thought and all things. I knew that wherever I turned my eyes, I would understand completely. I knew that I would keep this pure perception as long, and only as long, as my heart was pure. I knew that I was nothing, and immortal.

I left late in the evening and drove home with care. Alex was sitting on the half-finished patio steps in the moonlight, waiting for me. I knew at once that something had changed, and changed for ever.

I had lived for seven years in Alex's shadow. I was content with this: I had no liking for limelight. She was the talker, she was the doer, even if what she did was not always easy to determine. Quick of brain, lively of interest, warm of heart, with a smattering of information about almost everything and a complete originality of thought (resulting largely from a complete lack of education), she shone like a star in the obscurity of the local pub. There the men, mostly labourers or unemployed, who had gone there most of their lives to get away from their womenfolk and discuss the best way of growing beans or building a hedge or picking a runner in the three-thirty, looked first with resentment, then with admiration, and finally with a fierce protective love at this slip of a woman, five foot four, who smoked cigars and bought her round, and drove a Thames truck as well as any of them, and had about her a gentleness which they had never seen in their wives. Their wives, of course, hated her.

I was sufficiently sure of my own worth not to resent being eclipsed by Alex's personality. In any case, I did not share Alex's conviction of the innate superiority of the working class, and I thought she was welcome to the spoils. With our London friends I did sometimes feel I had been edged into a subservient position, and I reacted either by competing or by silence, depending on my mood. But I knew that it was as much my fault as hers. She removed from me the odious responsibility of being sociable.

Inequalities of personality were aggravated by the fact that when we began to live together she had a house and a private income and I, having given up a job to leave London, had nothing at all. The psychological structure thus established persisted long after her income stopped and we were both living on my earnings. But in a sense these considerations were all superficial. Alex dominated, and I did not challenge her dominance however disastrous the results might be, because she had a rare and precious quality. I could not name it, but when I met her I knew that, having found it, I must never let it go.

It was like a candle-flame that, however near to guttering, never quite goes out. It was at once an innocence, a wisdom and a strength. I had seen her draw on it to cope with situations in which I was utterly at a loss: Jacques nihilistic and blaspheming, with Manuela weeping in terror and the children white-faced against the wall; Manuela's brother, black eyes burning, covering sheet after sheet of paper with pencil drawings of landscapes made out of faces, never looking up, never lifting the pencil, for six hours; gentle William, devastating in his lobotomised simplicity, asking after five minutes' acquaintance if he could sleep with her; crazy Caroline, squatting on the unswept floor in her Highbury flat, working out numbers, working out the number of the house added to the numerical value of the street name plus the postal district, divided by the numerical value of her own name reduced to a single figure, because if the answer came out exactly she would survive the night in that house.

Alcoholics, drug-addicts, schizophrenics, the lost and the damned – to all these people, from whom I drew back in fear because I could not begin to understand the darkness into which they had fallen, Alex found something to say. Across that terrible gulf she would lean and hold their hands, and they would look up for a moment and hope.

It was a kind of grace. It came, obviously, from God, whatever that meant. Thus I acknowledged that Alex, however irrational, inconsiderate, wilful and self-opinionated, was better than me, and better in a way that transcended my scale of values. She had the true gold, the spark, the spirit. I bowed to it.

And now I saw that I had been mistaken. Oh, it was there. But what a small, threatened thing it was, and how unsure of its way. How weak she was, this woman I had thought so strong. How puerile was the wisdom that held them spellbound in the pub. I knew; and, looking at me as I sat by her on the steps that night, she knew that I knew, and buried her face in my shoulder.

All next day, and the day after that, we talked. I realised with growing dismay that she was in grave spiritual danger. I could see the light and the darkness struggle within her as she half-answered, parried or evaded my questions, or tried to translate what I was saying into something more congenial. She did not want to see Simon: she was afraid, as I had been. Or, rather, the darkness was afraid. I told her there was nothing to fear, but the dark thing writhed and lashed its tail and glared at me, and I knew that it was beyond my powers to remove it. The best I could do would be to hold her hand while one wiser than I brought her out of the shadows.

I came home from work on the Monday and saw the

Humber parked under the laurel tree. They were all there: Simon, Dao, and their three little girls, and Pete, Coral and the baby.

'Kay!' said Coral and hugged me. Dao, luminous with smiles, placed her hands palm-to-palm and inclined her head above them in the Eastern greeting. I responded, less gracefully, but from a full heart. Simon and Alex were talking in the garden. It was going to be all right, I thought, as I made the tea.

We sat in the sun listening to the bees among the roses, and smiled at each other. Simon said it had been agreed that they should move in at the end of the week. He thought there should be a trial period, and asked for suggestions as to its length. No one volunteered a suggestion, so Simon said five months. We agreed.

As Simon talked, I realised that what he had in mind was far more than a friendly house-sharing, far more even than a conventional commune. He wished to find out whether there was a new way for people to live together. A way that did not involve private will; a way that broke down the barriers between people until the will of the individual and the will of the group were one. A way in which communication flowed freely between people, unimpeded by motives arising from the self, so that a thing was no sooner thought than it was said, no sooner said than it was done, no sooner done than it was dismissed from the mind so that the next thing could be dealt with. A way in which there were no lies, no evasions and no secrets. A way in which there was no dwelling on the past and no dreaming of the future, but only total awareness of the timeless present. It was an amazing conception. Dimly I glimpsed the sort of power such a group would have.

So that was why he wanted so long a trial period. With such an aim in view, there would be many problems to be overcome.

But what was he saying now?

'One sees that in this beautiful place there is something wrong. There is something not straight. It is like a broken limb.

When a limb is broken you put a splint on it to keep it straight. Something strong and straight is tied to something weak and crooked, until the weak thing grows strong. That is what we are going to do here.'

I had some difficulty in believing that he meant what he obviously had to mean. I glanced at Alex, who was smiling serenely. She doesn't understand, I thought. I felt protective, and for a moment indignant.

'A five-month splint. The Bethany splint.'

Well, it was what I wanted, wasn't it?

2

THE ARK

Simon, sipping his peppermint tea by the kitchen window, said, 'The group has been in existence for a week. Are there any suggestions?'

'Yes. Another week,' said Coral with a broad smile.

She looked blissfully happy, sitting on the floor feeding her baby. We had all taken to sitting on the floor. It was the only comfortable way six adults and three children could fit into the long, narrow kitchen at Bethany, and in any case there were never enough chairs in the house for visitors because of Alex's deep-rooted hostility to furniture.

Alex and I had never encouraged sitting on the floor because, trodden constantly by three dogs, the floor had never been very clean; but now it shone with a lustre we dimly remembered from years ago when the lino had just been laid. Unlike Alex and me, Coral and Dao did not regard the fact that a thing would immediately get dirty again as a good reason for not washing it. The whole house sparkled.

'It's very nice here,' said Coral in her American drawl, and then smiled again at the inadequacy of the statement. I studied the slim figure, in white shirt and faded jeans, resting easily against the wooden cupboard. The lazy brown eyes and sensuous mouth were full of gentleness as she looked down at the baby and cupped her breast to help him. It was difficult to imagine hardness in that face, but Coral had hinted that there were many things in her past that did not bear examination. She was, I thought, to a greater extent than any of us, a refugee. She had stopped running, now.

I glanced at the others. Pete. Immediately I experienced the slight withdrawal I was never quick enough to stop. I had tried to like Pete, I had catalogued to myself his virtues and tried to return his open smile with an equally open one of my own, but it was no use. Confronted by Pete, my heart did not open up to welcome him, it closed like a clam.

What was it? His appearance? The black beard, hairy chest, powerful arms? Yes, he repelled me, even slightly alarmed me, as did all very masculine men, but I knew that I could have forgiven Pete his abundance of hormones were it not for the two other qualities he combined with them: a level of intellect which I despised and an intuition I had to respect.

How these two qualities came to co-exist in the same person I could only explain by Pete's long association with Simon. Pete was a simple, straightforward man, ill-educated and not very articulate, but on this ordinary material had been superimposed something of Simon's extraordinary perception and Simon's wide-ranging knowledge. The result was a man capable of remarkable intuitions and well acquainted with Eastern thought, who was quite unable to express himself in terms that could be understood. Sometimes I listened to Pete trying to express an idea, and it was like listening to a peasant who had once, long ago, seen a wonderful thing in a dream. Yet, at other times I was not so sure. Simon, Dao and Coral seemed to understand without any trouble what he meant. I had even seen Alex engage in discussion with him when I could not make head or tail of what he was saying. So perhaps there was something wrong with me?

The disturbance this idea caused me largely accounted for my difficulties with Pete. Objectively I acknowledged him to be a kind, helpful and considerate man: inwardly, the moment I saw him I recoiled. Physical distaste, sexual antagonism, intellectual disdain: it was a potent mixture, I thought, and none of it to my credit. I resolved to try harder to like him. If I indulged it, my stupid egotism could wreak havoc here.

My eyes moved to Dao, sitting comfortably in the lotus position with her children arranged around her skirts. I thought I had never in my life seen a face so beautiful: so eloquent and yet so contained, so serious and yet so full of laughter. She was so beautiful, so serene, this tiny Oriental creature, that at first I had found myself almost tongue-tied in her presence and had been as conscious of the size of my feet and the loudness of my voice as an adolescent. After a week of daily contact I was still shy of her, and she knew it, and across the supper table her laughing eyes would seek out mine and silently accuse me of running away. I couldn't help it: simplicity always frightened me, and here were wisdom, simplicity and beauty together. It was too much. She made me feel worthless. She made me feel like a child. She made me feel what I was – a devious, superficial, ungenerous and utterly imperceptive Westerner.

Simon had met her in Thailand, when he was working there for the British Council and she was teaching English at Bangkok University. He had played the flute for her in her village, and they had fallen in love. She came back with him to England. Simon was already married, although estranged from his wife, but the problem of a passport for Dao was simply if imaginatively solved – she married a college friend of Simon's who was also working in Thailand and who handed her over to Simon immediately after the ceremony. I blinked when I heard this part of the story: it seemed less than perfect. I then rebuked myself for my prudishness: what business was it of mine, and

21

what difference did it make? Did I want Simon to be a saint? I also made due allowance for the source of the information. It came from Manuela, who retailed gossip with such style that one was hardly conscious that that was what it was.

Simon, Coral, Pete, Dao. And Alex. I looked at Alex. She was sitting cross-legged against the pine chest in which we kept Wellington boots, of which there were always an inexplicable number. She sat, small, neat and upright, smiling at her folded hands. It was obvious that in a period of heightened emotion I had greatly overestimated her problems: there could be nothing seriously wrong if that look of peace was on her face.

Simon, Dao, Pete, Coral, Alex and me. Quietly, by doing almost nothing, we were going to change the world.

The world was crooked. The world was corrupt. The world was cruel. These things we took as axiomatic. However, unlike most groups which have taken it upon themselves to judge the moral standards of their contemporaries, we did not assume that the evil could only be eradicated by divine intervention. We believed, as do Buddhists, that evil is suffering and can be avoided, and that the natural inclination of man is towards good, which is happiness. We would withdraw initially from the world, not because we feared defilement, but in order to resolve our own problems, the better to help the world.

'It's like dropping a pebble into a pond,' said Simon on the first evening. 'The ripples spread out. Every action sends out ripples. Thought sends out ripples. When I drop a pebble, I have no idea where those ripples will go. Bad thought, bad action, where the ripples start, and ten thousand miles away the ripples end with human beings setting fire to other human beings' children.'

If the people who rule the world could listen to this man, I thought, there could not be a Vietnam.

'So my thought, my action, must be pure,' continued Simon. 'If I do the right thing, the straight thing, there are no harmful ripples. In a sense I have not "done" anything: I have simply

22

made an appropriate response. Now, a group of people consistently behaving in that way would create, in this chaotic and crooked world, a little pocket of stillness and sanity, an area where, in the best sense, nothing happened. And perhaps the ripples of that stillness would spread. And in time, perhaps, the world itself would be changed.'

I stared at my feet, too moved, too dazzled by his vision to meet another person's eyes. There was silence in the room for a long time.

'Doing nothing' turned out, in the tradition of all the best paradoxes, to be very hard work. This was only to be expected, since it entailed breaking the habit of a lifetime. It involved, for a start, a transparent honesty in one's dealings with other people. Honesty not merely in telling the truth, but in refraining from the minor manipulations, evasions and insincerities that constitute probably nine-tenths of ordinary social intercourse. I found it at first a constant struggle to anticipate and repress these verbal manoeuvres which had become so natural to me that often I was not conscious of the deviousness of what I was saying until some time after I had said it. But gradually it became easier, and the direct replaced the indirect response as a habit. My self-awareness sharpened until I could spot, not just the false response before it was uttered, but the impulse to the response, and beyond that the tawdry chain of mental cause and effect that gave rise to it.

Stripping away in this manner all superfluous utterance, we often found ourselves with little to say to each other, and would sit for long periods in a contented silence that communed far more deeply than words. 'Silence is good,' remarked Simon one day. 'Whatever breaks that silence should be better than the silence it has come out of.' Visitors to the house of course did not understand why, if there was nothing to be said, we said nothing. They would endure our smiling silence in growing discomfort and embarrassment until they eventually left in a state of mind close to fear. I felt sorry for them, but knew that by not compromising we had provided them with a rare opportunity. If they were too frightened to take it, that was their *karma*.

'Doing nothing' meant not interfering with other creatures, except when absolutely necessary in their own interests. Thus one would rescue a drowning wasp but one would never shoo a bluebottle from the room. One would try to do as little damage as possible to the world one lived in. A certain minimum of damage was unavoidable: one could not walk without trampling on millions of invisible organisms, or drive without smashing insects on the windscreen. Nevertheless one walked with care, mindful of the ground before one's feet, and one went out in the car only when it was essential. Above all, one was very careful what one ate.

We were all, of course, vegetarian, although Alex and I had renounced meat only within the last couple of years since meeting Simon. I had done so grudgingly at first. It was all very well for Alex, I thought: she had been brought up on a vegetarian diet. I hadn't, and I liked meat. Why should I give it up? But I did give it up, mainly because it seemed ridiculous for two people living together, sharing everything else, not to share the same food.

Having given up meat, I found myself developing a revulsion for it. I perceived each cutlet, joint and kidney to be part of a corpse, and was sickened by the cruel machine which bred and killed, bred and killed, year after year, uncomplaining thousands of sad-eyed animals for a populace too rich and fat and greedy to know or care what it ate. I saw with loathing the red pulpiness of the butcher's hands, the veined face and dead eyes of the farmer, the pallid grossness of people who day after day crammed their mouths and bellies with other creatures' death. I heard with incredulity the lamentations over the rise in beef prices, as if the price paid by the housewife were more important than the price paid by the bullock. Editing, as part of my job, the cattle market reports for the local paper, I gripped my pen in fingers trembling with anger and disgust.

And every now and then, unable to resist the lure of depravity, I would buy myself a Cornish pasty for lunch.

It was usually a gesture of defiance against Alex, after some trivial domestic dispute in the course of which I had been manoeuvred into acquiescence. There is not much meat in a Cornish pasty, but there is enough to make a V-sign. Even as I did it I knew it was unfair, that Alex had never tried to make me give up meat and that I was blaming her for a choice I had freely made. Even as the rank flavour flooded my mouth I knew that I did not like meat and that I was defiling my mind and body for no purpose at all. It was a gesture of independence remarkable only for its perfect stupidity. I always returned to the fold greatly irritated with myself after such an indulgence.

The other members of the group had progressed far beyond this stage, if indeed – which I doubted – they had ever been subject to dietary lapses. Abstinence from meat they pushed to its logical extension of abstinence from eggs and all things made with eggs. Now it happened that a new-laid free-range egg, boiled for four minutes until the yolk was just firm and eaten with sea salt and freshly milled black pepper, was one of my greatest pleasures. Indeed I was apt to reflect sourly, in the times of simultaneous abstinence from alcohol, tobacco, meat and sexual activity which life with Alex occasionally imposed, that it was just about my only pleasure. Moreover, we had our own chickens, and they had just come into full lay. Every day I would go out to the orchard, open the flap of the laying box, and fill a bowl with warm brown speckled eggs. They were not fertile, because there was no cockerel. There had once been a cockerel, but he had strayed too near the woods at dusk and met a fox, and left only a draggle of feathers to tell the tale. Observing that the hens seemed if anything rather relieved by his departure, we had not replaced him. The eggs, then, were innocent of life: they contained no baby chickens. Eating them was not an act of murder.

I put this to Simon as we washed our plates one evening. He considered it carefully.

'It's a very strong argument,' he said. 'On rational grounds, I cannot answer it.'

I waited.

'However,' he said, 'perhaps there is another kind of answer. "The heart has its reasons, which reason does not understand." Would you accept that?'

It was absolutely fair. It was also a challenge. His blue eyes rested on me, to see if I would take it up. He was asking me to make an imaginative leap. No one outside the group, of course, would have accepted that answer for a moment. I examined it and saw its profundity.

'Yes,' I said. 'Yes, that will do.'

The eggs, uncollected, were eaten by rats until the discouraged hens ceased laying.

Non-interference went much further than abstention from involvement in the grosser forms of killing. Size means nothing. Therefore if it is wrong to kill a bullock for its meat, it is equally wrong to kill a caterpillar on a lettuce. Accordingly, before vegetables were picked from the kitchen garden any feeding insects were carefully removed from them first. Often it was impossible to do this without damaging the insect unless one removed part of the plant as well, and thus the lettuce leaves that appeared on the table were apt to be a very odd shape and full of holes. The process was time-consuming: sometimes Dao and Coral would spend well over an hour preparing enough lettuce-lattice for lunch. This, of course, was not important. And, as Coral pointed out, the insects had as much right to a meal as we had, and how unkind to deprive them of it when it was really quite easy to tear off a small piece of leaf. I wondered whether city-bred Coral would speak in quite the same way if she had herself dug the seed-bed, sown the seed, thinned and watered the seedlings and carefully, on a cool evening, transplanted the young lettuces. I regretted the thought immediately: it was not how one felt that mattered but what one did;

and personal knowledge of a thing often made one unfit to judge it.

A consciousness of the immense gulf between the things taken for granted by the group and the things taken for granted by the world outside sometimes made my head reel. Returning home from work one day I found Simon, Alex, Dao and Coral earnestly bending over a sack of flour with matchboxes in their hands. The flour had been given to Simon and Dao by a friendly baker whose gift had subsequently been found wanting: there were weevils in it. Simon, Alex, Dao and Coral were catching the weevils in matchboxes, and proposed to take them out into the woods with enough flour to ensure immediate survival. After that, it was up to the weevils.

I went outside quickly before my smile was seen. For a long time I wrestled alternately with my sense of humour and my sense of logic, trying to force them to come to an agreement. They would not, I simply could not bring them to occupy the same mental space. I still had not resolved the problem a week later, when Simon found me on the point of lighting a bonfire with a pile of rotten floorboards. He looked at one of the boards carefully.

'It has woodworm,' he said.

'Yes,' I said brightly. 'That's why I'm going to burn it.'

'But there is woodworm in it,' he said.

I opened my mouth, and shut it again as I understood.

'Some people think it matters,' said Simon. 'Some people don't.' He walked away smiling, leaving me to reconcile the two warring halves of my brain.

'Doing nothing' meant not taking away the freedom of other creatures. Simon's eyes dwelt on the dogs as he said this, and they wagged their tails at him hopefully. He clearly considered them to be living in a state of spiritual slavery, but he did not say so, perhaps because nothing could be done about it.

He questioned the rules Alex and I had formulated years ago concerning dogs: no dogs to be allowed in any part of the house other than the kitchen, and dogs always to be shut in the kitchen when anyone left by car. The reason for the first rule was, I thought, obvious. The reason for the second was that my small terrier, Hoppy, was car-fixated and likely to follow any departing vehicle down the drive and on to the main road. Simon, Dao, Pete and Coral listened smiling to our explanations and appeared not to believe a word. I could hardly blame them. Where is the slave-master who cannot justify his actions in terms of the well-being of his slaves? Nevertheless I could not repress a grin when later, after the door from the kitchen into the main part of the house had been repeatedly left open, Dao found something unexpected in her bed. It was the leg of a long-dead sheep. I realised that it was a gift, but I was alone in this perception. The kitchen door was henceforth kept shut.

The goats posed more of a problem. There were three of them, and they provided us with milk. If they were not to eat every vegetable in the garden and every fruit-tree in the orchard, and then go off and do the same thing to the neighbours, they had to be tethered. The alternative was to fence them in, which would be expensive, difficult, and by the group's standards just as undesirable. The question was debated in the first few days of the group's existence and no solution was found. From time to time we would return to it, as to an itching scab. It was no answer to sell or give the animals away, for their new owners would impose on them the same imprisonment as we did: there were no wild goats in England. What was more, their new owners would undoubtedly apply the principles of commercial goat-keeping and slaughter any billy-kids they might produce. It was an impasse. We had to compromise, and show our regret by tethering them on pasture as varied and interesting as possible.

Having admitted a temporary defeat over the goats, we passed on to the ponies. The ponies were Alex's province, as the goats were mine, and I was glad to leave them to her since with the dominant one, Bishop, I existed in a state of perpetual war. If he could step on my foot or knock over my milk bucket or nip the top out of a tree I had just planted he would do so, and sometimes he managed to do all three at once. I loved Osmond, the nervous, fine-featured grey, who would come to me even across the stream if I called; but I could do nothing with Osmond if Bishop had set his mind against it. But Bishop listened to Alex. They understood each other, and she rode him bareback with an indolent grace that brought my heart into my throat.

Well, there was to be no more riding, that was clear. One did not put a piece of steel into the mouth of another being and climb on its back. Alex, who never rode for pleasure but only when there was no other way of getting Bishop home (he liked to visit Mr Webb's stallion over the hill), raised no objection, but I could see that, like me, she was wondering how the freedom of the ponies could be reconciled with the comfort of the humans. The ponies at the moment were kept in a field they could not get out of, and for good reason. Bishop had a disconcerting habit of pushing open the kitchen door in the mornings: if you let him, he would come in to breakfast. He also liked to eat the roses in the garden, break the cold-frames on the patio and take the wing-mirrors off cars. I said all this, and wondered, not for the first time, why the truth always managed to sound so silly in my mouth.

'Suppose,' said Simon, 'we remove the cold frames from the patio, make sure that the gate into the garden is kept shut, repair the latch on the kitchen door, make do without a wing-mirror, and set the ponies free.'

I knew it wouldn't work, and knew it had to be tried. We agreed.

'Doing nothing' meant keeping things simple. It meant doing only what was necessary. It meant, for instance, painting a window-frame to protect it from rain, but not merely to change the colour-scheme. It meant cutting the lawn if you wanted to sit on it, and not cutting it if you didn't. It meant cultivating, fencing, repairing and building only when these things were necessary to survival or to basic comfort, or when, if neglected, they would in the long term create even more work.

29

This idea of Simon's, that the necessity for work should be constantly questioned and that there was virtue in actually avoiding it, was familiar to me from his earliest visits and I had always had the greatest difficulty in accepting it. For I worked very hard. I milked and tethered the goats and fed the chickens in the morning before I went to work, and when I came home in the evening I would work outside for as long as I could before bringing the goats in and milking them again. At weekends I dug, planted, cut and cleared, put up fences and pulled down ivy, burnt up dead wood and tried to move all Alex's cast iron to the same place. From time to time I did some freelance work for a publisher. When Simon, Dao, Coral and Pete moved in I had just edited the manuscript of a book and was half-way through checking the galleys.

'You work very hard,' said Simon to me on numerous occasions. I smiled. After a while I began to hear the question in his voice when he said it.

Why did I work so hard? 'Because there are a hundred and one things crying out to be done,' I said. My voice was a little high.

'Crying out?' repeated Simon gently. The fields shimmered in the sun, asking nothing.

I knew, and fought the knowledge. My work was an evasion, an excuse. It enabled me to avoid the moment of quietness when I must ask myself who I really was and what I should really be doing. In vain did Simon tell me, over and over again, that I did not have to give up any of my activities, that all I had to do was *see* what I was doing, after which I could freely decide whether I wanted to go on doing it. I was afraid I might find that I didn't, and then where would I be? Or, more precisely, who would I be? What was I, shorn of my occupations?

The question pressed more and more heavily upon me until one summer's day when, tormented by Simon's insistence that I confront this problem which I did not know how to confront, I walked out into the blazing sun and climbed to the top of the haystack to sit and think. The heat, the light, the sweet smell of hay, the clamour of birds and insects, overwhelmed me and the knot in my head loosened. In a cool, limpid dream, the self I had been avoiding for so long appeared before me. I noticed that, while unique, it was at the same time exactly like everyone else's. I also noticed that it was quite transparent and had no innate qualities. That meant, obviously, that it could choose to be or do whatever it liked, and whatever it did would have no more connection with it than clothes have with the body they conceal. The unimportance of all my preoccupations was thus graphically revealed to me, and I never took them very seriously again.

My moment of vision on the haystack had been a year ago. I had lapsed a little, of course, back into my neurotic need to be doing things, but something once understood is never quite lost again. So at least I was saying to myself one evening during the early days of the group, when Simon suddenly raised his eyes to mine and asked, 'Why do you have a job?'

I felt my eyes widen as if at a blow. Three or four days out of seven I went to work and came home, the only member of the group to leave it.

'I have to earn my living,' I said.

'There are other ways of earning a living,' said Simon. 'We have been discussing today, while you weren't here, ways in which the whole group could earn a living. Growing herbs was one. Moving furniture was another.'

Simon had bought the Thames truck from Alex because we couldn't afford to repair it for its M.O.T. test. Now apparently there were plans for using it for furniture moving. I wondered if Simon knew that this would involve changing the tax and insurance. He was curiously unworldly at times.

'I think they're both very good ideas,' I said. 'But they'll take time to set up, particularly the herbs. And meanwhile I have to earn a living.'

'Ah,' said Simon, smiling. 'Kay will not give up her job until there is another one waiting for her. What a pity.'

How unfair, I thought; and then, how true. I liked to think

of myself as adventurous, but it was a fantasy. I would never do anything without a safety-net. The sole exception had been my decision to come and live with Alex: and I had been trying to curb Alex's taste for adventure ever since.

But wasn't it unfair, all the same? Alex had a very small income from the rents of some jewellers' workshops in London: it just covered the mortgage payments on Bethany. For the rest we were dependent on my earnings, since Alex flatly refused to make any more jewellery for the commercial market. It was soul-destroying, she said, and as I did not feel that my soul was destroyed by working for the local paper (which was not of the scandal-rag variety but more like a cross between the *Farmer's Weekly* and a Women's Institute news sheet), I thought it reasonable that I should earn the money. It was not a bad job, and there were times when it was almost stimulating. It was, moreover, harmless. The *Cornish Gazette* might not publish very much of importance, but at least it published no lies.

The job was harmless and it was necessary: why should I feel so defensive about it? Partly, I supposed, because I still clung to the middle-class idea that to work was moral and not to work when one could work was somehow immoral. I mocked this idea in others; now Simon was making me aware that I subscribed to it myself. I was aware, too, of a slight tension in the air over the very question of earning one's living, for what did they – Simon, Dao, Pete and Coral – live on? Pete, when Alex and I met him, had been working in a draughtsman's office; I assumed he was now on the dole. What about Simon? Did he have a private income? Or did this strange, powerful, gifted man line up with the unemployed dockyard workers every week and sign on? If so, what did they make of him? And was it right?

And underneath all this confusion lurked something much more important. I glimpsed it for a moment, then it flicked away and out of sight. I would have to come back and look for it.

Dao said, 'Kay will give up her job when it is the day for her

32

to give it up,' and on that note of acceptance the matter was left.

Fortunately, with so many things left pending, there were a great many issues on which action could be taken at once. Food, for instance. Here, 'doing nothing' resolved itself in the principle that Dao did all the cooking. This was at her request. She said she was so accustomed to doing the cooking for four adults and three children that doing it for six adults and three children would make no difference. She was also afraid that the children would not eat food cooked by anyone else, and in that she was probably right. Dao's cooking defied imitation. Supper consisted usually of a rich bean and vegetable stew, aromatic with coriander and garlic, served with brown rice and Dao's freshly-baked wholemeal bread. Lunch was usually salad. For breakfast there was muesli, porridge and fruit. It was a very simple diet and completely satisfying.

We washed up our own plates, cups and cutlery – even the children did. There was no exemption. Often, two hours after a meal had finished, I would come across Lily, the dreamy three-year-old, standing on a chair at the kitchen sink, gazing raptly at a trickle of water descending on to a long-washed plate. This small act of washing up was an application of the principle that one never asked someone to do something that one could do oneself. It was also efficient, and efficiency was important because it reduced work.

In the interests of efficiency we decided to pay a visit to a nearby town where it was possible to buy wholefood in bulk. We squeezed into the Humber, arriving breathless and full of a childish excitement. It was the first time we had all been out into the world together – how would the world regard us? It appeared to be nonplussed. The people we spoke to were taken aback and a little unnerved by the degree to which we functioned as a unit, and by the way we found quite ordinary things irresistibly amusing. Dao, trying to explain to the man behind the counter what kind of beans she wanted, was laughing until the tears streamed down her face.

We, on the other hand, were greatly struck by the world's drabness in contrast to the light we felt within us and saw emanating from each other. How the eyes of these people shifted away from ours, how their voices spoke anger, disappointment, fear and loneliness, behind the parade of words. How thin their lives were, how tragically small their aspirations. They had shut up their souls in an airless room, the better to make their way in a world of illusion.

We ordered several hundredweight of assorted beans, lentils, flour and dried fruit, and went into the park and ate ice cream. I discovered, incredulously, an animal's drinking trough bearing an inscribed dedication to a Thai princess who had visited the town. It seemed a clear omen.

The following day I did some arithmetic and found that Alex's and my share of the food we had ordered came to a sum greater than I was likely to possess when it was delivered. Simon noticed my preoccupation and asked me what was the matter. I had not discussed our financial affairs with him because I had considered them to be a personal problem between Alex and myself. I decided, now, that they could not be kept private. Something so fundamental to the running of the house, and holding such power over my state of mind, affected the group and was the group's business.

I explained to Simon that the running costs of the house together with the payment of various long-standing bills stretched our financial resources to the limit, and involved me in budgeting so stringent that it was a perpetual tightrope act. I explained that this week, for instance, out of my £24 wages I had to pay a £12 instalment on a £60 bill for builders' materials; next week I would have to pay something off the rates; the week after that there was the H.P. instalment on the car; the week after that I had to toss up between the electricity and the telephone, both of which would be cut off if the bill was not paid. Meanwhile we owed £90 to a local builder for work on the roof, we had owed £25 to the coal merchant for so long he had started charging us interest, and in a few weeks we would need more oil for the Rayburn, which would mean another bill of £70. Both Alex and I owed money to the Inland Revenue, and next month the Mini Traveller had to be taxed. I added that Alex did not seem to understand these things and left them to me. I said that in view of this I hoped he would understand why I was rather concerned about my ability to pay for the food we had ordered.

Simon was silent for a while after I had finished. Then he said, 'The running expenses of the house will be shared. The rates, the telephone, the electricity and so on – we will divide up the cost between us.'

'That will help,' I said. 'It means the problem won't arise in future. But I'm afraid it doesn't solve my immediate problem, which is how to pay the costs we've already incurred.'

'We will share them,' said Simon. 'Since we have come to share this house, we will also share its debts.'

I stared at him. He was offering to pay for telephone calls he had never made, electricity he had never used, coal which had never warmed him. I couldn't accept, of course: yet I saw that I could reasonably ask them to share the rates, which were paid in advance, and also to share the rental part of the telephone bill which was payable in advance. In that case, and with the money saved on food and the little extravagances with which Alex and I were wont to distract ourselves from our penury, I would be able to start paying off the builder and perhaps even . . .

Simon was watching me. 'In some communities,' he said, 'a certain person is chosen to be responsible for a particular aspect of life in the community. It is efficient. Everyone knows who is responsible for that particular thing, and can go to that person for information or for a decision.'

'It sounds a bit like school,' I said.

'Didn't you like your school?'

'I didn't like that part of it.'

'It is a question of whether one prefers chaos or order,' he said.

I grinned. 'I don't much like chaos, but I'm used to it,' I said. 'Perfect order repels me. I have a temperamental bias against it.'

'You'll enjoy it,' said Simon. While I digested this he added, 'I consider that the group needs a Bursar. I nominate you.'

Thus I, who could never add up a column of figures twice and get the same answer, became responsible for the group's finances. And thus the group became an organised entity. For Simon, having embarked on an idea, would always pursue it to its logical conclusion, and the logical conclusion of my becoming Bursar was that we should all become something.

I returned from work the following day to find that Alex had become the Farmer, Coral had become the Housekeeper, and Pete, who in the space of a week had already repaired the plumbing, the truck, and installed a new sink in the kitchen, had become the Maintenance Man. Dao of course was already Cook. Simon, at the centre of these activities, co-ordinating, advising, smoothing over difficulties, exposing and eliminating problems, chose for himself the title of Organiser.

The possession of a title did not mean that one had to do all the work the title implied, but merely that one was responsible for seeing that the work was done. For instance, we all helped with the housework, each taking a certain part of the house to clean every morning before breakfast, but Coral as House-keeper was responsible for seeing that no corners were neglected, that there were always enough dusters, and so on. Alex, as Farmer, was responsible for overall farming strategy and for checking that fences, gates and tools were in good repair.

My job as Bursar involved, initially, calculating the weekly running costs of the house and then, at meetings to be held every Thursday evening, collecting this amount from the group and ensuring that the week's expenditure was evenly borne. From the money collected for running expenses I paid bills as they became due. Proposals for major items of group expenditure were put to me for my approval, and I was supposed to see that we did not overspend. I was puzzled as to how I could perform this last duty without knowing what the group's combined income was, but while I was quite prepared to reveal my own income I met only an uncomprehending smile from Simon when I eventually put the matter to him, so I dropped the subject and assumed that I had somehow misunderstood him.

I had expected that we would split the costs three ways, taking Simon and Dao as one unit, Pete and Coral as another, and Alex and myself as the third. I was surprised to hear Simon say at the end of the first Thursday meeting that he thought there should be four paying units, myself and Alex being considered separately. Dao was surprised, too. She shook her head vigorously, without ceasing to smile.

'What I see,' she said, pointing round the room where we happened to be sitting in pairs, 'is there are two eating, and two eating and two eating.'

'That is not the correct way to look at it,' said Simon. 'It is a question of whether people are able to contribute.'

'But Alex hasn't got any money,' I said. 'The only money she earns pays the mortgage, and that's a contribution in itself.'

'Yes, but we pay the rent for the flat,' said Pete. 'If the mortgage is going to be counted, that ought to be counted as well.'

They had decided to keep the flat on and not sub-let it. It seemed extraordinary to me that Pete should place the flat, which they weren't living in and which was therefore an unnecessary expense, on the same level as the house, which they were living in and which was a necessary expense; but on the other hand if they relinquished the flat and the group experiment did not turn out well . . . I found myself in an unpleasant quicksand and withdrew, a little confused.

Alex put an end to the debate by saying that she was not able to make regular contributions, but she did sometimes have some money and would contribute when she could. That seemed to satisfy everyone.

Since the group was in every sense a new beginning, it was obvious that the house in which we lived should also be, as it were, made new. Obvious as it was, its necessity escaped me at first, and I watched with astonishment and some pain as, one by one, each room of my home was utterly transformed. Furniture was moved, or pressed into unfamiliar use; walls changed colour, floors changed carpets, ancient and venerable armchairs acquired bright and perky cushions. It seemed to be change for the sake of change – and so of course it was. A new way of life could not take root in old soil.

After the first shock had subsided I realised that my hankering for the familiar was a hankering for a dead past. I joined exuberantly in what had become a kind of festival. It was exhilarating to be in a house that hummed with activity and sparkled with cleanliness, where the windows, the brass doorhandles and the slate flagstones all shone as they had not done for years. It was a joy to be in a house that resounded with laughter, and was now being cared for as Alex and I had never been able to care for it.

We threw away everything for which there was no use – clothes that were never worn, books that were never read, implements that were never used, broken electrical appliances that only required a minor repair but had never been repaired because there was no need for them . . . all the accumulated junk of seven years. Alex and I flung ourselves into the task with a relish that at times bordered on hysteria, and laughed helplessly at the expressions that greeted some of our more extraordinary treasures. How could we explain to these rational people why the garage, instead of housing a car, housed a broken harmonium, part of a marble fireplace, three hundred Victorian glass bottles without stoppers, a box of old woodworking planes, twenty feet of cast iron railings, a forty-year-old motor mower, a 1914 jeweller's catalogue and six incomplete Cornish ranges?

I made it clear that the throwing-away would not extend beyond the big double doors to the contents of my study, since there was nothing in there that would not, sooner or later, be necessary to my work. Even so, looking around the room, I was able to pick out half a dozen books I had never liked, and dump them on the rubbish pile.

As room after room emerged in fresh guise it sometimes became appropriate to re-name them. The first one to be christened was the large front room in which we held our meetings and often sat and talked in the evening. It was a splendid, spacious room with a lovely curved wall in which was set a french window looking over the valley. Alex and I had always called it simply 'the front room'. Simon asked for suggestions for a new name.

'I suppose we could call it anything,' I said. 'Well, almost anything. I don't think we could call it the parlour.'

Simon thought for a moment. He said, 'I propose that we call it the parlour.'

I looked quickly at him. No, it was not a rebuke.

'The word means a place where people talk,' he explained to the others.

'It has connotations of lace curtains, and parrots, and anti-macassars, and long Sunday afternoons when nobody talks to anybody,' I objected.

'Then,' said Simon, 'we shall change the connotations of the word "parlour".'

After a few days it seemed remarkable that we had ever called it anything else.

The house was physically renewed, the people in it had been spiritually renewed. There burned in all of us a desire to renew the world. Perhaps subconsciously we felt there was an element missing. It was supplied by Alex.

One evening after supper Alex made reference to some recent prophecy that the industrialised world was heading for imminent disaster. 1975 would be remembered as the last summer of peace, she said. Alex was fond of quoting such prophecies, which ranged from economic collapse to global extinction, and as the years passed and the dates fixed for these catastrophes elapsed without incident her faith in them was by no means diminished. I connected this faith with her refusal to accept the Darwinian theory of evolution and her obstinate belief that the ancient history of the world had been concocted by a conspiracy of academics on the basis of a few mis-dated fossils. I dismissed the whole ragbag as the errancy of an undisciplined mind which had never troubled to read a serious history book, and from time to time we would quarrel bitterly over some obscure matter of archaeology far beyond the competence of either of us to determine, while I raged at her denial of reason, and she raged at my contempt.

In the past few weeks I had come to accept that I had been wrong in many things, and I had certainly never listened to Alex's wilder ideas with as much courtesy and open-mindedness as I did now. Nonetheless I was surprised by the alacrity with which Simon took up the point – almost as if he had been waiting for it.

'The industrialised world is coming to an end,' he said slowly. 'Yes, of course. One sees it everywhere. There is a kind of madness. But it is not only the developed countries, is it?'

He looked at Dao, and their eyes communicated a shared vision: Thailand, Cambodia, Laos, Vietnam. The fleeing peasants, the mutilated children, the chaos, the cruelty, the pervasive evil that was the same, whatever its guise, in every country. The evil that lived like a tapeworm in the mind of man.

'It is the whole world,' said Simon. 'The whole world is coming to an end.'

And we were the Ark.

3

ESTHER

Esther was dying.

She was eight, no more than middle age for an Airedale. It was cancer.

From time to time there seemed to be a slight improvement, and we allowed ourselves to hope: to hope that the second lump that had appeared on the lower part of her belly was not malignant, that the herbs Alex gathered for her daily in the hedgerows were working. Often, day by day, she seemed to be making progress. But looking back over the weeks we knew she was not.

Esther was irreplaceable. She was more than a dog: she was a gentle, humorous spirit sent to be a companion to human beings who did not deserve such straightforward affection. Generous, forgiving, she seemed to me to embody the spirit of Bethany, and I felt that when she died something of the place would die too: a special, lowly innocence.

Even Simon, who, while insisting that animals be respected, made it clear that they were not to be regarded as equals, recognised Esther's quality. He described her as a 'mature dog', meaning that she had developed to the limits of her nature. He inclined to the view that in her previous incarnation she had been human. The other members of the group also seemed to believe this – certainly Alex did. I did not. For one thing, try as I might I had never been easy with the doctrine of reincarnation: I found it intellectually repugnant. For another, if Esther had been a human being and was now a dog, presumably she had committed some very bad sins in her previous existence to merit this demotion, and I was sure that Esther's soul was unspotted. I also failed to see why one should assume that a bad human being would make a good dog. Surely a soul that made a bad job of being human would be likely to make a bad job of anything?

Esther bore her pain with dignity. Alex and I had decided, as soon as the first lump manifested itself, that having her 'put down' was out of the question. We had taken that decision in principle years earlier when two of our kid goats, clumsily de-horned by the vet, had suffered brain damage resulting in a gradual twisting-round of the neck. The spectacle was grotesque and evoked extreme reactions in visitors, who could not understand why we had not had the animals killed as soon as it began to happen. It was clear to Alex and me that the visitors were far more concerned with their own emotions than they were with the kids, about whom they had made the unexamined assumption that they were suffering so much they would rather be dead. Alex and I were not at all sure the kids were suffering, and even if they were, was death necessarily better than pain? How much did pain matter? How much did life matter? It seemed to us that no human could answer these questions, and that the average human, confronted by these deformed goats, would kill them because he could not bear the sight of them, and would call it pity.

We refused to do it. We helped the kids to feed, and waited until the day when they could no longer do anything at all to feed themselves. On that day, since they had ceased to be viable organisms, we called in the vet with a humane killer. For some time afterwards we suffered strange looks from people we knew.

We felt we had done our best to handle correctly a situation in which we had been at fault in the first place. We should not have had the kids de-horned. Henceforth, we vowed, no vet should set foot on the premises; if any disease arose among the animals, we would treat it herbally. However, we had reckoned without Esther. When an animal shows clear signs of a malignant growth, for which there is no known natural cure, what do you do?

We took her to a young vet whom we trusted: he had not been practising long, but was capable and compassionate. Or, rather, I took her. Alex had gone to London. I went home in my lunch-hour and took Esther to the surgery, and collected her at half-past five after the operation. Poor Esther. Barely conscious, drugged, shocked and sick, she opened her eyes as I entered the room and her tail thumped once on the floor. I carried her in a blanket into the back of the Mini and took her home. It was difficult, on my own, getting her out of the car, carrying her up the steps and into the kitchen and putting her down, all without altering the position of the hind legs, but I managed it. When Alex phoned that evening I was able to tell her that Esther had come through the operation well and was asleep in her usual corner.

Six weeks later, when Esther had apparently made a full recovery and was running about with the other dogs, we discovered the second lump. We knew then that she would die. There was no question of further surgery – she would not survive it, and in any case it seemed obscene to go on cutting parts out of an ageing animal. We did what we could to make her last days more comfortable, without relaxing the strict diet we kept her on in the hope that nature might still effect a last-minute cure. Alex, having recently read that violets had been known to cure cancer, searched for and picked them every evening and fed them to her. Gradually she declined, until she could only walk with the greatest difficulty.

The shift, subtle but unmistakable, into the last phase occurred about ten days after the group had been formed, and on that day Alex and I moved Esther into our bedroom. She lay on her blanket, patiently waiting. At intervals Alex would carry her outside so she did not foul her blanket. Simon watched, but said nothing.

The house was shipshape, we turned our attention to the land. Almost overnight, it seemed to me, the monster I had loved and struggled with became tame and obedient to command. Plants were hoed and thinned, seedlings were planted out, weeds were cut before they seeded instead of a week afterwards, little things I had always meant to do were done when I got home from work, big things I had never hoped to do became a real possibility. There was order. The plants glowed with health and pleasure. I wondered how I could ever have thought a solitary battle with fourteen acres preferable to the rewards of co-operation.

Alex was finding the same thing. I was well used to the spectacle of Alex, begrimed and oil-stained, emerging from underneath an ailing vehicle, cursing because she had been able to diagnose the fault but did not have the tools to correct it. This would not prevent her from trying, and I kept out of the way on those occasions because her wrath over a recalcitrant nut was apt to descend on anything in the vicinity which moved. But now it was Pete who lay on his back under the truck, while she passed him tools and made tactful suggestions, and gave me, as I passed, a grin which I perfectly understood.

The new sink was functioning, the Flymo worked, the truck could now be used for getting in the hay crop, and there was an acre under intensive cultivation. Soon we would start on the major tasks. One of the first was repairing the roof of the red barn. A gale had ripped off three of the galvanised sheets and dislodged one of the rafters: replacing it, while perched on a ladder, was far beyond the combined strength Alex and I possessed. And beyond that loomed the most formidable job of all: rebuilding the end of the house. Perhaps they would not want to undertake it. Yet if the group were serious in its aims the house must be completed. Not only for us, but for anyone else who, seeing the approaching deluge, sought shelter.

In the evenings we rested from our labours and talked. We would sit in the parlour, and if it was chilly there would be a log fire in the big fireplace. Simon would light some joss sticks and the air would be heady with incense. I had to overcome an initial prejudice against joss sticks, which I had always found to perfume the houses of habitual pot-smokers, and which I associated with the mental flabbiness that seems to accompany prolonged use of cannabis. In Simon's company the association rapidly weakened and I found myself enjoying the heavy scent. If no one else was in the room I would go up and sniff the blue smoke that curled from the glowing tip of the stick. I realised as I did so how much my lungs still craved tobacco. The smoke made me lightheaded: it seemed to be able to affect my state of mind. I wondered briefly whether it might be addictive.

Those early summer evenings we sat and talked about all manner of things. Having a taste for the abstract I was naturally more pleased when the conversation turned to metaphysics than when it revolved around the morality of daily life; but Simon, whose deft handling of abstruse concepts was beautiful to witness, regarded such speculation as unimportant and considered my interest in it slightly reprehensible. Indeed he once expressed himself very strongly on the subject, saying that I had the Faustus complex and was very fortunate in not being as clever as I would like to be, because that intellect allied to my lack of innocence would destroy me.

I was hurt by this aspersion on my intelligence, and was thereby forced to acknowledge the truth of what he said.

He also implied that my approach was not serious.

'You are quite happy to discuss any subject under the sun,' he said mildly to me. 'You will sit here in the evening and examine it from all aspects and pursue all its implications, and in the morning you will go off to work as if nothing had happened.'

It was damning. I struggled with it, and abandoned the struggle. I could not give up my job: not yet. The time would come.

The evening talks gradually became less frequent, until often a week would go by in which the only time we had all met in the parlour had been for the finance meeting. Part of the reason was that we began to find we had a lot to do in the evenings. Part was that Simon felt he should talk to us individually.

It began at the end of the first week. Simon suggested that as he had recently spent a great deal of time with Pete and Coral it might be a good idea if Alex and I, who had seen less of him, spent a couple of hours a week in personal discussion with him. My pleasure at the prospect of an hour's uninterrupted conversation with Simon was alloyed by the nervous suspicion that I would have to choose what to talk about.

The first conversation was revealing. I decided he wanted me to talk about a problem, and cast desperately about for one, finally coming up with my ambivalent attitude towards the room we were sitting in – my study. I thought it might prove an interesting line of enquiry, encompassing my difficulties in reconciling my academic leanings, which the bookshelves around the walls represented, with the way of life represented by Simon.

The opening did not lead where I expected it to. With Simon nothing ever did. He remarked casually that one never is happy in a room in which one has done bad things. This gave me a severe jolt. I had indeed done bad things in that room. I had killed bluebottles when they blundered infuriatingly round me as I was trying to write. The room was full of my anger and guilt. Too disconcerted to launch into the self-analysis I had envisaged, I found myself surprised into following quite a different tack, which led me, through half an hour's reluctant introspection, to a most unwelcome conclusion.

This was that for years I had been as unjust in my relations with Alex as I had always believed her to be with me. I undervalued what she had done for me: I saw the imperfection of the deed and not the generosity that inspired it. My study summed it up. When I first came to live with Alex, she had panelled and painted the walls of this room for me, and had brought down from London a second-hand filing cabinet which she had had re-sprayed for my use. But, being Alex, she had not quite finished the panelling on the walls – there was a small gap in the corner which required a board to be split, and she had never got round to it – and in the course of transporting the filing cabinet she had lost the handle and part of the sliding gear for one of the drawers so that it hung lopsided and could not be used. For years these things, neither of which I could rectify, had irritated me, and in the end had caused me more irritation than the gift had given me pleasure; and the more projects Alex undertook and left unfinished, each bequeathing its toll of junk in the garage and unpaid bills in the kitchen, the more the gap in the panelling and the lopsided drawer of the filing cabinet became a focus for my discontent. Thus her gift, springing from love, had turned sour because my own love was lacking. No wonder I was ambivalent about the room: it condemned me.

I thanked Simon and went to find Alex, who was working in the vegetable garden. I told her I had been unjust to her, and was sorry. She gave me a delighted smile. We had a long talk as we hoed the onions, and went into lunch holding hands like new lovers.

After Alex and I had had two or three talks apiece with Simon, Pete and Coral asked if they could have talks with Simon too. Simon smiled wryly, and arranged a timetable, which he wrote in the desk diary we kept in the parlour. We found the talks so beneficial that they became a daily feature. This took a considerable bite out of Simon's time, but he did not place any value on his own time. He only wished it to be well spent.

The daily talks had been continuing for about a week when their nature changed. This happened as the result of an experiment initiated by Simon, which was itself the outcome of a conversation we had before the group was formed.

We were sitting in Pete and Coral's flat. We had been talking for several hours when reference was made to a quasi-religious organisation which had a centre in the city, members of which were periodically to be seen touting on street corners for people to come and take one of their free 'personality tests'. I had once done so as a reporting assignment for the newspaper, without of course revealing my identity. The experience had been exactly what I expected: a questionnaire which asked ill-disguised leading questions; a bookshop in which one was pressed to buy as one waited for the results of the 'test'; a 'diagnosis' from the questionnaire which indicated that one should take a course at the centre in order to improve the quality of one's life. I went home and wrote a smug article on this money-oriented, fake-psychology-peddling cult. It was the same article the British press had been serving up for years. In a corner of my mind I was a little ashamed. It was too easy. There must be more to them than that.

And yet when the organisation was mentioned that evening two years later I dropped instantly into the same position of ridicule and dismissed them as charlatans. Simon looked at me with faint surprise.

'I've been to their centre and talked to them,' he said. 'They struck me as very energetic young people who would like to make the world a better place. Their eyes are bright, as if they have come through a difficult experience.'

I looked at the floor and blushed. It was true, but I had chosen not to see it. Their eyes had been bright. Not as bright as Simon's, but bright enough. Whether it was the glitter of delusion or the light of truth how could I tell, when I had not troubled to find out the first thing about them?

Simon then proceeded to talk about them, or rather about the idea on which their theory of psychology was based. Their

48

founder had discovered, he said, that in all human beings there existed a time-track on which was recorded everything that had ever happened to that person. It was analogous to the data-banks of a computer. All past experience was stored on the track, and all of it was accessible to consciousness, though sometimes only with difficulty. To regain an incident from the past all one had to do was command the mind to 'go back' to the incident and let it replay itself, which it would do with absolute fidelity. It was a process quite different from remembering; it was something everybody could do, and few knew about.

On most people's time-track there were gaps, said Simon. These occurred where the person had been unconscious, or when the incident was so painful, mentally or physically, that the mind had apparently obliterated it. Nevertheless these incidents were recorded, but they were stored in a hidden area of the mind from which they emerged at intervals when circumstances resembling the original incident occurred. At such moments the individual would find himself acting in an irrational way under a compulsion he did not understand. Some people's behaviour was almost entirely controlled by such compulsions. There was a way of ending the mechanism: one followed up the clues until one found what appeared to be the gap, and then one made the person go through the experience over and over again, until it was fully recalled and had lost its content of pain and its power to compel. This processing was the main technique employed by the organisation, and was carried out according to a strict formula by people trained for the purpose.

I was fascinated and repelled by this exposition. As a one-time devotee of science-fiction I was much taken with the idea of a sort of personal tape-recording, but the therapeutic application of it had a mechanistic ring I disliked, and the whole concept seemed to lean heavily on Freud while decrying psychoanalysis. I knew that Simon had no prejudices and was willing to take ideas from any source if he thought he could use them, but I was surprised that he should find this worthy of his attention. The jargon in which the technique appeared to be wrapped added further to my hostility. I gave the matter no further thought.

About a month after that conversation, and a fortnight after the start of the group, there was a telephone call for me at Bethany when, in common with nearly everyone else, I was outside in the fields. It was evening and the call was answered by Coral, who had not been feeling well and was resting upstairs. Simon, Pete and I came into the kitchen together to be greeted by a white-faced Coral with the words, 'There's been a horrible man on the phone.'

She turned to me, almost with entreaty. 'He said his name was Maurice and he was a friend of Kay's. Kay, who is he?'

I saw the whole ghastly situation in a flash and saw that there was no way of explaining it. Maurice was, indeed, a rather unpleasant character, particularly when he had been drinking, but on the basis of six years' acquaintance he was undoubtedly entitled to call himself a friend of mine. He was a strange man who had led a roving life, mostly as a diamond prospector in various parts of Africa, and he had now, at the age of sixty, settled in Cornwall to prospect for copper and change his sex. It was such an extraordinary combination that Alex had persuaded me to ghost-write his autobiography, which I did with increasing unwillingness as he became increasingly awkward, cantankerous and obsessed with himself. The confusion over his gender had naturally set up confusions over his sexual orientation, and he attempted to release the resultant tensions in a never-ending stream of sexual innuendo, suggestive laughter, and undisguised aggression. Yes, Maurice was tiresome. However, I thought a woman with any worldly experience at all should have had no trouble in dealing with him on the telephone. Coral was obviously more vulnerable than I had thought.

What concerned me most, I realised with shame afterwards, was my own image. Whatever Maurice had said to Coral had evidently given her the not unreasonable impression that he was a dirty old man, and why was such a person claiming friendship with a member of this very clean group? I knew I could never explain to them the split between my professional identity as a ghost-writer and my real identity as a member of the group. They would not believe such a split could exist, and perhaps they were right. Yet I must make some attempt, or to my known homosexuality, which I had always assumed they regarded as unimportant, they would add a presumed complicity with whatever this frustrated old man represented, and would arrive at the conclusion that I was sexually decadent.

I launched into an anxious speech but Simon cut me short. He asked Coral to tell us exactly what had happened, but Coral was almost incoherent. Pete tried ineffectually to comfort her.

Simon said, 'Shall we try an experiment?'

He made us sit down: we had been standing in a tense huddle by the door. Coral knelt on the floor, sitting back on her heels.

Simon said to her, 'Close your eyes. Now, go back to the beginning of the incident.'

Coral shut her eyes and concentrated.

Simon said, 'Are you there?'

'Yes,' said Coral.

'Where are you?' asked Simon.

'I'm . . . lying on my bed,' said Coral. 'I've just woken up. I've been woken up by the phone ringing.'

'Go through the incident until you come to the end,' said Simon.

Hesitantly at first, she did. At one point, when she had completely misinterpreted the meaning of something Maurice had said, I opened my mouth to interrupt, but Simon instantly silenced me with a movement of his hand.

None of us spoke or moved as Coral finished recounting the incident. She looked strained and distressed. Simon told her to go back to the beginning and go through it again. The second version was different: she remembered much more. She remembered, for a start, that she had been anxious about something – the baby – even before she'd answered the phone. In the third telling her tension rose to a peak and she covered her face with her hands and shuddered violently. The fourth time the tension had gone out of it: she seemed rather bored by the whole thing, and as she got to the end she laughed.

'Well, that's it,' she said, and spread her hands in humorous apology for making such a fuss. She was clear-eyed.

Simon observed her. 'Good,' he said calmly.

After Pete and Coral had gone to bed, Simon said to me, 'I'm sorry I had to stop you when Coral was talking, but I had no choice. You must never try to change someone else's data. Never. It is very dangerous. Do you understand?'

'Yes,' I said, rather blankly but at any rate glad that I had not incurred his displeasure. It wasn't true, though. I did not understand. I never did understand why one must not try to change another person's data, if the data are wrong.

We sat in the parlour, Simon, Alex, Pete and I. It was late, past ten o'clock. Dao and Coral had gone to bed. We were all usually in bed before this, because we got up well before seven. We four had not gone to bed because something important was happening. Pete and Alex were talking, and Simon and I were listening to them.

It was important because Pete and Alex did not talk to each other much, and there had been a time, a year ago, when there was something like open hostility between them. That of course had long since been resolved, but there remained a certain reserve between them which, while it could quite easily be breached, usually was not. This evening they were both trying very hard to communicate. It was difficult because of their residual resistance to each other, because of the abstract nature of the ideas they were discussing, and because Pete was so inarticulate.

I could not understand what he was saying. Not only could I not follow his thought, but every time he said anything I was assailed afresh by doubt as to what subject they were talking about. Sometimes it appeared to be the nature of happiness, sometimes it appeared to be the nature of the mind, sometimes it appeared to be a Buddhist idea which was not familiar to me, and sometimes it appeared to be a familiar and very elementary question of moral philosophy. I was quite prepared to agree that all these things might be related, might even turn out to be the same thing, but Pete was not making any order out of them that I could recognise. He was presenting us merely with a chaotic series of mental pictures. I felt a stirring of the panic that always afflicted me when confronted with mental chaos, but controlled it. I longed for Simon to make the single lucid statement that would pull all these wild fragments into their rightful places, but Simon said nothing. He listened. After a while I realised that he was listening, not to the words, but to the voices.

Alex, gently, patiently, was trying to weave sense out of it. She seemed to be succeeding, if the brightness of the smiles they exchanged was any guide, but I was too tired to judge. I knew that Alex often understood people's meaning when I did not, because I was trained to analyse words and that faculty is no use when you are listening to someone who does not use words in the proper way; whereas Alex, free of my assumption that a word must mean something, was intuitively open to the thought struggling to get out behind the words. But I also knew that Alex found Pete almost as baffling as I did. If she was making anything out of his utterances this evening it must be by the inspiration of charity.

At last she stood up, and we all said goodnight. I followed her out of the room, up the stairs and into the bedroom. Two steps behind her, I saw her fling herself with a cry on to Esther's blanket, and was just in time to see the dog's sad, grateful eyes close at the end of the long, long wait.

We buried her next morning in the spot where she had liked to sit, looking over the valley. One imagines that animals do not appreciate a view, but Esther would sit for hours, apparently rapt, gazing into the distance from that spot. I wept into the grave as I dug it, remembering her patience, and the times I had been bad-tempered with her. I wept for her pain and my callousness and Alex's sadness. For Esther had been Alex's dog, and when Esther was dying Alex had not been there. She had been downstairs, trying to help Pete make sense of himself.

I felt Alex's anguish more keenly than I did my own. She must have felt the same, because she came round the corner of the house and comforted me. Together we laid Esther, now cold and stiff, in the irregular pit I had dug and hacked, declining help, out of the stony soil. Together we heaped the earth and shale over her in a low mound and walked away.

As we went back to the house we found Simon sitting alone on the patio steps. There seemed something odd about him: his face was paler, it lacked its usual radiance. I sat down by him. He asked if he could help me. I said no. He had already asked me the same question several times and I had given him the same answer. We sat without speaking for a few minutes and I became aware that tears were trickling down my face again.

'Why are you crying?' asked Simon.

I started to answer, broke into a sob, and covered my face with my hands. After a while I said through my tears, 'Esther is dead and I loved her.'

Simon waited for me to control myself. Then he said quietly, 'No you didn't.'

I registered a dull shock, more of bewilderment than pain. There was nothing I wanted to say. After about a minute I got up and went in search of Alex.

We decided to go into the city. It was Saturday; we could do some shopping, have coffee in our usual coffee shop, and perhaps call on Manuela. It would cheer us up, and get us out of the house. We both felt a need to be away from the house, which was pervaded that morning by an unhappiness which seemed to have no connection with Esther's death. Pete and

Coral had had a disagreement and were making silent but audible statements about it, Coral from the bedroom and Pete from the toolshed; Simon was still sitting on the steps. In the kitchen one of the children was crying. We saw no point in adding our own unhappiness to the common pool. We told Dao we would be out for lunch, and went.

The city was stifling, and the heat, combined with the heavy-headed feeling that was the aftermath of tears, soon gave me a bad headache. I had a sense of dislocation from reality, as if I had walked into the middle of a film where there was no part for me and the other characters were not aware of my existence. The street in which Manuela lived, sunlit and dusty, was like a deserted film set. Then eight-year-old Ben came careering round a corner on his bicycle, scattering the pigeons and whooping with delight to see Alex.

Ben was Manuela's son by Jacques. She also had a six-year-old daughter by Jacques, Miranda. After Jacques' death Manuela had married a beautiful, melancholy Hungarian, by whom she had a baby son. Jacques had also left in her care his son Justin by his estranged wife. Justin was now fourteen. The three eldest children, who had lived with us at Bethany that desperate summer five years before, were handsome, articulate and imbued with a contempt for conformity that would ensure them incident-rich lives. They all loved Alex, as most children did, for Alex treated them as equals.

On this oppressive Saturday afternoon Manuela had gone to the shops with the baby, her husband had taken Justin fishing, and Miranda had gone to a friend's house to play, leaving Ben to ride his bike at the pigeons. He was particularly unhappy because he had expected to go camping with friends that weekend, and the arrangement had been cancelled. I felt sorry for him, remembering the bitterness of such childhood disappointments, but I was not prepared to hear him say eagerly to Alex, 'Can I come back with you? Can I come and stay the night?' and Alex reply, 'Well, I don't know. We'll have to see what Manuela says.'

Manuela, when she came home, was entirely in favour of a proposal which took a child off her hands for twenty-four hours.

'Where will he sleep?' I asked.

'I've got my tent,' he burst in. 'And a sleeping bag. I can sleep in your field.'

He wanted it too badly, it was already too late, for me to protest. I felt it was a mistake. We were no longer on our own, Alex and I: we were part of a group, and it was a basic principle of the group that no decisions were taken without a full discussion. In any community, it was always a violation of that principle that led to injustice. We could not simply turn up with an extra child, an extra mouth to feed.

Alex apparently saw no problems. 'Don't be silly, of course it's all right,' she said when I voiced my doubts. For a moment I was swayed by her certainty and decided that my reluctance to take Ben home stemmed simply from my own unease with children. In fact I approved of Ben, and if there had to be children around me I would have preferred them to be children of Ben's sort; nonetheless I was much happier when there were no children around me at all.

A moment later, seeing Ben let his bicycle fall with a clatter on to the path and rush off, shouting cheerful abuse at his mother, to collect his belongings, I knew my instinct was right. Ben's arrival would disrupt the group on a day when there had been enough disruption already. Why couldn't Alex see it? Simon and Dao's children were quiet, pacific children: they did not fight, or shout, or drop things with a clatter, or even drop things and not pick them up. Watching Ben, I realised for the first time just how quiet they were, just how little Bethany resounded to the normal rumpus of children. Simon's children had imbibed from their infancy a depth of peace which was not available to other children. Certainly it had not been available to Ben, his childhood dominated by a tempestuous Spanish mother. Ben would shatter the composure of Bethany. Ben was an outsider, a rule-breaker. In fact, I thought, he had a great deal in common with Alex.

The thought caused me a chill. It brought with it a perspective I had once had about Alex, but which over the weeks had shifted and faded so imperceptibly that I had hardly noticed the change. The contrast now was violently disturbing. I saw Alex, again, as someone who did not quite understand. She did not understand the rules of the group, and did not know she did not understand. I was sure something bad was going to happen.

We climbed into the Mini, where there was a prolonged performance over the correct siting of Ben, the tent and the sleeping bag. As we set off, Miranda came swinging down the road. Ben opened the back window.

'I'm going to Bethany with Alex, and Esther's dead,' he crowed.

Ben did not play much with Simon's children: he attached himself to Alex. She helped him put up his tent in the garden and he retired there, with a torch and book, apprehensive but determined, at nine o'clock, with instructions from Alex to come indoors if he felt cold or frightened. He did not.

His advent had already made a noticeable difference to Sarah and Lily. They were noisier and had become almost self-assertive. In the morning they came into our bedroom, a thing they had never done before, perhaps thinking Ben would be there. Sarah was trailing a pull-along toy dog on wheels, and I realised with surprise that it was the first time I had seen any of those children with a toy. I saw the change in them with dismay, and waited for someone to comment on it, but no one did.

The atmosphere in the house did not seem to have improved since the previous day. Pete and Coral avoided each other, Simon was remote, and even Dao's luminosity seemed dimmed. The only happy people appeared to be Ben and Alex, who were clearing nettles from the path into the woods, and even that came to an abrupt end when Ben tripped over a stone and fell headlong into a patch of nettles still awaiting the knife. He wept bitterly, and Alex cuddled him and applied dock leaves. They were in a private world, I thought. That day they formed an indivisible unit. Alex did not want to talk to me, any more than Ben wanted to play with the three adoring little girls who watched him from a distance and tried vainly to attract his attention. They shared something, an aloneless, that set them apart from everyone else.

Seeing the gulf widening between Alex and the rest of the group, I tried once or twice to point out to her that her behaviour was unsociable, but she did not seem to understand me. She said her responsibility was to Ben, who was a guest, and that anyway the rest of the group were quite happily going about their own business and what was I worrying about? I was not at all sure. It was so intangible. I knew a visitor to the house would see nothing wrong. I, with subtler sight, saw things terribly wrong, but perhaps my sight had become so subtle it was seeing things that weren't there?

Ben did not want his lunch. It was salad, with a lot of raw carrots and turnips. He ate some bread and margarine, and went outside as soon as he had finished it. Alex washed his plate.

In the afternoon they cut more nettles and went for a walk in the woods. Alex was going to take him home after supper.

Supper was bean soup with a stock made from nettles. There were a few nettle leaves floating in it. Ben studied them carefully.

'What is this?' he inquired at last.

'It's nettle soup,' said Dao, without her usual smile.

'*Nettles*?' repeated Ben incredulously.

Alex and I hastened to explain to him that the nettles couldn't sting you when they'd been cooked, but he pushed his bowl away and burst into tears. Sarah and Lily looked at him with interest, then at their own soup with doubt, and seemed on the point of doing the same, but, catching Dao's eye, thought better of it.

Alex comforted him, dried his tears, and said she would find him something else to eat in the kitchen.

'Please do not,' said Dao. I had never heard her voice so cold.

'He must have something to eat,' said Alex. 'He didn't have any lunch.'

'I do not do it for these,' said Dao. She always referred to her own children as 'these': normally I found it charming. 'I tell these they must eat what is in front of them, or not eat. Otherwise I will be in the kitchen all day, because they do not like this or they do not like that.'

Her words hung, uncompromising, in the silence. Alex said nothing, smiled reassuringly at Ben, and gave him some of her own bread. No one spoke for the rest of the meal.

I washed my bowl and went outside. I felt upset. Dao had been harsh, a thing which was in itself almost unthinkable. They had all been harsh, in that their silence had supported Dao. Yet they had been just. It was absolutely reasonable that a child visiting the house should be asked to obey the same rules as the children living there, in order that trouble might be avoided in future. But was it reasonable to expect a child to eat something which he thought would hurt him? Ben should trust us, of course. And yet, I thought, why should he, when of the whole group only Alex had troubled to be kind to him? But then it was only Alex who had invited him: he was her guest, not the group's. But what did that matter? We were supposed to love everybody, weren't we, and here we were discriminating against a child. Or were we, or was the discrimination purely mine, a pathological reaction to having yet another child around, yet another guest I had not myself invited?

My thoughts chased each other fruitlessly. I felt very lonely. I glanced once or twice in Alex's direction, but she was preoccupied with Ben and returned my look distantly. It was all I could expect. I felt alienated from the others, and although I longed for a kind word from Simon I was afraid to approach him.

In the end I went and joined him where he sat cross-legged at the edge of the field, gazing over the valley. The heat of the day had evaporated and it was a cool, slightly misty evening.

'It might rain,' I said. It had not rained for three weeks.

'Yes, it might,' he said with a smile. The smile said that anything might happen.

We sat and listened to the earth settling down. A few home-going rooks cawed. From the kitchen came a domestic murmur of Dao and her daughters. The chickens in the orchard were making the gentle throaty sounds that I loved, and there was a series of little flutters and bumps as they flew up into their hen-house for the night. I drank in the stillness, and marvelled that in this lovely place I could a moment ago have thought myself unhappy.

Shouting over her shoulder at the yapping dogs, Alex emerged from the garden, carrying the tent and an armful of treasures Ben had found in the woods. She was followed by Ben himself, half-enveloped in the sleeping bag which he was trying to fold up as he walked. The dogs played noisily around his feet. They all tumbled into the Mini, from which the dogs were then ejected. Alex took them back to the kitchen, shut them in, got back in the car, and with a wave in our direction started off down the drive in a cloud of dust and to the accompaniment of excited shouting from the back seat.

In silence Simon and I watched the little red car disappear round the corner.

'Why does she do it?' I said.

'She doesn't see,' said Simon.

'I thought perhaps it was me,' I said. 'I thought perhaps I'd got it all wrong and there was nothing the matter.'

'Nothing the matter?' repeated Simon with a ghost of a laugh. He might have been a general surveying corpses on a battlefield.

60

'For the past two days,' he said, 'it has been impossible to hear the silence for the trumpeting of human egos.'

I examined my soul. I could not at first find evidence of egotism in my behaviour. Then I saw that my wish not to bring Ben home had been a form of egotism. I had not wanted my grief for Esther intruded upon. That grief had itself been egotism, not real grief at all. It was my own shortcomings I had been grieving over. It was always myself: I could not keep myself out of anything.

Simon said, 'Why do you involve yourself?'

I was shocked. He could not have read my mind so literally. I stared at him.

He said, 'If it is nothing to do with you, why do you involve yourself?'

My mind wheeled in an arc like a buzzard and homed finally on his meaning, which, as I circled into it, became so beautifully obvious that I burst out laughing. He had presented me with the flipside of the mental process I had just been through. He laughed with me, not knowing what I was laughing at but delighted that it had made me happy.

I sobered up. 'You're right,' I said, 'I involve myself. I feel responsible. Particularly with Alex. Or rather, I *don't* in fact feel responsible, but I feel that I ought to, and so I involve myself even more anxiously.'

'But if it is Alex's business, why do you have to involve yourself?'

'I feel protective towards her,' I said.

'One protects children,' he said.

I could not answer him. The dogs gruffed and whined in the kitchen, wanting to be let out. Dao opened the door and they bounded out and streaked across the field, one blue-grey mongrel, one small terrier, barking exultantly, oblivious of the death of a companion the day before. Two dogs, free, simple.

'Why do you feel that you ought to feel responsible?' he asked.

I scanned for the reason and knew that I would not find it

that evening. It went deep. It was a chance in a thousand that I had brushed past the tip of it in my attempt to answer another question.

'I'm tired,' I said. 'Perhaps we can come back to it.'

He smiled, an approving smile, knowing that this was not an evasion but a decision to treat the matter with the seriousness it deserved.

'If you like,' he said.

Two days later the Sessions began.

'Locate an incident which might have caused this tendency to make you feel responsible when you are not,' said Simon.

His voice was quiet and held the power to command. We were sitting in the sun-dappled parlour. I closed my eyes, partly to concentrate, partly because of the brightness. My mind ranged back, selecting and rejecting, hesitant. Then it found. It was like a hawk stooping: there was no doubt.

'I have the incident,' I said.

'Go back to the beginning of the incident,' said Simon. 'Tell me when you're there.'

I was there. Standing in the doorway of Alex's workshop on a long-forgotten spring afternoon. Listening, puzzled and unhappy, as Alex railed at me. Watching the cold sunlight, broken up by the moving branches of the laurel tree outside, make patterns on the dusty machinery.

'It is seven years ago,' I said. 'I'm standing in the doorway of Alex's workshop, which is now part of the kitchen. Alex is angry with me because she says I'm not helping her. She says I am leaving her with the sole responsibility for the house. She says I'm not pulling my weight.

'The trouble is,' I continued, 'that it's true enough to make me feel guilty, but it isn't really true. I haven't got a job, but then neither has Alex. She's supporting me, but it isn't costing her anything in terms of effort. In any case she says she isn't asking me to get a job. She wants me to take responsibility, she says. But responsibility for what? She doesn't expect me to mend the roof. What does she expect me to do? I thought it was all right for me to live here and clear the brambles and work in the garden and do a bit of freelance work and enjoy myself, but apparently it isn't. Something more is being required of me. I don't know what it is.'

The workshop faded from my mind and I was standing in a field: one of the lower fields that led to the river. I was gazing at the hedge. It was an old Cornish stone hedge, overgrown with grass and weeds and crowned at intervals along its curving length with a number of trees, ending with a fine beech. I loved the hedges at Bethany, I delighted in their ancient mingling of the man-made and the natural. Looking now at this hedge I saw that my innocent relationship with it had been destroyed. I could no longer enjoy it, because I was going to have to use it. I was going to have to trim it back and put a fence along it and turn it into an efficient hedge. And when I had done that, it would have ceased to be a hedge. It would have become what already I saw in it, a wall.

'And so my attitude to the place altered,' I said. 'It became something I had to worry about. And because there was not very much I could do on my own, I worked very hard doing things which I knew were not particularly important. All to discharge a feeling of responsibility which I did not feel to be quite genuine.'

I sat back in my chair, very surprised. In ten minutes I had discovered the cause of a habit which had dominated my life for seven years.

Or had I? There was something more. Why had I been so susceptible to that accusation of Alex's, which I could see even at the time rested on flimsy foundations?

Simon saw it, and did not attempt to take me through the experience again. 'Is there an earlier incident which you associate with the idea of responsibility?' he asked.

It came almost at once, and I fought to dismiss it. I did not want to look at it. I knew from the violence of my reaction that I must.

I was back at school, boarding school. I was in sixth form and I hated it. I hated it for its tedium and lack of privacy, but most of all because it imposed duties on me which I did not want to fulfil. All my schooldays I had flouted authority: now, as a sixth-former, I was authority. I could not cope with it. I did not want to tell the younger children to be quiet, brush their hair and behave themselves. I did not want to because I did not believe in the virtue of doing these things. And I did not want to because I was afraid they would laugh at me.

Sitting tense in my chair in the parlour, I found myself once more, sixteen and bitterly alone, standing irresolutely in the sixth-form study when I should have been upstairs. I should have been restoring order in the dormitory, imposing silence on chattering juniors and braving their whispered sarcasms. Instead I was leaving it to my fellow sixth-former, an earnest girl universally mocked and despised. I left it to her every night. In consequence her public standing was as low as mine was high. No one saw that I, the rebel, the individualist, the free-thinker, was a hypocrite, a coward and a fake.

I shuddered. I was very cold. I came out of it slowly, feeling drained. I knew that I would have to go through it again until the pain was discharged, but that behind it lay a dark mountain of unsearched misery that would have to be explored, mapped and understood before I was a whole human being and could call my mind my own.

4

SOURCES

It was about this time that something strange happened.

I came into breakfast and found a roomful of silent, still people. Simon, instead of occupying his usual chair at the head of the table, was sitting in a chair several feet away near the window in an uncharacteristic attitude: it was almost a slouch. His face was pale and withdrawn. No one was eating.

'What's the matter?' I said, to the room in general.

'You know,' said Simon without looking up.

It was like a physical blow. I had no idea what he meant.

'I'm sorry, but I don't,' I said.

Alex came in.

'What's going on?' she said.

Simon looked up, and his eyes fastened coldly on hers.

'You know,' he repeated.

Alex drew in her breath sharply as if to say something, then looked at me. I shrugged.

We sat down and helped ourselves to muesli, and tried to eat it. After a while the others ate too. The chink of spoons sounded deafening.

'Won't you have something to eat, Simon?' coaxed Dao.

'No thank you, Dao,' he replied with his normal courtesy.

Whoever had caused this, it wasn't Dao.

After a while Pete put down his spoon and said, 'Are we going to repair the orchard wall today?'

'It's too late,' said Simon.

I felt dread settle into every crevice of the room.

'Too late for *what*?' said Alex.

Simon stood up. 'It's too late,' he said, and walked out.

The only thing I was sure of was that this nightmare had nothing to do with me. Doggedly I finished my muesli, washed the bowl, and went upstairs to change. I had to go to work. To my surprise I heard the Humber start up and go down the drive while I was in the bedroom. I went downstairs to find everyone in the kitchen except Simon. He had gone to the city, said Dao. Simon, who never went out. Alex and I exchanged glances.

'What's it all about?' I asked.

There was no reply.

'Is it something we've done?' said Alex.

Coral said, 'Simon didn't say what was the matter.'

Alex and I walked out on to the patio. It was a beautiful morning. The exhaust fumes from the Humber still hung faintly in the air.

'Have you done anything to upset him?' asked Alex.

'No,' I said. 'Have you?'

'No.'

We stared down the drive.

'Bit heavy,' I said.

'Mmm,' said Alex.

Pete and Coral joined us, Coral holding the baby.

'Well, I think that's quite extraordinary,' said Alex. 'People don't behave like that.'

'Not without giving a reason,' I said.

'Even with a reason,' said Alex.

'Oh, well,' I said. 'If that's how he feels . . .'

Pete said, with a puzzled air, 'You seem to be saying that Simon is in the wrong.'

Alex and I turned on him in unison.

'Well *we* aren't,' we said.

Pete smiled gently, and spread his hands in a gesture which plainly signified that we should think again. He walked off, still smiling, to the toolshed.

Dao had come out as well, the children pattering behind her. Alex and I turned to her as to our last hope.

'Dao, what is going on?' said Alex.

She was silent for a while, and I feared she would give us the same answer as Pete. But she was thoughtful, a little subdued. The children hung about her, thumb-sucking, absorbed in another world.

She said slowly, 'Simon does not have the same needs as other people. He does not need things. But he must have mental nourishment.'

I had difficulty catching the last word, which she pronounced uncertainly.

'His mental nourishment comes from love. Simon has a great need of love. When he feels that is lacking, he . . . oh, he becomes sick.'

She smiled dazzlingly, and made the quick, graceful gesture of apology that accompanied all her efforts to explain something difficult in a language unsuited to spiritual nuances.

Alex and I stared at her, at each other, at the landscape before us. It could not be clearer, or more impossible to grasp.

I thanked her, and went to work.

In the evening as soon as I got home I went to find Simon. He was sitting in the parlour. He looked tired and unhappy. This man who had given me so much: it wrenched my heart.

I did not know what to say to him. In the end I stumbled out a statement that if I had upset him I was sorry, that the last thing in the world I wanted to do was cause him unhappiness. Then, greatly daring, I kissed his forehead. He said nothing.

'Will you come in to supper?' I said. The bell had gone. 'Please.'

He gazed at me, and suddenly smiled. He stood up.

'Very well,' he said. 'Let us both go in to supper, Kay.'

We went.

It was all over. What had it been? Alex and I did not discuss it: we were too glad it was past. In time I did the only thing I could do with it: I dismissed it from my mind. There was plenty to think about.

Step by step I was being drawn back into my past. It was like entering a cavern. I had no map, no idea of where I was going. I followed the path, and after a while it was no longer possible to turn back.

What had I done? My mother, who was supposed to be brushing my hair, was almost beating my head with the hairbrush. She was crying. She was asking how she deserved such a child, such an evil child.

My stomach knotted. Simon's voice, emotionless, seemed to come from far away.

We were pursuing the theme of responsibility. Asked to define the word, I had said 'moral accountability', and Simon had asked me to locate an incident where the idea of moral accountability was associated with pain. My mind with scarcely a moment's pause had taken me to a scene twenty-five years ago. A frightened child on a kitchen stool; a desperate, tearful woman. A scene only half-understood.

'I can't remember what caused it,' I said. 'I don't know what I'd done.'

My incomprehension was an echo of the incomprehension I had felt then. Whatever I had done could not merit the word 'evil'. My mother simply did not understand.

'Go back to the beginning of the incident,' said Simon.

She did not try to understand. Everything was black and white for my mother. Everything was straightforward. For me, at the age of eight, it was not straightforward. I stole things, all sorts of things, I could not stop doing it. My mother found out and cried. She took it personally. She was right to do so: it was a rejection.

'Oh God,' I said, and twisted in my chair.

'Go back to the beginning,' said Simon.

'I feel guilty,' I said. 'Terribly guilty at upsetting my mother so profoundly. And I can't cope. She has called me evil.'

I paused.

'She says I'm a secretive child and I tell lies. It's quite true. I'm secretive because I have no friends. I'm not allowed to play with the other children in the street because they're rough. And I lie . . . I lie because I can see no good reason for not doing so.'

I had been through it six times, there was no more emotion to be discharged from it. I sat quietly, feeling very sad.

'Is there an earlier incident which you connect with the idea of moral accountability?' asked Simon.

I could have picked half a dozen, but it was not the memories which came to hand that I wanted. I wanted the thing which was so important that for twenty-five years the mind had walled it up in a cell where it could do no more harm. I waited.

It stirred in its cell, and I had it. I wished it had been something else.

I was watching my father wash his face and hands in a bowl in the kitchen sink. He had taken his shirt off, and I looked at his thin shoulders with distaste. He had just come home from work; he was tired, but before he could rest he had to do something for me.

'I've stolen something from school,' I said. 'It's an ornament, a little lighthouse carved out of stone. It has to be returned, but my mother doesn't want me to get into trouble. So my father is going to walk up to the school this evening and throw it over the wall into the flower-bed.'

I stared at the red-necked figure in trousers and vest washing the grime of the day's work from its hands.

'It's very odd,' I said, 'but I don't feel at all guilty about stealing this lighthouse. I feel it's quite unimportant. What I feel most strongly at the moment is anger. That they're interfering again.'

I came back to the present, puzzled at my reactions.

'Go back to the beginning of the incident,' said Simon.

'My father doesn't like me,' I said after a moment. 'And I don't like him.' I paused. 'I'm jealous of him, that's why. And he seems to despise my intelligence, which I can't understand because I know he isn't particularly clever. So part of the reason why I'm angry is that I don't want to be in his debt.'

I finished speaking rather abruptly, with a feeling that it would be a mistake to spend any more time on this incident. As I turned away from it, something came into my mind so forcibly that I spoke without meaning to.

'I wanted to be bad,' I said. 'That's the point.'

Alex's brother Philip called to see us and brought his latest fiancée. He was thirty-nine and she was twenty-four, but Philip, suntanned, muscular and unimaginative, both looked and thought like a much younger man. The girl was ordinary and adoring. They might suit each other very well, I thought, if Philip was sensible this time. Something always went wrong with Philip's plans for marriage, and he exhibited an inability to learn from experience which amazed me.

Alex did not like her brother. Beyond a certain facial resemblance they had nothing in common. I could not make up my mind how he regarded her. At times he seemed solicitous and anxious to help, doing odd jobs for her which required little time but a lot of strength. At other times he was inconsiderate and gratuitously rude. Alex said that whenever he did things for her there was an ulterior motive, and this appeared to be true. He had, for instance, spent several days painting the front of the house after it was stripped of its rendering; it happened to be the summer that Jacques and Manuela stayed with us, and Philip had taken a very strong fancy – unreciprocated – to Manuela.

Relations between Alex and Philip had sunk to an unprecedented level of hostility within recent memory, but since the start of the group Alex had resolved to be friendly, and in response to a cautious overture Philip had paid this visit. I could see that Alex, although civil, wished he hadn't come. If he was aware of her coolness he didn't show it; he seemed much at his ease, chatting to Pete and Coral, and glancing from time to time, half-puzzled, half-entranced, at Dao. At ease, that is, until Simon entered the kitchen. At the sight of him something seemed to happen to Philip: he quivered, like an animal sensing the presence of a natural enemy. They had never met before: it could only be fear. Simon's eyes struck fear into many people.

Alex introduced them and there was an exchange of courtesies in which I had a vivid impression of Philip in headlong flight with no pursuer. Dao must have perceived the same thing, because a few days later she asked Alex whether she had said anything to Philip to prejudice him against Simon. Alex was justifiably surprised.

I drifted off to the fields. I did not feel inclined to talk to anyone that afternoon. I had a lot on my mind.

'I can't remember writing it,' I said. 'And yet now it's been discovered I recognise it with a sort of surprise, as if it was something I thought I'd only dreamed about, and it's turned out to be real.'

'It' was a small black notebook. It contained a record of the most appalling crimes and atrocities the imagination of an eight-year-old could invent. I had committed them.

'I'm not surprised by my mother's reaction,' I said, 'but I feel that it's none of her business. It was a game and she's taking it seriously.'

Simon directed me to go through it again.

'My parents don't know who I am,' I said. 'I've always felt that. I feel I know things they don't know. And I feel that I'm important in a way that wouldn't mean anything to them.'

'Go back to the beginning of the incident,' said Simon.

I was finding it hard to breathe.

'I feel exposed,' I said, and paused to gulp in air. 'I feel something is terribly unfair. And of course I feel humiliated. Because I'd like to play king, and I'm just a child.'

My forehead was clammy. I had nearly got to the core of this awful experience, the thing that had never been understood.

'Go back to the beginning,' said Simon.

'I have cut myself off from the human race,' I said. 'My mother's reaction is that I'm a monster. But that's what I wanted. That's what this notebook was all about. It was completely mad. It was about power and cruelty.'

Then at last I remembered writing it, and was overwhelmed by an emotion so painful, so disturbing, that I had to fight for breath. It was an emotion grotesquely out of place in childhood. It was an emotion I knew, and could not identify.

'When I put down my pencil,' I said, 'it was like waking from a beautiful dream. There was a moment of intense sadness.'

I felt again the deep, uncomprehended anguish that followed the exhilaration of writing in the notebook.

'It was like a drug,' I said. 'These exploits of mine had to get worse and worse. I went from excess to excess. I killed thousands of people, in the most unpleasant ways I could devise. I crucified them, I burnt them alive. For some reason they were usually women. And babies. God, how I hated babies.'

With the eyes of an adult I surveyed the torment of a child, and still could not understand. The horror and the beauty, how could they be the same? I shut my eyes and tried not to think.

'It was like flying,' I said suddenly. 'I used to dream a lot about flying. It was the same feeling.' A startled moment later I added, 'There's a very strong sexual element in it.'

I opened my eyes and sat back in my chair. I had found it. I felt exhausted, but physically lighter. I breathed deeply for a while. Simon waited.

'I don't know what it means,' I said at last. 'I know it's right, but I'm no wiser. There's something impenetrable there.'

The bell rang for supper. I heard the click as Simon put away his pen. We smiled at each other and walked towards the house.

Alex had decided to go to London. She had received a terse letter from her bank manager requesting specific proposals for the reduction of the interest on £18,600. She would go to see him, and would also see various other people who might be of assistance in selling a roofless property which nobody wanted to buy. She departed turbulently, after losing, bewailing and finding again the ten-pound note with which I provided her for the journey, at half-past six in the morning.

I was not sorry that she would be away for a few days. I had no room in my mind for the demands of a personal relationship. I was in a dream, sleepwalking through the days towards the hour in the evening when I would sit down with Simon and resume my journey through the dark cavern that held the secret of my childhood.

Then as I walked pensively through the fields waiting for that hour, I realised that I already knew it, and stood amazed at its simplicity and my obtuseness.

'I spent a large part of my early childhood in a state of bitter anger,' I said. 'I felt I had been cheated. The reason was that I wanted to be a boy.'

The tension in my stomach had gone, and I spoke confidently. I had made a vital connection, and it illuminated everything around it.

'It wasn't envy,' I said. 'It was a passionate yearning. I couldn't understand why I wasn't a boy. When I was very little I believed God would one day turn me into a boy if I was good, but eventually I realised it would never happen. I felt it was a terrible injustice. I looked at the little boys I knew and it seemed to me that most of them didn't deserve it.'

I was conscious of smiling wryly. I had never quite lost the feeling that the male in general was not worthy of its biological privileges.

'So,' I said, 'I tried to be as much like a boy as possible, but it didn't work. I wanted to wear jeans – or whatever they were called in those days – but my mother didn't approve of trousers for little girls. And I wanted a toy revolver.' I stopped, momentarily assailed again by that desperate childhood lust.

'No one would give me one,' I said. 'It became an obsession. In the end, I took some money from the hallstand and went to the toyshop and bought a black toy revolver in a holster. I couldn't wear it openly, of course, I had to wear it under my raincoat. It was discovered and I had to send it as a Christmas present to my cousin. He probably had a dozen of them.

'By the time I wrote the notebook,' I said, 'I'd more or less given up trying to acquire a gun. I'd always thought the notebook was an expression of alienation and something to do with my relationship with my parents, but I've realised that it wasn't. It was a sadistic fantasy based on the childish equation: male equals big and strong equals cruel. My dislike of babies was simply a rejection of the maternal role, of course. I still don't like children much.'

Simon wrote busily. He took notes during all the Sessions now. He spent most of each day writing at speed. I thought it must be very tiring.

He asked me what physical feeling I associated with the experiences I had just described.

'Being bottled up, caged in,' I said. 'A feeling of rage.'

He told me to locate a particular incident when I had felt that. I hesitated. There were so many. I selected the one that seemed to have the strongest emotional charge.

'I'm six years old,' I said. 'I'm standing looking in a toyshop window at something I want which will change my life. I know I can't have it. There is no good reason why I can't have it. Nobody understands why I want it. I hate them.'

I stopped abruptly. I was looking at an expensive toy revolver with an imitation ivory handle. It was the biggest and

74

best in the Lone Star range and I looked at it every day on my way home from school. Every fibre of my being yearned towards it. I felt that it was already mine. Yet as I thought that, that it was mine, I felt a strange dissatisfaction.

I, as adult, examined this dissatisfaction and saw that it was not the normal boredom that ensues on getting what one wants, nor was it a consciousness that the thing was a toy and not a real gun. It was the tip of an insatiability. As I saw it, I experienced an avalanche of comprehension. For I was prepared to do anything to obtain this revolver – lie, cheat, steal. And as the years went by I did precisely that: I lied, cheated and stole. I had never made the connection, because I had never stolen anything I really wanted. Instead, I had . . .

I slammed my hand down on the arm of the chair with the force of the insight. '*That's* where it started!' I exclaimed.

Mindlessly I had accepted the dictum that the kleptomaniac is looking for love, and blamed my compulsive childhood thieving on loneliness. I had been looking for nothing of the sort. With newly-opened eyes I scanned the wretched catalogue of things I had stolen from relatives, school-mates and shopkeepers – the little lighthouse, dozens of pens, pencils and crayons . . . I remembered stealing money from my mother's purse to buy a cheap fountain pen I didn't want; I remembered the strange episode in which I had stolen a pound note from my grandmother and obliterated the memory of the theft, so that my first consciousness of it, and all I could subsequently recapture of it, was the moment when my fingers contacted in my raincoat pocket a stiff papery cylinder which my mind desperately interpreted as a toothbrush. I had coveted and by devious means obtained another child's plastic retractable dagger, and the last thing I had ever attempted to steal was a model soldier with a rifle. All this, and a six-shooter too. A parade of phallic symbolism almost embarrassing in its orthodoxy. Seldom could Freud have been so simply and triumphantly vindicated.

I put my head back and laughed.

Sophie came for two days. Sophie was the four-year-old daughter of Harriet, who was Simon's ex-wife. This did not mean that Sophie was Simon's daughter: she was assumed by Manuela, Alex and me to be Pete's, since Pete had for a time lived with Harriet before he met Coral. The reason for Sophie's visit was that Harriet was going into hospital to have another baby. Gordon, the friend of Simon's who had married Dao for him, telephoned to ask if we could look after Sophie until Harriet was home again. I wondered who was the father of the baby, and rather hoped it was someone I hadn't heard of.

'Bottled up, caged in, in a rage,' said Simon. 'Is there an earlier incident when you felt that?'

It would have to be much earlier to be any use. I had discovered a great deal, but the source lay much further back, in my first years, before I went to school. I pushed my mind back beyond the point at which it could remember.

I was sitting on the kitchen floor cutting holes in my father's socks. I had a green sock in one hand and the scissors in the other. I was consumed with rage about something. There was another feeling which I could not identify. Having cut the heels out of several socks I folded them up and put them back on the dresser.

I went through the incident several times but could get no more out of it.

'Is there an earlier incident?' asked Simon.

When else had I felt this baffled rage?

From the fringe of memory a dim picture came: a child, three and a half years old, looking at a Christmas tree on which were hung toys more suitable for a baby. The picture sharpened. One of the toys was a rattle in the form of a pink plastic telephone. I saw my mother, her face strained, sitting in an armchair. My father was not in the picture.

'I feel these toys are an insult,' I said. 'I must have expressed my dissatisfaction because my mother says, "If you behave like a baby you'll have baby's toys." I have some inkling what she

76

means. I think I have been behaving badly recently. I've started wetting the bed again. But I have a strong feeling that it isn't fair.'

I paused. 'They're not being honest,' I said. 'I feel I've been tricked.'

I could not account for this last perception. I waited for the emotions to clarify.

'I feel terrible,' I said, 'belittled. Angry. But the strongest feature is that these toys are simply nothing to do with me. They're for someone else. My parents do not know who I am.'

I left the incident with a feeling of irritation. It seemed both enigmatic and trivial. I returned to the incident of the socks, which now seemed to hold a new element.

'It's very confused,' I said. 'It seems the right thing to do. I know it's destructive, and I know that something terrible will happen if I do it. And at the same time, as I cut into the fabric I have the extraordinary feeling that I'm doing something helpful.'

Yet the motive was spite. I was intensely angry, and the cutting of the socks brought an emotional release I could still feel. The anger was the same in all the incidents I had been through: it was the anger of impotence. It was caused by an initial frustration, compounded by many repetitions, and rendered almost intolerable by the frustration of the need to communicate. Through all the incidents ran the theme that I could not communicate my real nature. With surprise I realised that I had last felt this anger very recently.

'It's the rage I still feel when someone won't listen to me,' I said. 'When their refusal to listen amounts to an attempt to change my identity. It happens often with Alex. I become incoherent with anger, because she is trying to tell me about something that is happening inside my own head.'

I paused. 'I suppose that's what is meant by trying to change someone's data,' I said.

There was a phone call to say that Harriet had had a baby boy.

It was her fourth child, the others being Sophie and two sons of Simon's, aged respectively twelve and nine. The boys were physically graceless, as was their mother, but highly intelligent. I had once seen Simon, Harriet and the older boy, Martin, together, and been struck by the child's originality of mind and by Simon's lack of warmth towards him. Simon had said afterwards that Martin had serious problems of ego. I had noticed that he required a very high standard of behaviour from his children. I reflected that it must be difficult having an apparently perfect being for a father.

I did not like Harriet, although we had a lot in common. She, Simon and I had all read the same subject at the same university, although they had been there six years before me. Harriet and I shared the same combination of an orderly mind and a lifestyle which hovered perpetually on the brink of chaos. I could not decide why I didn't like her: every time I thought about it there seemed to be a different reason. When I caught myself mentally accusing her of both puritanism and promiscuity I realised that my dislike was not rational and I had better look elsewhere for its cause. In the event I never bothered.

She and Simon had separated because of mutual incompatibility of temperament. (My words, not his: the only time he ever referred to it in my hearing was to pay Dao a gentle compliment, saying what bliss he found it to live with someone who left him in peace.) He had given Harriet the cottage in which they'd lived, a few miles from the city, and since then he and Dao had never had a permanent home. When I met them they were living in a cliffside chalet overlooking the Atlantic. The view was breathtaking, and so, in winter, were the winds.

The chalet belonged to Gordon, the friend who had married Dao. They moved out of it after the Buddhist equivalent of trouble with the neighbours: the man next door, after a few conversations with Simon, had become angry and hit him. Simon had not attempted to defend himself, but had decided to move since his presence obviously upset the man. This information came from Manuela, supplying, as always, the apocrypha to Simon's canon. I could not fathom her attitude to Simon: it seemed to be a mixture of respect, impatience, affection and mockery. I had once heard her say, 'When I think of Simon I feel so sad,' with the unmistakable and extraordinary implication that there was something wrong with him. I concluded that Manuela had never properly listened to Simon because in her mind she was still listening to Jacques – Jacques as he had been before alcohol and drugs claimed him. I concluded also that she was a little in love with him. Surely few women who met Simon could not be in love with him. Men, too. Why else did Gordon do so much for him? And there was the dog-like fidelity of Pete.

For the first time I allowed myself to consider the question of whether I too was falling in love with Simon, and was dismayed to feel my heart quicken at the thought. I had never been in love with a man: I had thought myself not capable of it. I liked male company, I approved of the balanced detachment and range which I considered typical of the male intellect at its best, and I admired many personal qualities in the men I knew; yet there was a way in which men were not quite real to me, not entirely dimensional, and I could not believe that they had emotions as profound as a woman's. I could not take them completely seriously, and the more physical my commerce with them became, the more I despised them.

Simon, in this sense, was not a man to me; he transcended the category. Not merely did he demand to be taken seriously: he was my touchstone of seriousness. I was saturated with his ideas and his presence. He had broken every defence I had. Of course I loved him – in the sense he demanded. Was it possible that the steady warmth of this affection had aroused from its slumber a sexual love which he did not ask for and would not want?

I knew it was a mistake to think about it, and I continued to think about it. It had the heady sweetness of all forbidden thoughts, with a strong spice of fear. After a while I was unable to stop thinking about it, and I was beginning to feel the first stirrings of jealousy towards Dao. With the jealousy came guilt.

I told myself that the psychological self-exposure involved in the Sessions was bound to set up an emotional tension between me and Simon: I could hardly be blamed for it, and it was something he ought to be prepared for. But I realised that it was at least as likely that my self-exposure was sexually motivated, that I was using the Sessions to achieve a precarious intimacy with him. I was carrying on a flirtation with him through my past. It was in very bad taste, quite apart from being dangerous, and I knew I should stop it. I couldn't: it was too piquant. Besides, the discoveries I had made in Sessions were real and important. I had to go on until I found the thing that had started it all.

'Nearly all of it is now very clear,' I said. 'I tried to cheat in all sorts of ways – by escaping into fantasy, by trying to steal the thing I wanted, by simply pretending that I had it – but it didn't work. What isn't clear is the original event. At some point I discovered that I wasn't like a boy, and that must have been traumatic.'

I was very calm. The previous evening, after the end of a Session, I had realised something so luminously simple that I marvelled I could have missed it for so many years.

'In my Session yesterday I said I'd started bedwetting when I was about three and a half,' I said. 'It went on for well over a year, and it wasn't only at night. My mother used to get very upset. I've never known why I suddenly regressed like this, because there wasn't, as far as I know, any disturbance at home which would account for it. Then last night I recaptured how I felt on those occasions, when I knew it was going to happen; and the feeling was an absolute panic-stricken refusal to go to the lavatory.'

No doubt about it, it was a striking insight. And it brought me to a point from which I could, I was sure, reach the final enigma of my childhood in a single step. I thought I knew the direction in which it lay.

'I had a little boy-friend,' I said, 'Johnny. He was almost the same age as me. Our mothers were friends. I remember an occasion when I was at his house, and we were playing in the sandpit . . .'

Simon broke in and made me run the incident properly.

'I'm playing in the sandpit,' I said, 'and his mother comes up and asks me if I want to go to the toilet. I do, but I say no. It gets worse, but I still refuse to go, and finally the inevitable happens. Then we go in for tea, and his mother notices. She can't understand why I didn't tell her. And I don't know either. I just felt compelled to say no.'

'Go back to the beginning,' said Simon.

This time I recaptured the fear – the fear that the wet patch I was sitting on would be discovered. Then I got a vivid picture of the green bathroom door and the green and white squared lino, and was gripped by a colder fear. Whatever happened, I could not go in there. Someone was saying something to me. I concentrated.

'Yes,' I said. 'His mother's saying something. She says, "Are you sure you don't want to go, Kay? Because Johnny's going." '

I stopped. 'Good God,' I said, in amazement at the literalness of the subconscious. I didn't want to go because Johnny was going. There it was.

But why?

'Is there an earlier incident?' asked Simon.

Of course there was: *the* incident. I could feel it, but I could see nothing. I knew it was to do with Johnny, but it was an incident that had never been consciously held in the memory. I waited. It struggled towards me, appearing slowly like an animal emerging for the first time from the mud in which it has always lived. It became bright and sharp. I was in Johnny's garden again. I must have been very small because the grass came up to my shoulders. Johnny and I were there alone. It was early evening.

'We've been playing,' I said. 'I say I'm going in, to go to the lavatory, and he says, "Why don't you go here?" '

I couldn't see what happened next: it was as if the reel had stuck.

'Go back to the beginning,' said Simon.

It was very confused: a series of impressions. Hesitantly I said, 'I take my knickers down and he looks at me in amazement and says, "You don't do it like *that*!" – and demonstrates. I am very hurt at the contempt in his voice. And very envious.'

A tremendous sigh escaped me.

'Go back to the beginning,' said Simon again.

But this time it was quite different.

'He's challenged me,' I said. 'Who can pee the furthest, or something like that. Obviously he doesn't know that girls can't. I am wondering how I can evade the challenge without being humiliated.'

I could see no more, but I knew that I had not managed to evade it. The humiliation, the exposure of my inferiority, had taken place then in that garden.

'I've been tricked, betrayed, conned,' I burst out. 'I am at a terrible disadvantage and nobody has prepared me for it. The worst thing is the feeling of betrayal. My parents made me believe I was someone special, and all the time I was inferior. They don't even understand how terrible it is. I can never trust them again.'

I came back to the present with a faint dissatisfaction. I had expected to find, at the end of my quest, some event of haunting lucidity, alight with the strange logic of the subconscious. What I had found was the logic of suburbia. It was so predictable that I could have made it up. An uncomfortable feeling grew in me that perhaps I had made it up. And if I had, what else had I made up? Surely only a colourful detail here and there, to make a better story of it. The progression from incident to incident was real. Yet I wondered if it was inevitable. Would other incidents have done?

Well, I would have to rest content with what insights I had gained. The series was finished. I had said so: and in any case, Alex was due back.

The diary was kept in the top right-hand drawer of the carved oak sideboard in the parlour. Simon had bought it, so that, he said, everyone could write in it what they felt. Since, if we had something to say, we usually said it openly, most of the entries were records of things done, decisions made, or major items of expenditure. However, interspersed among these sober entries, which were usually in Simon's hand or mine, appeared others of a more poetic nature by Dao, Coral, and sometimes (rather shyly) Alex.

Sometimes there was nothing on the page except, in the top right-hand corner, a note of the weather by Simon. However, the page for the second Thursday in June was almost filled.

First, in Dao's surprisingly bold writing, whose only hint of un-Englishness was the little spiral, like the start of the treble clef, with which she prefixed her capital I's: '5.30 a.m. saw the red car. Very nice indeed. It means Alex has come back.'

From these two lines could be deduced several things: that Dao got up early, that she was fond of Alex, and that Alex had returned after Dao had gone to bed. In fact Dao habitually went to bed shortly after eight o'clock in the evening, at the same time as the children, and she was always up before anyone else. She liked to get up before six and meditate for half an hour on the grassy slope in front of the house. Then she brought us tea, or whatever we liked. Most people liked a herb tea, but I was reluctant to wake up to anything but Assam. Dao herself rarely drank anything but boiled water which had been allowed to cool until tepid: occasionally she would squeeze a drop of lemon juice into it.

Underneath Dao's entry Simon had written in his neat hand: 'Simon, Pete, Dao, Coral and the children went to see Harriet and baby at the hospital.' On the next line Coral had written: 'Afterwards, went to Manuela's.' And then after a space, 'The

atmosphere in the city is poisonous and the people are suffering.'

The lower half of the page was taken up with Simon's notes
on the weekly finance meeting. These meetings always followed
the same form. I would open the proceedings by stating how
much had been spent in the past week. Shopping for the group
was done by whoever happened to be going into town (in fact
I usually did it in my lunch-hour), and the expenditure was
written in the cash book. Every Thursday I added up the total
expenditure and divided it by three or four (depending on
whether Alex was paying a share that week), and people who
had done shopping were reimbursed or asked for the balance
according to whether the amount they had spent was more or
less than their share. I also collected money for the running
costs of the house. This money, the kitty, was kept in a tin box
and from it the bills were paid.

The arithmetic involved was not complex but it was enough
to oppress me, and after the first week I bought a battery for
Alex's pocket calculator. I put the battery down as group
expenditure, on the principle that it was in nobody's interests
if the Bursar got her sums wrong.

Having given a statement of expenditure and collected the
money for the kitty, I would raise any other matters relating to
the finances. When the financial business was completed Simon
would take over the meeting and ask if anyone else had anything to say. When everyone had finished, Simon himself
would speak.

His chairmanship was superb. By turns patient, humorous
and incisive, he guided us through an agenda which, item by
item, he reduced to its essentials. Every view was equally
weighed and no suggested course of action was dismissed
simply because it was inconvenient. He made sure that a decision of some kind was always taken, and was taken with the
full, considered assent of all members of the group. There were
no majority decisions: if anyone disagreed, the matter was
examined until a course was found that satisfied everyone. It

was no small achievement. In any normal committee it would be impossible: it was made possible because we had no personal ends to pursue.

Simon's notes for the second Thursday evening in June ran as follows: 'Finance meeting,' followed by the sum we had spent that week. It was rather higher than usual because Alex had bought food in London which we could not obtain locally. Under this Simon had written 'Agreed': and three items. The first two were 'Hay and hay barns' and 'Roof'.

The hay was a yearly ordeal for Alex and me. Would we be able to get a contractor to harvest our modest six acres of hay when all around us were farmers struggling to get a hundred acres cut, turned, baled and under cover before it rained? Somehow it was always managed, and each time it seemed a miracle.

This year matters were in the hands of the group. Pete opened the discussion by asking, 'Why do people cut hay?'

Alex explained that if you didn't either graze a grass field or cut it for hay the field would quickly revert to weeds and brambles and eventually scrubland. We considered whether there was anything wrong with scrubland and decided there was not, but that equally there was nothing wrong with hay either, and that as the hay was there it would be a waste not to cut it since the goats and ponies would be glad of it in the winter.

We discussed briefly whether it might be possible to process grass into milk without first drying it and feeding it to a goat, and then, by logical progression, whether it might be possible simply to eat the grass. I said I had tasted fresh hay and it was very palatable, but I did not think the human digestion could cope with it. The latter part of this statement was challenged, and Simon said it would simplify life considerably if we could come in to supper and find a bale of hay on the table. Having noticed how Simon's jokes had a way of turning into realities I did not find this as amusing as the others.

The decision was therefore taken to cut the hay and Alex was asked to find someone to do it. I then raised the question of where we were going to store it. The red barn would hold ten tons, but half of it was unusable because of the huge gap in the roof and the other half was filled with timber and building materials. We would have to use the coach-house. One end of it was almost entirely occupied by a decaying pine dresser which had once been used as a rabbit-hutch, and the other end housed gardening tools and Alex's collection of non-functioning electric motors. There was a loft over, but its floor was rotten. There was nothing for it but to find somewhere else to put the rabbit-hutch, the gardening tools and the electric motors.

The second item, 'Roof', was music to me in its terseness. It meant that they had decided to start work on what Alex and I dryly referred to as 'the west wing' (the group had adopted the phrase without a smile).

The question of what to do about the west wing, or whether to do anything at all, had rumbled on for weeks. Now a decision was being requested by Dao. She was worried about the structural condition of the bedroom in which she, Simon and the children slept: it adjoined the west wing and had an inch-wide crack down the wall. It was quite safe, because Alex had had a steel tie put through the house to hold it; but Dao, with the safety of her young at stake, was not to be reassured.

Another disadvantage of the bedroom was that the section of roof above it was only partially slated and the room tended to be damp, which was not important in mid-summer but soon would be. An unsatisfactory discussion had already been held on the subject, opened by Pete with the question of why people slated roofs. He could see no reason for not patching up the leaks with anything that came to hand, and Simon observed that there were several sheets of galvanised iron lying around.

Alex rather tartly remarked that the house was a substantial one and with luck would outlast us, and we ought to be thinking about its next occupants as well. At this point Dao said that, far from being substantial, it seemed to her to be in immediate danger of falling apart. Simon mildly remarked that houses were only a lot of stones piled on top of one another and sooner or later the stones would again assume a horizontal position, and the timing of this event should not arouse emotion. For several hours after this exchange I observed between Dao and Simon what was known in the group as a 'communication break'.

When the group first formed Alex had suggested that we should finish the west wing for Simon and Dao to live in. Although accepted in principle, the idea had not been seriously developed. Dao now revived it, and, looking at it, we saw what an excellent idea it was. There was a lot of work to be done, but it could be done before the winter. All the external structural work had been completed: it was just a question of finishing the slating, glazing the windows, and putting in a new floor and ceiling. Part of the wing was already fit for occupation: that was my study, a nervous outpost of civilisation in a waste of sawn timber, bags of nails and sacks of petrified cement. I would of course vacate it as soon as the rest of the wing was completed, but meanwhile it was too small a room to be useful to anyone but me.

It was agreed to make a start on the roof of the west wing the following day. The first thing to do was erect scaffolding. While Simon and Pete were doing that, Alex, Coral and I would sort the slates into sizes. Hearing the plans made, I could scarcely believe that a problem which had oppressed me for so long could be so quickly solved.

The third decision was expressed simply as: 'Partnership from June 30th'.

The idea that the group should be legally constituted as a partnership had been put forward by Alex at an early stage. It fulfilled a number of purposes: it gave us a solid base on which to organise our financial affairs, including any commercial undertakings in which we wished to engage; it defined the basis on which we were living together and assured equal rights to everyone; and (with luck) it would mean that the house could be regarded as belonging to the group rather than to Alex, which would make it more difficult for the bank to force its sale.

Alex's trip to London had not, needless to say, solved the problem of the roofless property and the £18,000 overdraft. She had managed to stall the bank manager for a little longer. She spoke briefly about the situation in reply to a question from Pete. With problems on all fronts – architects, solicitors, builders, district surveyors, quantity surveyors, planning officials and vindictive neighbours all adding their quota of obstructiveness – it was by now so unbelievably complicated that I could only with difficulty keep up with it myself, and that was with the aid of background knowledge and regular bulletins from Alex.

I could see that while Simon grasped the situation perfectly, Dao, Pete and Coral were completely out of their depth. After several more questions, to which they received answers that confused them further, they subsided into a puzzled silence. I was sorry that Alex had not managed to communicate, but secretly relieved that I was not the only person to be baffled by the labyrinths into which she got herself.

While in London Alex had spoken to her solicitor about the formation of a partnership, and he had said that all that was required was for the prospective members to agree to form one. With the consent of all parties, the partnership then came into being. However, if any member withdrew, the partnership then automatically ceased, and had to be reconstituted.

The simplicity of it was part of its attraction. It was really no more than a formalisation of the group in terms which the world would understand. For tax purposes it would have to be formed before the end of the month. We agreed to hold a meeting on the 29th of June to discuss the details, and to constitute the partnership on the day following.

It was hot and sultry the afternoon we sorted the slates. Coral helped for twenty minutes, then went in to feed the baby and did not reappear. Alex and I made stacks of long and thin, short and fat, squared and irregular, Welsh and Delabole, while

Pete and Simon put up the scaffolding. I admired the ease with which they did it – ease, that is, compared with the way Alex and I did it, with Alex crouching on a pole twenty feet up, cursing like a navvy as she just missed locating the end in the socket, and me, never happy with heights, trembling on a pole ten feet up as a hundredweight of iron swung six inches from my ear.

I found it difficult to keep my eyes away from Simon for long. Even as, with my back to him, I measured the slates and shifted them around, I could feel his presence behind me. In the space of a few days I seemed to have fallen under a spell, and I could not decide whether it was for good or bad. Obviously my being in love with him might prove very disruptive unless handled with discretion, but for me it was surely an important achievement? It signified a freedom I had thought I would never attain. It was a gift he had made me: he had shown me that I was as able to love a man as a woman.

What about Alex? I did not think about Alex, or indeed about anyone else. It seemed irrelevant, and in any case I did not feel capable of answering any of the questions raised by my emotional state.

One question though I would have to answer: was I going to tell him? In ordinary circumstances, since I had no wish to supplant Dao even if I had been able to, the answer would have been no: but these were not ordinary circumstances. In the first place, absolute truthfulness was the bedrock of the group; in the second, Simon missed nothing and would eventually ask me what was wrong; in the third, even if he did not, he would inevitably ask me at the beginning of my next Session, as he always did, 'Is there a present-time problem?' and to lie in a Session would be like lying in the Confessional – pointless, and a blasphemy. I would have to tell him, and how could I dare?

'My brain feels as if there's a cement mixer inside it,' I said.
I had been sitting dumbly for nearly ten minutes while my

thoughts tumbled in all directions and Simon waited, to my left and slightly behind me, pen poised.

'Perhaps I should come back when I have something to say and won't be wasting your time,' I said.

After another long silence Simon said, 'Is there something you don't like?'

I admired the penetrative power of this question even as I tried to evade it. I evaded it by saying nothing.

In the end I said, 'I'm having a bit of trouble with my emotions.'

'Okay,' said Simon. 'So, is there something you don't like?'

I considered very carefully. 'I don't think so,' I said.

'I will read you a list of emotions,' said Simon. 'Tell me if you are experiencing any of them.' He paused. 'Anger.'

'No,' I said.

'Jealousy.'

I swallowed. 'Yes.'

'Hatred.'

'No.'

He named in addition, fear, envy, cruelty, misery and apathy. I said no to each, and laughed wryly at the last. He asked me to name any other emotion I felt. I postponed it as long as I could, until it could be postponed no longer.

'Love,' I said.

After a moment he said, 'The emotions I have just named are known as mis-emotions: they are unreal and negative. The one you have named is not a mis-emotion.'

'Oh,' I said.

'Is the emotion you are experiencing connected with some-one present or not present in the group?' he asked.

'Present,' I said. 'You're present all the time. That's what makes it so difficult.'

We were sitting in the field, usually noisy with insects, but I could hear no sound.

Simon said, 'We can pursue this subject as a Session, in which case I can only ask you questions; or we can conclude the Session and discuss the subject. Which do you want to do?'

'Discuss it,' I said.

He wrote something in the notebook, drew a line and put the book away. He began to talk. He told me that the root of my trouble was that I had never denied myself anything and therefore my ego was uncontrollable, and that this was the result of being brought up by parents who alternately over-indulged and frustrated me (he had obviously gathered a completely different set of data during my Sessions from those I thought I was presenting him with). He told me that I cared nothing for the group and was quite prepared to break it up. He told me, lastly, that my fault was the most serious fault of all – the perverse refusal of help offered, the knowing choice of wrong. It was in all likelihood this fault which was referred to in the Bible as the sin against the Holy Ghost, he said: the sin that could not be forgiven because it denied the possibility of forgiveness. He said this in a quiet, speculative tone, offering it as something that would appeal to my intellect as well as being morally improving.

I heard all this as if from a great distance. As I thanked him, Dao rang the bell for supper.

I do not like to think of my behaviour during the next two days. I behaved like a rejected adolescent, alternately sulking and trying to attract Simon's attention. I succeeded in attracting it, but it profited me nothing. In an access of self-pity I retired to my study and listened to Wagner: Simon, hearing the turbulent music, strode into the room and, without forfeiting a scrap of his good humour, had me out working in the garden within two minutes.

Plunging then to the opposite extreme in an attempt to please him, and out of a need to punish myself, I worked ridiculously hard the day we brought the hay in, driving myself to lift, carry and throw the bales until my shoulders and arms felt like water, and my fingers were numb from the twine, and my eyes were red with dust. Simon said nothing except, towards the end of the day as I sat exhausted on a bale, 'Some people work too hard, for reasons they are aware of.'

He behaved towards me as if the incident had not happened. As the days went by I began to forget that it had. He proposed a new subject to be covered by everyone in Sessions: drug experiences. Mine were modest by contemporary standards: the only drugs that had ever caused me trouble were tobacco and alcohol. We covered them in the first two Sessions and I made surprising and delightful discoveries about each.

It was a good time. A threatening shoal had been avoided, and we were in untroubled waters. Then early one morning there was a telephone call for Alex. Her father had died of a heart attack. She left at once for Jersey.

5

THE FULCRUM

Alex's relationship with her parents, when I met her, was polarised into love bordering on hero-worship for her father, and a sustained low-key anger bordering on hatred for her mother. Over the years her feelings mellowed but did not change their nature, and making due allowance for the emotional pitch of the relationship, I thought there was a great deal of sense in them.

Her mother was the most frightening woman I had ever met. Her forthrightness was attractive until you glimpsed the mountain of arrogance that lay behind it. She was capable of great generosity, and of an equal ruthlessness. She had never been anything but kind and courteous to me, but I had seen beneath this surface a depth of suppressed violence and a controlled irrationality which paralysed my response to her. The irrationality had not always been controlled: Alex's childhood had been haunted by the fear that one day her mother's fits of black despair would become permanent madness.

Her father, by contrast, was a quiet, mild and reasonable

man, an English gentleman, who had spent a blameless life in insurance and acquired a useful instinct for stocks and shares, but whose real interests lay in organic husbandry, fringe medicine and the innocuous foothills of the occult. He was a great reader of the works of Immanuel Velikovsky, and I held him largely accountable for Alex's regrettable conviction that all written history was a pack of lies. He was a religious man, in a diffident way. Through him Alex had inherited a distant strain of Jewish blood of which she was apt to boast, and a family crest about which she was reticent although her brother Philip wore it on a signet ring. There was an estate which had once belonged to the family in Norfolk; it had ceased to belong owing to the misplaced gallantry of an ancestor who had fought too well for Cromwell in the Civil War and been dispossessed at the Restoration. Alex had once shown me a picture postcard of the house – a pleasant place suffused with the ripe glow of ancient brickwork, surrounded by oak trees.

It was an unusual family. Both parents had a striking independence of mind, which they had imparted to all three children in quite different ways. It manifested itself partly in an inability to settle down. Alex's restlessness took the form of constant changes of direction and a very low boredom threshold, which ensured that she tired of tasks almost as soon as she had started them. Her sister, Celia, was forever embarking on new business enterprises, none of which ever fulfilled its promise. Philip, at an age when most men are frowning over their adolescent sons, was still looking for a suitable marriage partner.

Alex connected the dislike she felt for Philip with the fact that he was, as she maintained, 'just like my mother'. I could not see the resemblance, but then, apart from the occasional rudeness which I took to be normal between brother and sister, I had never seen Philip when he was behaving in the way of which Alex so bitterly complained. From direct observation I would almost have judged him to be an amiable, handsome fool, a man in whom puritanism replaced real moral sense and who was out of his depth in all the serious matters of life including relationships with women. Almost, but not quite, because every now and then I glimpsed something else, a spitefulness, a slyness, which lent credibility to Alex's furious denunciations of him. She said he was a betrayer, a snake in the grass. She had never forgiven him for a crucial breach of confidence many years ago which could only have been committed out of malice, and had resulted in her parents' realisation that she was homosexual. Not, said Alex, that she minded them knowing, but she certainly minded them finding out in that way.

There had been many other, smaller incidents when Philip had contrived to stick a knife in her back, but the major recent offence was the roof. Philip, a fine carpenter and fresh from building his own house, had undertaken to do the dormer conversion of the west wing at Bethany. At the last minute he had decided not to do it, and had telephoned to say so only the day before he was due to start. The timing made it impossible for Alex to find other builders in time to qualify for a local authority grant, and the event had cast a blight over the whole west wing enterprise from which it had never recovered.

Alex, still bitter more than a year later, blamed Philip solely for the dilapidation of the west wing, and in moments of passion was apt to blame him for the dilapidated state of the whole house and even for her financial problems over the property in London. Listening to one such outpouring I was at a loss to understand how she could involve him in the London fiasco, until she reminded me that at one point he had been going to do that job as well. As I pondered this she added thoughtfully, 'I suppose I did let him down over that. I was going to take him into partnership, and I changed my mind.' She paused, then said: 'Thank God I did.'

My uneasy feeling that in Alex's relationship with Philip lay more than met the eye was crystallised by this remark. I had known, and forgotten, the quickly-dropped scheme that would have made Alex and Philip equal partners in the London property, she to put up the money, he to do the work. I had known and forgotten that Alex had put this scheme to Philip as one that was sure to make an excellent profit and might lead to even more profitable co-operation in the future. When nothing came of it I assumed that it had been dropped by mutual consent. Now it appeared that Alex had simply changed her mind. Alex was always apt to change her mind on any issue, no matter how firmly it seemed to have been decided and no matter what was involved for other people in a change of plan. She did not seem to understand that the right to change one's mind is limited by other people's right to know what is going on. So, Alex had changed her mind about the house in London, and six months later Philip, bearing no outward sign of a grudge, had changed his about the west wing. There was no doubt that Alex was perfectly aware of the connection.

It did not make Philip's behaviour any better; in fact it seemed to make it worse; but it did introduce a justification for him from Alex's own behaviour. I began to wonder how often Philip's meannesses had been, not, as I'd assumed, wanton, but the revenge of a weak man on a stronger, younger, cleverer sister who had trampled on him. Every one of the incidents I could recall was susceptible of this interpretation: every one was the sequel of an incident when Alex had wounded Philip's pride. The original incident of the breach of confidence was a prime example, for Alex had been having an affair with a woman with whom Philip fancied himself in love. Philip at the time had been an immature twenty-five: he must have hated his sister with all the fervour of his young puritanical heart.

Where did the truth lie? In Alex and Philip were expressed two conflicting views of life: hers founded on freedom, tolerance and the pursuit of intangible goals; his founded on self-discipline, hard work and a respect for conventions. He found her lazy and unpredictable: she found him stupid and mean-spirited. Whenever I tried to weigh their respective rightnesses I found the balance tipping heavily in favour of Alex, if only because her view of life was larger than his. But I realised that the tipping of the scales resulted from the centre of balance I had adopted, and that this followed a subjective preference. What would happen if I shifted that centre, adopting a less sympathetic criterion? I could get no further with this question, because I did not know what to take as my fulcrum. After all, what I was attempting to weigh was two interpretations of the world, and over what truth could I weigh them which did not itself belong to one or the other?

I was less disturbed by the metaphysical difficulty of these thoughts than by the bright light they cast on Alex's character. In that light the shadows danced alarmingly. In time Alex's relationship with Philip came to symbolize for me everything in her which caused me disquiet.

Now her father was dead. She caught a plane to Jersey, to stand beside Philip at her father's grave.

Looking back, I am amazed at how little I understood even then. Simon did not want Alex to go to Jersey, did not think it necessary. I thought this harsh. I was a little upset because in the diary, when he might have written, 'Alex's father died', he wrote, 'Alex went to Jersey to see her mother'.

He did not want her to go because there was no point. There was no point in any of Alex's forays into the outside world. There was no point in going to help her mother, because her mother could not be helped. And there was no point in going to bury the dead, because the dead will bury their dead.

At the time I had temporarily lost sight of what the group meant. If I hadn't, I would never have made the mistake I made three days later, the evening Alex came home.

Alex's absence, since the question of which slates to put on which part of the roof had not been fully resolved, meant that the slating of the west wing could not be started, so instead Simon and Pete began to demolish some of the rotten timber inside. A bolt was put on the double doors so the children could not go into the danger area, and the house echoed to the wrenching-up and throwing-down of floorboards. I worried about my study, and crept off to inspect it when work had finished, but apart from a fine deposit of plaster-dust over everything it was unharmed.

Demolition came to an abrupt halt the day after it had started when Coral found Bishop on the patio poking his velvet nose into the baby's pram. The ponies had been brought down from the upper field where they were fenced in to the lower, unfenced fields around the house, so they could roam freely and enjoy the benefits of human company. Bishop, as usual, had taken things too far. Coral was almost hysterical at the idea of 'what could have happened'; indeed such was her distress that I wondered if she thought horses were carnivorous. When I came home from work the next day a strong wooden fence had been erected all the way round the patio and Pete was making a ten-foot gate to go across the top of the steps. Pete was also tiling the surround of the new sink he had installed, and putting up a large herb-rack in the kitchen. The herbs were to be stored in glass sweet-jars, which could be bought cheaply from sweet-shops. It was one of my jobs as Bursar to locate and purchase sweet-jars in my lunch-hour. Alex collected most of the herbs, and had promised to label them for Dao.

Pete worked very hard. I never saw him when he wasn't working. Once on the patio I heard him remark to Coral – in a tone of perfect good humour, as if mildly surprised by it – that he didn't seem to have any time at all. I sympathised. I never had any time either. Every moment of my day, from the time I got up, milked the goats and hoovered the stairs before going to work, to the time I fell into bed, was completely occupied. Not even in my lunch-hour at the office did I have time to sit over a cup of coffee and think. I wasn't tired: I had never felt more full of energy. And I certainly wasn't unhappy to work. It was simply that I had no time to think.

It seemed to me that everyone else in the group must be in the same situation, and Simon most of all. He was now doing Sessions with all of us, since Dao had asked to have them as well. And the Sessions themselves, since an hour was frequently too short to pursue an incident thoroughly, had been extended to an hour and a half. Simon was therefore spending seven and a half hours every day guiding and taking notes while we put our souls in order, in addition to what other work he did on the house and the land. Whatever his reserves, I thought, it must be a strain on him.

And was it necessary? I remembered how we had agreed that the ideal was to do as little as possible, how Simon had said with a smile that he looked forward to the time when the sound of the hammer was heard no more, and I wondered how we had got into a situation where the sound of the hammer never ceased. The house, the barns, the fences, the hay, the scaffolding, the roof . . . we hadn't stopped for weeks, and nearly every day new suggestions were made and Pete added a few more items to the list in his maintenance book. What had happened to those marvellous talks, those magical times when we had sat for hours after a meal, or in the parlour in the evening, or on the patio in the sun, and listened to Simon, and explored the universe with our minds?

Thus I reflected. And, since we always said what we thought, I said it.

Again the defence. I persist in attributing to myself the best motives, to believing that it was all a misunderstanding.

But of course he understood. He has always understood. I have never known him wrong.

And even if he had, in this case, slightly misunderstood, it wouldn't matter. Because his rightness would always, in sum, exceed mine and the excess would swallow up, as it were, any small wrongness. That was why I submitted.

We sat, then, in the parlour, I in my usual chair in the corner, the high-backed Victorian armchair which, like everything else at Bethany, struggled to maintain its dignity in spite of a broken spring. We always sat in the same places: Coral and myself on either side of the fireplace; Simon directly opposite the fireplace with Dao sitting next to him, surrounded by the children; Alex between me and Dao, and Pete between Coral and Simon.

Coral fussed a great deal over the baby during meetings, but Simon said nothing about it, although he tolerated no interruptions from his own children. If they were disruptive – which was rare – he asked Dao to take them to bed. Since the meetings were in their nature meetings for and about the group, there was no question of the children not attending. At the start of this particular evening the group was incomplete because Alex was away. It was the only time anyone missed any part of a Thursday meeting.

The atmosphere of those meetings was something I had never experienced before. It was a little like being in church; but the peace that filled the room had nothing to do with rituals: it was a peace that came from living truthfully. It was the peace of perfect communication. Simon never tired of stressing the crucial importance of communication. He seemed to attach a mystical value to it, which I did not quite understand at the time. I did, later. Perfect communication is Communion.

So there we sat on that ill-starred Thursday evening, and I announced that we had spent just over £41 in the course of the week. There had been several abnormal items of expenditure: roof battens, a pitchfork, and a quantity of pinhead oatmeal. I was just dividing the sum by three and wondering if I could pay my third and also repay the £20 I had borrowed from the kitty to get Alex to Jersey, when I heard a car come up the drive. Alex was back.

I suppose I had expected her to look upset. She looked distant, but serene. She returned our smiles calmly and took her place in the semi-circle. We went on with the meeting.

Alex said she could pay her share of the expenditure this week as her mother had given her some money. I did my arithmetic again, and it was agreed to pay the phone bill. We were running short of flour and oats, and Alex, who had not contributed to the bulk food purchase a month earlier, said she thought the food merchant would probably barter a sack of each for a small antique sewing machine of hers which had caught his eye when he delivered the initial order.

This offer was accepted with approval, and Simon said there must be a lot of things we could barter if we looked around. In time we might find we could do without money altogether.

We agreed that we could not go on doing without baths altogether. The water situation was becoming critical: there had been almost no rain for six weeks and the spring that fed our tank was running low. A bath drained the tank completely, so no one had had a bath for a fortnight. In any case no one felt like having a bath because, since the Rayburn was on all the time for cooking, the hot water was so hot it came spitting out of the taps half steam. You couldn't add cold water to it because the constant emptying of the cold water pipes had dragged the scaling of rust from their insides and the cold water was now permanently orange. It was surprising how disturbing the idea of sitting in orange bathwater was. The hot water came out comparatively clear, presumably because the sediment had had time to settle in the boiler.

Dao, who at first had been loud in dismay at the peculiarities of the plumbing system, now accepted them with humour, but Coral was not resigned. Indeed, we would all have liked to plunge into a cool bath after a day's work in the fields. We discussed, not for the first time, installing a shower, and realised again that a shower would work directly off the existing water supply and merely provide us with the same choice of clear scalding water or orange cold water.

Simon then remembered that a portable shower for campers was manufactured: it used only a gallon of water, which could be drawn off from the hot tap and allowed to cool. It was obviously the answer, and I was requested to find out the price.

The next item was the ponies. It seemed that Bishop had decided Coral was fair game. Reading galley-proofs in my study that afternoon, I had been disturbed by a movement outside the window, and, looking out, had seen Simon running full pelt down the drive. I wondered what could be happening to make Simon run, and then I heard a whinny and knew. Bishop and Osmond had decided to join Coral as she took the baby and the three children for their afternoon walk while Dao had her Session. Bishop had teased, Coral and the children had panicked, and Bishop had gleefully chased them all the way down to the gate. It was useless to say to Coral, 'Never run away,' just as it was useless to say to the rest of the group, 'These ponies are like that: I tried to tell you,' so I said nothing, and the situation was resolved by Alex's volunteering in future to escort the four o'clock walk.

The last item was the west wing. There was hardly any discussion: we were agreed that it should have top priority. Simon wrote it in the diary.

Then looking quickly round the group he asked, in his level, courteous, chairman's manner, 'Has anyone else any suggestions to make?'

I waited for a few seconds, to give other people a chance. No one seemed to have anything to say.

Slightly nervously – it was, after all, quite a bold statement – I said, 'Yes, I have. I think we're working too hard.'

I was surprised by the silence. I had expected some kind of recognition. There was nothing.

I continued.

'All these projects,' I said. 'We're all doing something all the time, we never stop. We never seem to have time to talk any more. At the start of the group there seemed to be much more time. We used to sit around and talk; it was good, we all benefited. We don't do that any more.'

My voice had risen and I had trouble keeping it steady. There was no feedback at all: not the slightest hint that they knew what I was talking about. Simon was frowning.

Alarmed, I blundered on.

'Only the other day I heard Pete saying there never seemed to be any time.'

'Don't speak for others,' said Pete.

I felt as if I had walked into a tank.

'I'm sorry,' I said. 'I know one shouldn't speak for others. I was just trying to make it clear that I wasn't speaking purely on my own behalf: I thought I was expressing a view which was probably shared by other members of the group.'

'Don't speak for others,' said Simon.

I realised I had made a terrible mistake, but I didn't know what it was. There was silence in the room. I glanced at Alex, sitting a few feet away; she was looking straight in front of her.

I waited.

But Simon was waiting. What was he waiting for? There was nothing more I could say. After a few minutes of that silence I would have been unable to speak even if I had found something to say. The silence was iron; it was ice; it was stronger than all the souls it contained.

It lasted for ten minutes by my still-ticking watch.

Simon said, 'Has anyone else anything to say?'

Receiving no answer, he stood up and walked from the room.

He wanted to bring me to my senses, I suppose, and knew that only the strongest measures would do it. I held out against him a long time. I felt an injustice had been done me. I hoped in the morning things would be different.

We went off to bed in silence, except for the smiling 'Goodnight' which usually said so much, and tonight seemed to say nothing at all. I wanted support from Alex, but she was withdrawn. She said that in Jersey she had made some important discoveries which she had come back wanting to share with the group, and instead had found herself in the middle of a distressing situation which I had provoked. We slept in the same bed, not touching.

In the morning things were not different. I spoke to no one and no one spoke to me. At about nine o'clock the bell in the hall was rung. Normally the bell was only rung for meals: if it was rung at any other time it was a summons to a meeting. Dao was calling a meeting.

We sat again in the parlour. Dao said she had called the meeting because something was wrong and she thought it should be settled. Simon asked of the group what was wrong. There was a long silence.

In the end I said that Dao was obviously referring to what had happened the previous evening when I made a suggestion and it was badly received by the group.

Simon said in a cold, puzzled voice, 'When you did what?'

I faltered. Surely that was what had happened?

'I made a suggestion,' I said. 'I thought we were all working unnecessarily hard and I suggested that it might be a good idea if we had a bit more time to . . . well, sit and talk.'

Again the complete silence, as if I had not said anything. Or as if they were waiting for me to say something in a language they could understand. On every face was the same faint smile of patience, and behind it an endless gravity.

I began to feel very afraid.

Simon waited to see if something would come out of the silence. Nothing did. After a while he picked up the thought again.

'You know what you did,' he said to me.

'No, I don't,' I said.

'You don't know?' His voice was incredulous, contemptuous.

I grasped the arms of the chair to steady myself, and kept my voice quiet and level.

'No,' I said, 'I don't understand what has happened.'

It was true. In a few minutes I had moved from absolute certainty about what had happened to utter doubt. I knew I had said what I remembered saying, but I knew nothing else. I did not know what I had meant when I said it. I did not know what effect I had intended, or what effect my words had had. I felt I was alone in a dark place. From long habit I looked to Simon to guide me, but remorselessly he threw me back on myself.

'You know,' he insisted.

Surely I had tried to help. No, I could no longer cling to that idea, which now seemed ridiculously inadequate. My motives must have been selfish. Yet I could not see how. What could I gain? It occurred to me that I was looking at the wrong thing, but I did not know where else to look.

In the midst of my confusion I felt a resentment. For surely this was monstrously unfair? Simon had turned the full force of his rejection on me in punishment of an error so small it merited no more than a stern word. Indeed I still did not know what the error was, but I was sure it was superficial, no more than a misunderstanding.

And then Simon did the thing which I had sometimes seen him do before, and which is the most frightening thing I have ever seen in my life.

He goes back into his mind. His body hangs limp in the chair: if you struck him he would not feel it. All the force of his being now drives the mind, which, at a speed reflected in the strange flickering of his eyes, scans . . . what? Information. He is reading information. Information stored somewhere I cannot reach, in a form I cannot imagine. Faster and faster the mind flickers, searching, comparing, checking, rejecting, refining ever further until the analysis is complete.

Still now, like a blue lance, the eyes pierce mine.

'What have you done?' he says.

A banal question, a question often asked of children. The primal question, the question asked of Adam and of Cain.

Let the question sink into you, do not fight it. Let it sift down through the layers of your mind, through the thickening layers until it is lost to sight and can only be sensed, and then is lost altogether. It becomes the most terrible question in the world.

I could not answer. I sat, drained, in the corner of my high-backed chair while Simon spoke.

I don't remember what he said. It didn't register. His words

105

surged over me, making no sense. I knew they were addressed to me, but they seemed to have nothing to do with me. At one point he rebuked me for fidgeting, because I was moving the toe of my right shoe slowly in a small circle.

A little later he asked if the others wished to say anything. Coral said gently, 'You see Kay, when you love people you don't want to hurt them.' I smiled at her, with not the glimmering of an idea what she was trying to say.

The meeting broke up in an impasse. People went back to their work. I walked out aimlessly into the fields.

Several hours went by. The bell rang for lunch but I didn't go in. I couldn't face them. Literally, I didn't know how to face them: I did not know what face to present to them, because I didn't know who I was. My centre of identity had been broken by Simon's question.

I found myself by the ruined cottage. It was a spot I particularly liked, at the top of a sheltered slope and overlooking the wooded part of the valley. People didn't usually go there. The field was uncultivated and given over to dock, bracken and a spreading colony of raspberry canes. I leant against an ash tree and let my gaze wander over it. I saw that it was beautiful, and that I had no part in it. It was sealed off from me.

Alex walked past. I said something to her: she stopped, grudgingly. I said, 'I'd like to talk to you about what's going on.'

She was preoccupied and unsmiling. 'I'm sorry, but I don't think there's any point,' she said. 'In any case, I have my own thoughts to think about.' She walked off abruptly towards the woods.

Only the tension in my stomach and the constriction across my forehead told me it was really happening. My mind had stopped working. Every time I started it up it whirred furiously for a few minutes, scattering thoughts instead of relating them, and then cut out again.

I forced it into life once more. What was I going to do?

I had been rejected by the group. They had, as it were, withdrawn my membership. I had a choice to make: I must go or stay. The more I thought about it, the more impossible it was to do either. If I were to stay, I must immediately heal the breach between us: it would have to be done by me, since they would not, however long the situation continued, move from their position of monolithic rightness. But I could not heal the breach without confessing myself guilty of whatever it was I was supposed to have done, and I still did not know what it was. I did not feel guilty, just hurt and bewildered. My mind formed the words 'hurt and bewildered', and I caught a glimpse of myself as a pathetic victim, and then of myself watching this creature with pity and approval, and recoiled in disgust. If I was still writing dramas for my ego, perhaps everything Simon had said about me was true. I tried to concentrate on what he had said about me, but it had gone, leaked out through the holes in my head.

I returned to my dilemma. Should I leave? At once, with a cold claw at my stomach, the question became, could I leave? This was my home. It was more than that, it was my world. If I left it I would die, deprived of vital nourishment. In any case, where would I go? To obliterate the pain of this leaving I would have to go far away; but I had no money for travel or lodging, and my job was here. Should I then just move out of Bethany and find somewhere to live nearby? The idea was grotesque, and more painful than the idea of going away altogether. I forced myself to think about it; about the mechanics of finding somewhere to live, probably in the town where I worked because I would have no car; about coming home to an empty room, and making tea for one. I told myself it did not have to be as bleak as that: I could make new friends, go to the pub in the evenings, do all the things I was not free to do now – stay in bed late, read, listen to the radio, eat eggs for breakfast. The small stirring of excitement produced by these ideas was immediately quenched by a recognition of their paltriness. Certainly I would be free. Free, in a desert, to choose whether I died of thirst, despair or loneliness. I knew the world outside the group: it was a grey, disjointed, senseless world, a world of cardboard through which its inhabitants moved like puzzled ghosts. How could I imagine that I could go back and live in that featureless, sunless place?

Yet the group, outside which I could see no possibility of life for myself, had rejected me, like an organism rejecting an unhealthy cell. The organism would not re-admit me until I was again in harmony with it, and that meant accepting a guilt I did not feel. I wondered briefly whether they would let me live somewhere on the land, in a caravan perhaps, as a sort of friend of the group but not part of it. I saw that the idea was ridiculous. 'He who is not with me is against me.' Either I was part of the group, or I wasn't.

Up by the house I heard Pete calling something cheerily to Coral, and my heart ached in its isolation. From inside, the group appeared to be a centre of radiation, pulsing outwards its warmth and light; but from outside, this magic circle presented the appearance of an unbroken wall.

Why had they done this to me?

I brooded again on what had happened, and, finding no answer, concluded again that what had really happened could not be what I thought had happened. Yet what else could have happened? I examined it again, over and over, and still I found no clue to what had taken place in that fractured moment after I said, 'We're working too hard'. The answer must lie in what I'd said, but although by now I could see many things wrong with the statement – a cocksureness and insensitivity, perhaps even an echo of the old desire to gain Simon's attention – I could not see anything sinister enough to merit his devastating response. It was an injustice, it must be: and yet if so, it was a terrible one. I did not want to think Simon unjust even in a very small way – I simply could not tolerate the idea of his being guilty of an injustice as great as this. But there was no third possibility. Either he was guilty of a terrible wrong, or I was. I had to admit that, on the past records of both of us, the likelihood of my being wrong was considerably greater.

I would not have minded discovering that I was in the wrong; indeed I would have welcomed it. But I could not honestly come to a conclusion for which neither my reason nor my intuition showed me any evidence. It was a deadlock on all levels, and somehow I had not only to resolve it, but resolve it at once. It would not loosen with my inaction but become more rigid, and it would extend its sphere of paralysis until I could not act at all.

There was only one thing I could do. Simon had refused to tell me what had happened, but I must make him tell me. Otherwise, for the rest of my life I would never be able to move beyond this point.

I went to find him.

He was on the landing, about to go up the second small flight of stairs to his bedroom.

'Simon,' I said timidly.

He looked down at me and smiled.

'Yes, Kay.'

'May I talk to you?'

We sat on the floor of the landing, he with his back against the bathroom door, I with my back against the opposite bedroom door.

He said, 'What do you want to talk about?'

I said, 'I've come to ask you if you will please explain to me what has happened, because I've thought about it for hours and I still don't know.'

His blue eyes rested on me with just a trace of humour. He said, 'Why have you thought about it?'

I thought, and smiled. 'I don't know how else to approach it,' I said.

He waited long enough for me to realise that I had just told a lie. Then he said softly, 'What happened?'

I was back again in the mists. But this time I knew which direction I should follow. Somehow I was in the wrong, for I had lied and there would be a reason.

109

Lifting the lie to see what lay underneath it, I found that I had constructed a double defence: against seeing the problem, and then against seeing the only way in which it was possible to see the problem. Presumably I also had a third defence against seeing that I had done it, and so on.

Simon now was forcing me to see what had happened.

I saw the group assembled in the parlour, smiling at the satisfactory completion of an evening's business, an evening's communication. I saw Alex, pensive and peaceful, and Simon, looking just a little tired, about to tuck his pencil away in his pocket. I saw myself, absorbed in myself, about to impose my personal view of reality on them.

I heard my voice, self-confident and stupid, making assertions, and the amazed silence that followed it, a silence in which became dreadfully clear the distance which separated this member of the group from the others.

I saw, as the time passed, how this member, though now conscious of being out of communication with the group, refused all offers of help, rejected all clues to the nature of the situation, and took refuge from imagined hostility in a fancied incomprehension.

I saw how the member's resistance to understanding the situation increased to the point where Coral's statement, in which the issue was presented in its simplest possible terms, had been seen as a riddle.

And of course it really was that simple. My self-absorption had been lack of love. Lack of communication was always lack of love. I had cut myself off. In a group such as ours there could be no greater offence. It was an act against the group. I remembered that Simon had accused me of being against the group and I had protested that I didn't understand what he meant. 'You mean you *won't* understand,' Simon had retorted.

I recalled the recent occasions when I had felt hostility towards the group or individual members of it. I had been irritated by Coral, for her excessive preoccupation with the baby, her lack of interest in any tasks that were not directly concerned with the household, and her naivety, which seemed to me to be a pose. I had been shamed on more than one occasion by Dao's directness and had once deliberately refused an invitation to talk to her because I was afraid of contact with a being so innocent and so discerning. I had felt flashes of dislike for Dao's children, particularly Sarah, the beautiful unsmiling five-year-old whom I had several times caught throwing earth at the chickens and reprimanded with a gentleness I was far from feeling.

I had experienced antagonism to the group as a whole on almost every occasion when their opinion had differed from mine on the subject of the animals. I had never succeeded in ridding myself of the idea that experience with animals conferred wisdom on the matter, even though I would readily have agreed that those with the greatest experience of animals are the greatest exploiters of animals, and therefore the least able to see what an animal is.

My irritation had reached a peak with the incident that involved Coral, the children and the ponies. I had somehow managed to tell myself that it was their own fault if they were chased by the ponies and that an unnecessary amount of fuss was being made about it. The fact that three young children had been in physical danger and that the baby in the pram might even have been thrown out and killed I had dismissed as unimportant, preferring to regard the incident as a rather amusing vindication of my view that the ponies should be fenced in.

My selfishness, my cruelty, momentarily sickened me so much that I covered my face with my hands. Behind that wall of selfishness I had sat at the group meeting, and wondered why I could not see what was going on.

I uncovered my eyes. 'I see,' I said.

'What do you see?' asked Simon, and I told him. It wasn't enough, of course: Simon always pushed one further, further than one thought one could possibly go, beyond logic, beyond experience, into a region where the investigating mind was as

111

sharp as a blade of light and as subtle as the mothlike ideas it darted among, and where even to glimpse an idea was to milk it of its burden of truth. In this quicksilver region I lost and found myself many times in the three hours of our talk, and, when at last we came back to our starting-point, I felt as though I had been made new. My understanding seemed limitless, my love unbounded.

There was just one small point on which I had a reservation. I thought that Simon had not been quite fair in his assessment of my behaviour at the meeting: he had ruled out any possibility of my having had an altruistic motive, and I thought there had been at least a slight element of concern for the well-being of the group. I started to say so.

'I agree that you're almost entirely right . . .' I said.

He transfixed me with his gaze.

'Entirely right,' he said, and waited.

I wavered. It was such a small point. I was sure he was right. Of course he was right: it was just that I couldn't see it. Surely, if I trusted him, I could afford to make this small leap of faith?

'Entirely right,' I said.

6

THE ROSE-GARDEN

Simon suggested that, since I had upset four other human beings, I should go round and apologise to them individually. It was a little difficult, particularly with Pete, but they smiled at me very warmly. Afterwards we seemed more united than we had ever been: it was as if the experience had purified not only me but the whole group.

In this confident frame of mind we started on the task that had become a symbol of the group's unanimity – the slating of the roof of the west wing.

Simon (when he was not taking Sessions) and Pete nailed the slates on, sometimes assisted by Alex, who as usual was unable to concentrate on one job for long and periodically went off to attend to another part of the roof, or inspect a chimney stack, or secure a loose window-frame. I could see that Simon and Pete were perplexed by this and unaware that Alex was making a rare effort: she was at least confining her activities to a single area. I had grown so used to her restlessness, and to persevering with my own work irrespective of it, that I had forgotten how disturbing it could be.

My job was to get the slates up to the roof. I hauled them up on a pulley to the top stage of the scaffolding in a makeshift basket that Alex had constructed out of an old window-frame. After a while, realising that I was far more likely to be decapitated by a descending slate as I stood on the ground than I was to fall off the scaffolding, I mastered my fear of heights sufficiently to climb the ladder without my knees shaking and to walk about at the top, handing up slates. I suddenly realised that I was not afraid any longer, and that probably I never had been. It had been an idea. I stood at the end of the scaffolding and gazed over the valley, exhilarated by this new freedom. In time, I thought, I shall be afraid of nothing: I shall be completely free.

I was feeling freer every day. It was the Sessions. Every day I made new discoveries, and each discovery brought a liberation, peeling off a crust of habit, lifting an unnoticed weight. One by one the tensions of the present dissolved as I tracked down the old fears and resentments that lay behind them. It didn't seem to matter where I started: every path, however unpromising, held its little crock of gold at the end.

For instance, I had discovered something quite important about my liking for tea. Tea was one of the drugs on Simon's list, and as we came to it I realised that it played a more important role in my life than alcohol or cigarettes had ever done. Them I could give up: my tea I could not.

I isolated an incident, a year previously, when a cup of tea had been particularly important. I had been feeling depressed and ill and was unwilling to get up. Alex dragged me out of bed and insisted that we talk about something I did not want to talk about – it threatened my peace of mind and indirectly our relationship. I refused to confront the issue and we started to argue, and the argument became a major row about our whole way of life. Alex was shouting at me, it felt as though she was hitting me. I started to cry. As I cried I began to see that what she was trying so violently to tell me was true. I stopped crying and we talked. Alex became gentle. She made a pot of tea. It was the best tea I had ever tasted.

Looking at the scene, I could see that the importance of that tea lay not in the fact that Alex had made it, nor in the fact that it was a token of communication. The importance lay in the fact that it was tea. I had never liked tea until I met Alex, and then, because she was always making tea, I had started to drink it. Tea-drinking had become a central ritual of our relationship. And now, at the end of a quarrel which had apparently blown that relationship wide open and obliterated all the familiar landmarks, we were still sitting in the kitchen drinking tea.

Tea was a statement that nothing had changed; and indeed on that occasion nothing had changed. Our relationship had continued as before − slightly dishonest, slightly cynical, slightly cruel, just like everybody else's relationships. For a moment we had had the opportunity to re-make it, and lacked the courage. And tea for me was still a statement that nothing had changed. While all around me were drinking herbal teas or sarsaparilla, I drank Assam with milk and two spoonfuls of sugar. It was a last-ditch attempt to preserve my old identity.

Once I had seen it I was free of it. I realised that tea was in fact a rather drab drink. I abandoned it forthwith for peppermint, with a slice of lemon and sweetened with honey.

It was one of many little things that were steadily increasing my understanding. With understanding came clarity. It was the clarity I had experienced several times before, notably on the evening when I went to the city to see Simon. Then, because it was based on an intense experience and not on an inner discipline, it had only lasted a few days before being eroded by mundane exasperations and failures. Now, at last, it seemed to have come to stay.

It was as if my mind for nearly all my life had been functioning at half-throttle. Now I found I had at my disposal a truly efficient mechanism which could think with a speed and sureness I would once have considered astounding, drawing on sources of information I often did not know I possessed, and making connections that in earlier days I would have regarded as brilliant. Very often, however, it was not necessary to think at all. One simply looked. The mental energy seemed to translate itself into terms of sight, so that one saw and understood in a single act.

One saw what people were thinking: it was nearly always some kind of fear. One saw the wounds in their hearts as plainly as if they had been scars on the face. I was filled with pity for the people I met, pity which I could not communicate. They seemed to recede from me as I looked at them. They seemed physically smaller than me: I had the impression that I was looking down on them from a height of several feet. They seemed unreal, and I understood that indeed they were. By the manner of their lives they had abandoned the reality for the illusion, and the illusion was what they had become.

I knew that spiritual insight must in the end confer psychic power, but until a certain incident occurred at Bethany I did not realise that I already had it.

Two visitors arrived one evening. One was a girl whom Alex and I had known for several years and on whom Alex had once expended a lot of time, trying to persuade her into the paths of vegetarianism and right living. The attempt had been dropped when Alex realised that Tessa's wide-open eyes concealed a complete lack of scruple and that she was less interested in Alex's ideas than in her brother. Philip at the time was a not infrequent visitor at Bethany. The friendship, such as it was, had not completely died, however, and Tessa still sometimes came to see us. On this particular evening she had brought with her a young man I had not seen before. I looked at him and felt as though I were falling into a deep, dark pit.

For a moment I thought that he had no eyes. Then I realised that I was seeing, for the first time, either pure evil or pure madness – I did not know which. From the sockets of his eyes there radiated a dense blackness which obliterated nearly a third of his face. I tried to pull my mind back to an ordinary perception, and glimpsed, as in a snapshot, a thin, nervous, moody young man standing on the patio. I asked him a question. He did not reply, but stared at me. The coalpits opened again.

He asked if he could go into the kitchen. It was an odd request, as we were all out on the patio, but I said yes. I had forgotten that Coral was inside. She came out very quickly.

'Who is that man?' she whispered to Simon and me. We were sitting side by side on the bench.

'A friend of Tessa's,' I said.

'He's . . . Simon, I don't like him. I don't think he ought to be in the kitchen on his own. Can you ask him to come out, Simon? Please?'

Simon, without moving, said, 'Kay, will you ask him to come out, please?'

I went into the kitchen and said quietly, 'I'm sorry, but would you mind coming outside again?' I stood aside so he could come past me.

Then something so extraordinary happened that I could hardly believe it. He backed away, down the kitchen, opened the window and climbed out of it.

He had not been able to come past me. Something had made him so afraid that he had had to escape through the window.

Conscious of the unbridgeable gulf that now existed between us and the outside world, Alex and I let many friendships lapse. Invitations were declined, letters went unanswered because there was nothing to say. The world, however, did not understand that we had renounced it and continued to knock at the door. We coped with the summons with varying degrees of success.

I got home from work one day to be told that the bed in my study had been made up for an overnight visitor who was expected late in the evening. She was a friend of a London friend of ours called Nick, and was coming to inspect an old showman's caravan which Alex and I had acquired years previously; she was thinking of buying it and taking it back to Wales.

The caravan was in an advanced state of decay and we had never told anyone it was for sale; and neither Alex nor I had ever heard of the girl, whose name apparently was Brenda. It all sounded rather odd.

'You know what I think it's about?' Alex remarked to me. 'This girl is having Nick's baby, and is putting pressure on him, and to keep her quiet he's going to buy her the caravan and tuck her away in Wales. You remember he was looking at it last time he came down here.'

It was a wild conjecture, but I did not dismiss it. Nick, who was loosely associated with television, had an even looser personal life. He had a charming, defeated wife. Alex, moreover, was sometimes clairvoyant.

Brenda arrived at about half-past nine, and as she walked into the house I felt the temperature drop from summer to autumn. She was about twenty-four, and she wore her unhappiness like a winding-sheet. Only Simon, Alex and I were still up. We gave her something to eat, and sat down to talk to her.

She told us about herself and the purpose of her visit. She rented a Welsh farmhouse from two young men who now wanted to move into it, which meant that she had to move out. However, they did not mind if she continued to live on the land. She wanted to stay there because she was growing herbs. She was very interested in the curative properties of herbs and intended to make a study of them. Before going to Wales she had lived with a group of friends in London and they had made gardens on the bomb-sites. It was creative.

Her fingers picked nervously at the shawl trailing over her black dress as she spoke. Why was she wearing black?

She had a cat, she said. Cats had a special kind of intelligence. In earlier times this had been understood, but we had now lost nearly all the ancient knowledge. A few people were trying to revive it.

118

I felt the hair on my arms prickle. Simon said nothing. He had not said anything since she arrived.

I said, 'The caravan is in a very bad state of repair, you know. It needs a great deal of work done on it.'

'Oh, that doesn't matter,' she said. 'These friends of mine who are moving into the farmhouse have offered to do it up for me.'

'You'd be better off buying a newer one,' I said.

'Well, you see, someone else is going to pay for it. I don't want to land him with a bill for something expensive.'

Alex's eyes drifted to the girl's stomach, which to me betrayed no evidence of a secret.

'I hope you don't mind me asking,' she said, 'but are you pregnant?'

'Yes,' said the girl. She was astonished. She recovered herself. 'That's why I want to find a caravan as soon as possible, before it gets difficult to do things.'

'But how are you going to get our caravan to Wales?' I asked. 'It can't be towed, and it'll cost a fortune to take it on a low-loader.'

'I've got a friend in Devon who works for a haulage firm. He can take it up for me for nothing.'

The silence settled like fine ash.

Simon said, 'Do you mean you are going to live on someone else's land, in a caravan bought by someone else, restored by someone else, and transported by someone else on someone else's lorry?'

He did not know Nick, and therefore did not add, 'with someone else's husband's baby.'

She went white. She said, 'I don't look at it in that way.'

'Is that what you intend to do?'

A pause.

'Well, yes, I suppose so.'

The silence returned.

After a while Simon said, 'Why do you make yourself so unhappy?'

I felt her fear.

'I don't know what you mean. I'm not unhappy at all. All my friends say I'm a very carefree person.'

'Your friends are dishonest. You are dishonest. You have just told us as much.'

She struggled like a fly in a web.

'My friends aren't dishonest. They just want to help me.'

'And in return you give them what?'

'I help them too, believe it or not. I like to help people. That's why I'm studying herbs.'

'You think you can tell what's wrong with people, and heal it with herbs?'

'Yes.'

'But what is wrong with you?'

'There's nothing wrong with me.' Her eyes were glassy, her fingers trembled as they picked at the shawl.

Alex said, 'You have to confront your own problems first. Until you do, you can't deal with anyone else's. You'll always be planting flowers on bomb-sites.'

The struggle went on for over an hour. Inch by inch Simon and Alex pushed her back towards the abyss into which she must fall. Finally, on the edge, she used her last defence. She covered her face with her hands and blacked out her attackers. She sat silently, shivering a little.

Simon stood up.

'Good-night,' he said, and went upstairs.

Alex picked up the girl's plate and cup and took them out to the kitchen to wash. I looked at the huddled figure before me. Slowly, without uncovering its eyes, it reached a hand into the shoulder-bag on the floor, groped until it found something, and brought out two pills, which it put into its mouth and swallowed. So much for herbal medicine.

Until that moment I had been undecided. I knew that the normal rules of hospitality must be thrown aside if any real attempt were to be made to help this girl. I knew that; but the girl didn't. Young, pregnant, and probably tired from a long journey, she had been subjected to a shattering experience for which nothing could have prepared her and the reasons for which she would not understand. Now she was going to have to spend the night, alone, in an unfamiliar house, in a room which was not even within earshot of anyone else – it was sealed off by the great double doors. Who knew what terrors would visit her in that room? If, at her age, I had been through what she had just been through, and had had a bottle of sleeping-pills with me, I would have swallowed every one.

I stood up and touched her on the shoulder.

'I'll show you your room,' I said. 'It's a bit spartan, I'm afraid, but the bed is comfortable. The doors may creak a bit in the night, but don't let it worry you. It's a friendly house really. In spite of appearances.'

She stared at me, with a confusion of hatred, suspicion and gratitude. She followed me to the study, and I said good-night to her. I told Alex what I had done, and why.

I did not see her in the morning before I went to work. When I came home I was told she had left soon after me, with hardly a word to anyone. She did not want the caravan. I wondered if she would ever understand what had happened to her.

'It's a great pity,' said Simon.

I met his eyes, and shifted mine away.

'If you had left her alone,' said Simon, 'if you had allowed her to experience the climax she was ready for . . . But you had to intervene. You had to intervene because you yourself were afraid of what might happen at that moment of emotional release. What a pity.'

It was true, and the damage could not be calculated.

In the same week, Charles telephoned from Sussex. Charles was an ex-public school bachelor, a director of a small firm which manufactured expensive sports cars for the export market. He was the stereotype of the xenophobic, Philistine Englishman from his greying sandy hair to his carefully casual suede shoes, and it was his great misfortune that he had been in love with Alex for the past ten years.

It was a relationship that mystified everyone, for she combined all the qualities that exasperated him, and she gave him not the slightest encouragement. In fact there were times when I thought she treated him very badly. She resented him: she resented his tenaciousness, his proprietorial attitude, his emotional demands. She put up with these things because she saw the desperation behind them and because over the years she had become irritably fond of him. And because he was charming, witty and rather rich.

It was difficult to make the mental separation between Charles and his money because he used it in his relationships. He bought people, even those he had known for years, cementing their obligation with small gifts, dinners in the best restaurants, trips abroad. It was Charles who had taken Alex to the south of France for a week when Jacques and his family were at Bethany. Alex found this ceaseless bribery difficult to cope with and eventually succumbed, as did everyone. There seemed no reason not to: after all, the only return he asked was her company. And yet it was not as simple as that: he was also asking that she share and approve his way of life, and every time Alex saw him she knew that once again she had accepted the bargain, and hated him for it.

She discharged her unease in small acts of social cruelty. He took her to lunch in a chic restaurant which had just opened in north London: Alex refused an aperitif and demanded beer, which they did not have, and then rolled herself a cigarette, scattering Golden Virginia all over the pink check tablecloth. It ruined the treat. Knowing that he wanted to take her somewhere special for the evening, she would suggest a preliminary drink in the local pub and there engage in conversation with the most truculent drunk she could find, until she wearied of paining him or until so much of the evening had elapsed that his plan was no longer feasible.

I had witnessed many such incidents, for Charles always

treated me with scrupulous courtesy and would take us out to dinner together. Sometimes I ventured to reproach Alex afterwards for her behaviour. Her reaction was violent: she would accuse me of taking Charles's side against her, of betraying her. After a few explosions of this nature I kept my thoughts to myself. She reacted in the same way when I did not completely agree with her view of Philip. Her almost hysterical anger on these occasions seemed to be the expression of a paranoia implanted in childhood, when – so she told me – she had always been the odd one out in every situation, and the thing she had come to dread most was betrayal by the few people she trusted. Anything, I decided, was preferable to awakening that paranoia.

Alex justified her treatment of Charles by saying he was a manipulator. This was true: he did attempt to manipulate people through his money. However, it seemed clear to me that he used money because he thought he had nothing else to give. He was all surface and *savoir faire*; his assured manner masked a deep nervousness, his dry wit a terror of having to think about something serious, his presents an inability to love. There was no doubt that he thought he loved Alex, but I did not see how he could love someone whom he did not understand in the slightest and with whose deepest needs he had no sympathy.

Alex said it was not love but an obsession; and indeed what but an obsession could make a man cling for ten years to a woman he desired and would never attain, a woman with whom he played a sophisticated, self-mocking parody of the disappointed lover? Only once had I seen him drop that mask. He used sometimes to come and stay with us at Bethany, and during one of these visits Simon turned up. After a few vain attempts to attract Alex's attention, Charles had retired to bed, feigning a sudden chill, and stayed there for two days. He knew nothing about Simon but he had intuited that here, at last, was the man who could take her away from him, and he had not been able to cope with his jealousy.

123

Charles telephoned from Sussex, wanting to speak to Alex, one afternoon when Alex was in the middle of a Session. Sessions were never interrupted for any reason. It happened to be a day when I was at work. Coral answered the phone and asked him to ring back at another time, not between four and six o'clock. Two days later he rang again, at five-fifteen. Coral again answered the phone and, apologetic, said she could not fetch Alex but would ask her to ring him.

I could imagine Charles's reaction to being told that Alex was on the premises but could not speak to him. 'You'd better ring him,' I said to her, 'or he'll be down here.' I could not imagine anything more disastrous. Alex didn't. Alex had a rooted objection to making phone calls which, combined with her rooted objection to doing what was expected of her, ensured that she almost never rang anybody back. I waited for the inevitable third, angry call. It came the following Monday, to my office.

He was very near hysteria, the clipped voice sharp and jerky. 'I'm sorry to trouble you at work, Kay, but it seems the only way I can get hold of anyone. I'm extremely worried about Alex. Is she all right?'

I felt immediately his antagonism to whatever was happening at Bethany and the unspoken demand that I share it. I was determined not to compromise.

'Worried?' I repeated. 'I don't know why you should be worried. Alex is very well.'

'I've telephoned twice and been unable to speak to her.'

'Well yes, she . . . couldn't come to the phone, that's all. She was doing something.'

'Something so important that she couldn't leave it to come and speak to me?'

'Yes.' How, in a busy newspaper office, could I tell him about Sessions?

'I don't believe it,' he said. 'I may tell you I've been round to see Harry, and he's told me a number of things I don't like the sound of.'

Harry was the friend in whose house Alex stayed when she went to London.

'Oh?' I said.

'He says that when he last saw Alex, a few weeks ago, she was behaving very strangely and saying things that were quite out of character. As if she was repeating someone else's words.'

'Oh really!' I said.

'He was extremely disturbed by it. It appears you've got some sort of commune staying with you . . .'

'We're sharing the house with some friends,' I said. 'It's a sort of experiment in group living.'

'Well what am I supposed to think, when some strange woman answers the phone and tells me that Alex is not allowed to speak to me?'

'I'm sorry, Charles, but you have yourself to blame,' I said. 'If you'd rung back at the time you were asked to, instead of at the time you were asked not to – '

'I've got a company to run,' he snapped. 'I ring Alex when I can. I don't expect to be told that unless I ring at a certain time she'll be forbidden to come to the phone.'

'Oh, don't be ridiculous.'

'It's not at all ridiculous. I tell you, Kay, after seeing Harry it has seriously occurred to me to wonder whether Alex is being kept a prisoner in her own house, and whether her friends ought to rescue her.'

I was suddenly flooded with anger. I said coldly that he was suffering from delusions and should take a grip on himself. There was a moment's profound silence. Nobody spoke to Charles like that.

'You assure me that Alex is all right?' he said at last.

'Perfectly all right,' I said. 'She's never been happier.'

'Then I suppose I have to accept it,' he said. 'Thank you. Goodbye.'

I was shaking a little as I put the receiver down. I felt bruised by his desperation and fear. However, I was pleased with the firm way in which I had handled the conversation.

The world was full of Charles and his kind, I reflected, and although deserving of pity they did a great deal of harm. They devoted themselves unceasingly to seeing that no one ever got out of the trap in which they were caught themselves.

I reported the conversation verbatim to Alex, who to my amazement accused me of rudeness. The idea that she had caused the situation by not telephoning Charles herself did not seem to have occurred to her.

I did not think very much about my relationship with Alex, beyond registering the fact that it had changed. It had lost a certain quality of humorous complicity, which I sometimes regretted while recognising that the regret was sentimental – I was regretting the loss of an intimacy which had been based on lack of respect.

Viewing our past relationship with unclouded eyes, I saw just how mutually disrespectful it had been. How we had used each other, hidden behind each other, lied to and, in our different ways, bullied each other for years! And in spite of this we had been proud of our relationship, proud of what we called its honesty, proud that it had endured when all around us the relationships, marital and non-marital, of our friends were breaking up in storms we had weathered. The stability we had been so smug about had been founded on apathy and fear. In such a relationship there was no room for love.

Now that I was free to love this person with whom I had been living for seven years, I found her changed. She had abandoned old habits, interests and friendships with apparently no trouble at all, and the wildly fluctuating needle that had registered her life-direction had come to rest, pointing confidently away from the past. The volatile, difficult, whimsical Alex had gone, and there was a new Alex, serene, controlled and smiling. I was ashamed to find that I did not like this new Alex as much as I should have done, that I sometimes hankered after the old Alex I had fallen in love with, the Alex who had been so exciting and so unhappy. But I was not even consistent, for on the occasions when Alex did relapse briefly into something like her old self I became acutely disturbed.

I was puzzled by this perverse ambivalence, but dimly recognised the same mechanism at work when Simon pointed out to me that Alex and I were never happy at the same time: when one of us was happy the other would be having a difficult day. His interpretation was that we did not want each other to be happy. I rejected this, but could not find another explanation. I sometimes felt that Simon was over-harshly critical of our relationship. Alex indeed had once told me that she thought he disapproved of it, but I regarded that idea as nonsense. Simon, I thought, could not conceivably subscribe to contemporary prejudices about homosexuality: his concern was with the content of a relationship, not its form. In any case, if a homosexual relationship is defined by sex, ours wasn't one. We had stopped making love six months ago, out of boredom. Not, of course, that Simon knew that. Alex wanted to tell him so, but I indignantly forbade her. It was no one else's business, I said. I was secretly a little upset by her attitude, which amounted to a rejection of the sexual side of our relationship. I was content to let it lapse, but not content to see it condemned. Alex had always been a latent Puritan: now she declared herself. We went on sleeping in the same bed, out of habit, and because we liked it, but there was no denying that much of the intimacy had died between us.

It was inevitable, it was perhaps desirable, and in any case it didn't matter. Our relationship now flowed as a current within the stream of the group, and what mattered above all was that it should flow harmoniously, so that the progress of the group was not impeded. I was made very conscious of the disruptive effect a lack of harmony could have by the periodic tensions that occurred between Coral and Pete. Little was said on these occasions, but a chill descended on the house and the group was fragmented until the breach between these two individuals was healed. I saw that such tensions resulted from

127

the disrespect of familiarity, and thought it was a good thing that there should be a little space between Alex and myself.

So, at least, my reason thought. My subconscious apparently did not, and took action in its own way.

It happened the day the dustbins were emptied. I usually took them down to the road in the back of the car on my way to work. On this occasion the large dustbin had been filled with bits of scrap iron, broken tiles and all sorts of rubbish, and was too heavy for me to lift. I asked Pete to help me get it into the car, and as I set off down the drive I wondered how I was going to get it out at the other end. By sliding it and wriggling it I almost managed, but there was a moment when I had to take its weight, and at that moment I knew I had done something very stupid. My back began to stiffen, and by the end of the day it was as much as I could do to get up from my desk.

I hoped I had merely strained it, but when two days later it was no better I accepted the obvious and made an appointment with the osteopath. That left me with another five days to get through. I was trying to carry out my usual duties, but cleaning the stairs was very difficult, and just getting up in the morning took about ten minutes. I mentioned at supper the first day that I had hurt my back, but I had clearly been too casual about it because the very next day Dao asked me to take the big iron casserole out of the oven for her and seemed surprised when I apologised and said I couldn't. After that I didn't like to mention it again.

Alex of course knew I was in pain and offered to massage the area for me, but I refused because I didn't think I would be able to bear it. One afternoon I was so tired that I went up to the bedroom and lay down for half an hour, risking Simon's displeasure. He disapproved, quite rightly, of people retiring to bed feeling sorry for themselves, and in spite of the shaft of pain that shot through me as I sat on the edge of the bed trying to take off my shoes, I could not quite rid myself of the suspicion that that was just what I was doing.

However, at the finance meeting when I had to get up from

my chair to collect the money, I could conceal my disability no longer.

'Why are you walking hunched up?' asked Simon sharply.

I explained that I had hurt my back.

'Touch your toes,' said Simon.

My forehead went clammy. 'I can't,' I said.

'Try,' said Simon. 'See how far you can get.' The pain took my breath away, but I found I could bend quite a lot more than I had thought. I also found, under his unremitting direction, that I could shrug my shoulders, move my hips and do a number of other things which I had assumed would break me in two. After an hour of concentrated anguish and embarrassment – I was performing these antics as a solo in front of the assembled group – I was, to my surprise, fairly supple and in much less pain.

I kept up the exercise during the following days, and by the time I went to the osteopath I was wondering if in fact there was anything wrong with my back. The osteopath was in no doubt. 'Sacroiliac,' he muttered, and banged and kneaded my shivering skeleton into what I belatedly recognised as the right place. I was relieved at the vindication, but at home no one seemed much interested.

By that time I had realised why I'd done it. It was a classic case of an injury with a psychological cause. Two years previously I had hurt my back while digging the garden. Alex had been out at the time, drinking in town with someone with whom I knew she was contemplating an affair. It was her one infidelity. I had done it to claim her attention then, and I had done it again now.

This realisation came to me in a Session, but I kept most of it to myself, considering it to be too personal for Simon's ears. He knew that something was missing, and the Session ended on an unsatisfactory note. It was the first time I had not fully expressed my insight, and I was disconcerted to find myself on the brink of manufacturing an insight for his benefit. I wondered if I had begun to invent discoveries when there were none to be made. However, what concerned me even more was that he should not interpret my slight awkwardness at the end of the Session as a communication break.

Since the very life of the group depended on communication, a communication break, even a minor one, was potentially a very serious matter. Simon was therefore quite right to pursue them as vigorously as he did, but I thought that sometimes he detected them where they did not exist, and in doing so created them. I could recall at least one such occasion, and on that occasion, when Simon had insisted for ten minutes that he felt a communication break within the group and every member of the group denied having had one, I offered myself as a sacrifice and said that it was mine.

I said I had been out of communication with him earlier in the day when we were moving the rabbit-hutch out of the barn. This was true, but it had been a split-second's resentment, immediately repented, when I thought he was making fun of me. It had not been a real communication break, which entailed the blocking of one's responses towards another. I knew that every other member of the group, if questioned, would have to admit to half a dozen identical falls from grace, committed and remedied, in the course of the day. But I saw that Simon's insistence was creating a tension far more dangerous than the will-o'-the-wisp he was pursuing, and since it did not seem to matter much what had started the pursuit, I volunteered to be the person through whom the tension was discharged.

The partnership meeting should have been a joyful occasion, a culmination. Work was proceeding well and harmoniously. Four rows of roofing slates had been put up, the herb rack in the kitchen extended, and more vegetables sown. The patio fence had been boarded to make it doubly animal-proof, and in their new security sunflowers smiled by the steps from earthenware pots.

To conserve water – there had still been no substantial rainfall – all waste water was now collected in large metal barrels which Alex had obtained for next to nothing from a local factory. Pete had made a notice board and fixed it to the kitchen wall; it bore Session times, telephone messages, requests for shopping, and a list prepared by Alex for Dao's benefit of the mineral and vitamin constituents of various foods. Alex had appointed herself the group medical officer.

'The place looks nicer and nicer every day,' Dao wrote in the diary. We gathered in the rose-garden at three o'clock on the afternoon of June 29th to discuss how to give the group a legal form.

Dao and the children were a little late in appearing. As we waited for them I looked round appreciatively at the garden. We were working so hard that almost the only time I spent in it now was when I cut the grass. It was a charming, unkempt garden, sweet with the scent of the old-fashioned shrub roses I had planted for Alex. They were the only roses she liked, and I understood why. They sprawled in superb profusion, the crimson Gloire de Dijon, the delicate candy-striped Versicolor, the lovely peachy-pink of the thornless Zéphirine Drouhin. The last I had planted in a corner of solid rock; it had taken me two days with pick and shovel to gouge out the cavity it now grew in.

However, in spite of the name chosen for the garden by Simon (to Alex and me it had always been simply 'the garden'), it was not the roses that dominated, but the low-curving quince tree, almost sweeping the ground with its fragile black fingers, which each year long before the other trees were awake announced the spring with an unfurling of mossy yellow buds. I had a special affection for this tree: its faith touched me, its generosity humbled me. It was old now, and needed propping up, but still its skirts broke the angularity of the garden with a graceful counterpoint and seemed to curtsey to the spiring pittosporum that fluttered small fastidious leaves just behind it.

Dao and the children arrived and settled down on the grass.

We waited for Simon to open the meeting. I had brought a notebook and pencil, in my capacity as Bursar. I now saw that Simon also had his notebook and clipboard, and felt embarrassed. I should have realised that he would take the notes. I hoped he wouldn't think I was being officious, or implying a criticism of his competence. I was so preoccupied with this ridiculous anxiety that I missed quite a lot of what was said in the first few minutes, and my sense of dislocation lasted for the rest of the meeting.

Simon said it had been agreed that we should form a partnership, and wrote down the names of the members. We agreed that the children were too young to be members. Simon then asked what we were going to call ourselves. We had already spent several hours discussing this and reached no conclusion: we simply could not find any name that seemed to convey our vision of the group.

In the end Simon, who had been thinking for some time, said, with the air of someone suggesting something entirely new, 'I propose the name Bethany.' It was a name we had discarded right at the beginning as being too familiar. Simon, as always, was inviting us to re-examine our preconceptions. The name was perfect.

What were to be the partnership's sources of income, Simon then asked. There was a silence and we all studied the grass. I said there was my job, and Alex said yes, but surely I wanted to give that up soon. As a matter of fact I didn't, I was going through a phase of enjoying it, but it seemed an inappropriate moment to say so. Simon said we should be discussing ways in which the whole group could earn a living. We reviewed the possibilities, of which growing herbs was still the favourite. We had planted a lot, but they took time to grow.

Alex mentioned her own income from letting the workshop premises in London. It was only £8 a week and just paid the mortgage on Bethany. She wanted to give it up, she said. She thought there was probably nothing wrong in making a profit out of rents, but she didn't want to be involved in capitalism herself. She proposed to write to her tenants asking them to take over the lease themselves.

In the startled silence that followed my mind raced. It would be an enormous relief to me if Alex disburdened herself of the business, because while the tenants were far from conscientious about paying their modest rents on time, the quarterly demand for Alex's lease payment on the whole building came in with terrible regularity, with the result that four times a year when the mortgage had been paid there was a frightening deficit in Alex's already grievously overdrawn bank account. (Alex had three bank accounts and shuffled her debts in a never-ending rob-Peter-to-pay-Paul between them. The branches she patronised had, I noticed, a remarkably fast turnover in managers.) It would also mean there would be no more querulous letters from the Borough Council about the lack of separate lavatory facilities for male and female employees. Altogether the property was a recurring headache I would be delighted to be rid of. Nevertheless £8 a week was £8 a week, and I wondered where in future it would come from.

I was faintly irritated at Alex's assumption that the decision was hers alone to make: I felt she should have phrased it as a suggestion rather than a statement of intent. I felt, too, that her approach was childish, and I wondered for the hundredth time why Alex persisted in seeing herself as a businesswoman when she was the most hopelessly unbusinesslike person I had ever met. I looked at her face, flushed with youthful enthusiasm, and then at the other members of the group. Dao and Coral were smiling, but in response to Alex's mood: they had not grasped her meaning. Simon and Pete were frowning slightly. I felt a chill I had felt before.

Simon made no comment on Alex's announcement. Instead he went on to consider what assets the partnership had. There were, for a start, three vehicles – the Humber, the Thames truck and the Mini. Alex said that her friend Harry in London, to whom she had several years ago given her old Mini van when he was experiencing hard times, was now enjoying better times and wanted to give it back to her. It would need a little money spent on it but was basically sound, and would enable us to sell the current Mini. She thought the latter would fetch about £400 if smartened up. We agreed to start immediately on smartening it up.

I thought Alex's estimate of its value was wildly optimistic: it was very little less than we had paid for it two years ago, and since then it had been knocked around, neglected, used for transporting hay, goats and cast iron, and driven daily over the mud-filled ruts of our abominable lane. The interior light had been broken by a drunken Scotsman, the passenger window-catch by a drunken Cornishman and the wing-mirror by the ponies; moss grew along the rear window-frames and there was no carpet on the floor because Alex had taken a dislike to it and thrown it away. I mentioned some of these imperfections, but Alex brushed them aside. A few days' work was all it needed, she said.

Then there were the various items of machinery, starting with the rotovator which had never been entirely satisfactory and now only worked when it felt like it, and then never for more than ten minutes at a stretch, after which you had to let it rest for half an hour. Alex thought that this rusting, temperamental creature could, 'if we got it serviced', be valued at £180. Admittedly prices of garden equipment had risen steeply in the past few years, but the machine had only cost £120 new. She was equally sanguine about the value of the veteran motor-mower we had bought for a few pounds in a Dartmoor village years ago, brought home at great hazard in the boot of a Ford Anglia, and never persuaded to work at all. 'It's an antique,' she said. 'People collect them, you know.'

I was used to Alex in this mood and knew there was no point in contradicting her. When she was convinced of the value of an object no amount of evidence to the contrary would change her mind. She habitually asked too much for the odds and ends she advertised in the local paper, with the result that she never sold them and I had to pay for the advertisement. On the other hand, when buying she would expect to get things much too cheaply. It was not that she wanted to make a lot of money on the transaction, because she abhorred profiteering and would often give quite valuable things away. It was simply that she was unrealistic about money. In some way it frightened her; whenever she had it she had to get rid of it, spending compulsively until it was all gone. If she was unable to spend it fast enough she would lose it out of her back pocket. She did not understand what money was, and held it at everything but its true value.

The list of assets grew long and impressive, and when we totalled it up it came to about £4,000. It seemed to me that the exercise was rather pointless because surely we did not intend to sell most of the things that were listed. However, Pete was thinking along different lines, because suddenly he said with a delighted smile, 'But there's a house!'

Simon smiled. Dao and Coral laughed at their own foolishness in forgetting the biggest asset of all. I was too taken aback to say anything. Surely the house, which was virtually in hock to the bank, could not be given to the partnership just like that? The complications were immense. I also felt a momentary flush of anger. Alex might well want to give the house to the group – she had indeed said as much – but I did not think it was Pete's place to assume that it was already theirs.

Simon said, 'How much is the house worth?'

I looked at Alex. After a slight hesitation she said, 'As it stands it's probably worth about twenty-two thousand.'

'But surely – ' I said.

'There are certain difficulties about making the house over to the partnership,' said Alex. 'The bank has a charge over it, which means that I'm not free to do what I like with it.'

'A charge?' said Dao. 'What is that?'

Alex started to tell her, and, seeing the incomprehension only deepen in Dao's eyes, went back to the beginning and tried yet again to explain how she had come to owe eighteen and a half thousand pounds to the bank. My mind drifted away, reluctant as always to enter the maze, and snapped back to attention again to hear Alex saying that she thought it was nonsense that individuals should own houses, charge other individuals for their use, and make money out of buying and selling them.

'Houses belong to the people who live in them,' she said.

She added that banks however did not understand this, and she would have to find out exactly what her position was as regards giving Bethany to the partnership.

Simon, who had been listening attentively, wrote 'House, £22,000' in the notebook. We agreed that the partnership would start the next morning, and that in my lunch-hour Simon and I would go to see the manager of the local Barclays Bank and open a partnership account. We would show him the list of assets.

'Perhaps he'll give us a loan,' said Coral innocently and missed, in the ensuing laughter, its depth of irony.

Simon asked everyone to sign the book. I wondered privately what the bank manager would make of us. We had chosen Barclays because neither Alex nor I had ever had dealings with that bank.

Coral went in to make us all a drink. We sat quietly on the grass listening to the humming of the bees. It seemed to have been a very successful meeting. Yet there had been something wrong. There was a shadow in Simon's eyes.

Normally we helped ourselves to breakfast when we were ready for it. But next morning Simon seated himself at the head of the table and asked us all to come into the room.

'I would like everyone to be here,' he said. 'I have something to say.'

There was a solemnity in his manner that disquieted me.

He waited while we assembled. Then he said, 'I find that I do not want to be a member of a partnership. I do not want to be part-owner of a house. And I do not want to go on being Organiser of this group.'

136

7

TROUBLE

It was as if, just before the assault on the summit, the leader had abandoned the expedition.

I did not understand what had happened. We sat at the table, shocked and silent. Finally Pete spoke.

'I don't understand,' he said.

'I do not want to tell people what to do,' said Simon. 'I don't think this group needs an Organiser. You may not agree, in which case perhaps someone else would like to be Organiser.'

The idea was so preposterous that no one attempted to reply.

After a while Simon said, 'The fact that I have stopped being Organiser doesn't mean of course that you have to stop doing your jobs. You may decide to stop doing them, or to carry on. You must make up your own minds.'

He smiled equably, picked up his spoon and began eating his muesli. I struggled to eat mine. Pete and Alex were thoughtfully chewing theirs. Coral fed the baby, Dao attended to her children. We sheltered from the silence.

I realised that we were being required, as individuals, to

take an important decision. No one else seemed aware of this responsibility, or that it could not be deferred. I cleared my throat and said, 'It seems to me that we need someone to look after the money, so I shall continue as Bursar unless someone else would like to be Bursar. Or unless people feel that we don't need a Bursar.'

No one said anything, but they all smiled encouragingly, which I took to mean that I should carry on. I waited for other people to speak on their own behalf, but they all finished their breakfast in silence and one by one went out to the kitchen, leaving me alone with Simon. He was peeling an apple.

By this time I had achieved an interpretation of his behaviour. As I got up from the table I said, 'I'm glad you're off the hook.'

I meant that as Organiser he had presumably found himself, in the interests of the group, assuming a position of authority which conflicted with his principles, and that I was happy for him that he had resolved the dilemma.

He looked at me strangely, without warmth.

'I wasn't on a hook,' he said.

It was an unmistakable rebuke. I went outside and saw to the goats. As I was about to leave for work Simon came into the kitchen with a pile of the exercise books he had used for taking our Session notes.

'I'm returning these to you, as they're your property,' he said to us. 'It's up to you what you do with them. You may well decide that the bonfire is the most suitable place.'

He could not have expressed his contempt more clearly. I was shocked. I had regarded the Sessions as one of the most valuable experiences of my life. I wondered at that moment if I knew anything about Simon at all. I remembered several occasions in the past when I had not understood his behaviour. I had felt on those occasions as if I had suddenly seen that I stood on the edge of a precipice.

I went to work, telling myself that things would be clearer when I came home.

I sought out Alex immediately on my return and asked her what had happened during the day.

'Nothing,' she said.

'But surely you discussed it. Decided whether you were all going to carry on.'

'No,' said Alex, 'nobody said anything.'

'But that's extraordinary,' I said.

'Yes,' said Alex, 'I know.'

I could not understand it. The ground had been taken from under our feet, and everyone was continuing as if nothing had happened. The only reference to the event was made by Dao, who said something wry about lost sheep. She continued to cook, Coral to housekeep, Pete to fix and mend and Alex to inspect the crops, just as if the centre of the structure had not dissolved away. But the fact that it had was made painfully apparent whenever a question came up that required arbitration or a decision. Instinctively we would wait for Simon to pull the threads together; and he would smile, and say nothing.

I was dreading the Thursday finance meeting and was committed to it. It was as bad as I expected. I had never chaired a meeting in my life, and the contrast between my amateurishness and Simon's mastery was so painful that I rushed through the essentials in five minutes and sat back in my chair, hot with embarrassment.

'That concludes the financial business,' I said. If anyone else would like to say anything, please go ahead.'

After a pause, Simon stood up. 'Thank you,' he said, with a polite nod in my direction, and strode from the room.

As the days passed we settled down again. Outwardly, except that there were no Sessions, very little had changed. Yet I felt that something of fundamental importance had happened and had not been confronted.

Simon's abdication was recorded in the diary by Dao with the words: 'The Organiser has left. A friend comes.'

But on the page for the previous day, below 'Partnership

139

meeting in rose-garden', Simon had pencilled the cryptic entry, 'Comm. B'.

Communication break. Whose, and with whom?

The potato patch had not been watered for six blistering weeks. The trough that fed the top field only held enough water to keep the smaller and more vulnerable plants alive, and transporting water in buckets from the house to supply ten fifty-foot rows of potatoes was not a viable proposition.

One evening I saw Pete and Simon deep in conversation over an old copper boiler they had found in the nettles by the cottage. Half an hour later as I was thinning the turnips I heard an engine labouring at full throttle, and turned in time to see the truck, with Pete clutching the copper boiler clinging on the back, and Simon grinning at the wheel with a cabfull of excited children, rounding the steep corner into the field.

They had filled the boiler with twenty gallons of water, quite a lot of which was still inside it when they lurched to a halt and started looking for the end of the hosepipe. The hosepipe was a hundred feet long and slightly too wide for the outlet of the boiler, so that Pete had to crouch on the truck holding the boiler at a steady angle while Simon held the end of the hose in place and all the rest of us manipulated its almost interminable length along the potato rows.

Everyone helped, even Coral, who did not normally venture among the vegetables, and after about ten minutes nearly everyone was helpless with laughter. As the water level in the boiler fell the flow along the pipe diminished, until Pete was wrestling with the boiler at shoulder-level to increase the gravity-feed while Simon struggled to keep the hose falling off, and in grudging recognition of these efforts a trickle of lukewarm water sauntered out and vanished instantly into the ground. At the end of it Simon was soaked, Pete was soaked, the children were soaked, and the potatoes remained surprisingly dry. Two days later it rained in torrents.

The day before the storm we had repaired the roof of the

barn. It had gaped reproachfully for months. When Simon said after breakfast, 'I suggest that today we repair the red barn,' I was delighted. Yet that was the day when I first felt it: the trouble. There was something different about Alex. Or rather, there was something ominously familiar.

We were up on the roof of the barn, she sitting astride the ridge, I perched on a ladder, clearing away the ivy. I was still not entirely happy at the top of a ladder, particularly when leaning far out to the side to wield a heavy sickle, and the heat from the metal roof struck up at my face and made me feel faint. I was making a poor job of it and Alex was chaffing me, as she used to do in the old days when humour was as often as not a mask for contempt. Conscious of my clumsiness, I retaliated petulantly. It was a relief to climb down and let Simon and Pete come in to shift the rafter.

The thunderstorm broke at about ten o'clock at night. The lightning lit up the whole valley; the thunder seemed to tear the sky apart. Coral appeared, white-faced, at the top of the stairs, beseeching Pete to come to bed. We all went to bed, although there was no point in trying to sleep. Alex and I lay awake for hours, united again in our joy of the rain and our dread of what it would do to our leaky, long-suffering house. In the event not too much came through, except in the parlour where the French windows had never fitted properly and there was a small flood on the floor. In the morning the world was intensely green. I stood outside and listened to the deep breathing of the grass.

It was the next night that the ponies got out.

I had just fallen asleep, and it was some time before I could make sense of the sounds that assailed me. There were feet on the stairs, a loud opening and shutting of windows, and Simon's voice, uncharacteristically agitated, asking for either Alex or me to get up. 'You needn't both get up,' he was saying, 'but can one of you come quickly.'

I pulled myself back to consciousness. No need to ask which of us was going to get up: Alex had a remarkable capacity for sleeping through disturbances. I struggled out of bed and into my clothes and followed Simon's voice.

'The horses are in the top field,' he said. 'Someone must have left the gate open.'

The vegetables were in the top field and the ponies could not be allowed to stay there. It was a nuisance, but I didn't really mind – it was such a beautiful night. But Simon was upset: it showed in the odd jerkiness of his speech. I was puzzled, but I dismissed it from my mind. The important thing was how to get the ponies out. Trying to catch them was out of the question – I would simply end up chasing them, and chasing them would either result in wholesale destruction of the vegetables or in the ponies' breaking through the fence into the woods, after which they might wander for miles. I would have to call them, and they might or might not come. I hoped Simon would leave it to me: if he was with me they would certainly not come.

He followed me in the direction of the field. I turned to ask him to stay behind and in the moonlight saw to my horror that he had picked up the big rake.

'What have you got that for?' I asked.

He stared at me. 'To drive them out,' he said.

'I should put it down,' I said. 'These ponies can be led but they can't be driven.'

I had never spoken to him like that. The terse words echoed in my mind as I walked up the field and started calling.

They didn't come. I could see them, two pale shapes against the shadowy hedge. I called again. They shifted a little, and watched me.

Oats. They would come for oats if I rattled a bucket. I went back to the barn to get some. I saw Simon standing on the patio, watching me. I went back up the field with the bucket of oats and shook it, and called again.

There was a stir of interest, but they didn't come.

Then I heard Alex's voice. They heard it too, and moved a few paces forward. Bishop whinnied.

142

Alex took the bucket from my hand and walked on into the field, giving the musical call that I could never quite imitate. There was a drumming on the ground and the grey shapes swept towards her, then pulled up abruptly and nuzzled and jostled to get into the bucket. Slowly Alex began to walk back down the field, and they followed her. We went through the gate, and shut it.

'Thanks,' I said.

Simon had gone.

In an attempt to dispel the disturbing quality of the incident, I apologised to Simon the next morning for speaking to him so sharply.

All Simon replied was, 'Someone left the gate open.'

My feeling that something odd had happened was confirmed by a look at the diary page for that day. Almost at the bottom of the page Dao had written, 'It's been a peaceful day,' and directly underneath it, in Simon's hand, was written 'Thunder and lightning'. It was so pointed as to be unkind. It was also unfair: the thunderstorm had raged the previous night, and had been all over by the start of the day. I wondered what was troubling Simon, that he should find a symbol in the storm and express his disquiet in so uncharacteristic a way.

It was the last thing Simon wrote in the diary, except, three days later, the solitary word, 'Trouble'.

I did not know what had caused it. All I knew was that suddenly Alex was behaving in the most extraordinary way.

It had started with what I could only describe as an insensitivity to the feelings of the group. Somehow she had lost the wavelength, and everything she said and did was slightly discordant.

She complained to me about the way Pete and Simon were slating the roof. They were doing it all wrong and breaking a lot of slates, she said. I heard this with a shiver of disbelief. Alex had never been satisfied with any building job done for her. As each new builder appeared on the premises with his barrow and plastering board she had enthused to me about his skill and honesty, then in a few days had begun to find fault, and by the end of a week would be raging at his incompetence. It made no difference whether he was a master craftsman or a weekend plasterer from the Gas Board: Alex would declare he had botched the job and cheated her. I did not know enough about building to be able to judge, but it seemed to me that in this endless procession of workmen there must have been some who had been dismissed without cause. I did not understand why Alex was incapable of having a satisfactory relationship with someone working for her, but I came to foresee and dread the bitterness in which these relationships always ended. However, it had never occurred to me that the same poison could begin to work in her relations with Pete and Simon, who were our friends, and were going to live here, and were doing it for nothing.

And she was always going out. She had always liked going out in the car on her own, and had made numerous trips to buy odds and ends for the building and to collect watercress and wild herbs, but now she was going out every day on errands which seemed less and less necessary. It was as if she wanted to get away from the house. The implications were very disturbing, and I knew that Simon was unhappy about it. 'Why does she want to go out?' he said to me. 'There is everything here one could want. I walk down to the road with the children and I have no wish to go any further. I would never go out at all if I didn't have to.'

I remarked to Alex that her absences were becoming pronounced, but she reacted impatiently. She pointed out that Simon went to the city regularly once a week and Pete sometimes went twice, once with Simon in order (we assumed) to draw their Social Security, and once with Coral to the flat to do the washing in the washing machine. 'Which is quite unnecessary,' added Alex. 'And you go to work three or four days a week, which gets you out of the house. So why should I be expected to stay here?'

144

'But why don't you *want* to stay here?' I persisted.

'I like to be on my own sometimes,' said Alex. 'I like to get away and think.'

Think. About what? Her tone forbade me to ask her, but it was of the utmost importance. 'We shall have no secrets,' Simon had announced at the start of the group; and, barring those things which were properly private, we had none. We were transparent to each other. Alex now had ceased to be transparent. She had deliberately withdrawn communication, in order to concentrate on thoughts which she would not share. The thoughts themselves might be harmless enough, but the exclusiveness with which she invested them was dangerous. In any case, why wouldn't she share them? I suspected that she was indulging in an introspection that was not only pointless but unhealthy, because it was food for the ego. I hoped she would take the sensible course and talk to Simon about whatever was on her mind, but far from wanting to talk to him she seemed actually to be avoiding him; and he, since there were no longer any Sessions, lacked the framework in which the problem would formerly have been tackled, and had to wait for her to broach it.

When one's eyes are turned inward, one cannot see other people. Alex did not see the puzzlement on the faces of the group as she talked to them about her property problems one sunny morning on the patio. The conversation had been set off by the arrival of another letter from the bank manager. The overdraft had reached £19,000, and a man whom Alex had believed to be seriously interested in buying her roofless building for a luncheon club had turned out to be interested only if he could buy it at site value, which was a quarter of the sum Alex needed. Alex's thinking about the problem had now become quite tortuous: she wanted to form a syndicate with various friends and acquaintances, who between them would put up the money to pay off the debt and convert the building into a series of rented *pieds-à-terre* for businessmen. Alex's contribution to the syndicate would be the building itself, since

145

she had no capital; but the difficulty was that most of the friends whom Alex hoped to interest in the venture had no money either, and Alex was now engaged in working out ways in which they could raise their part of the investment, and calculating the return they might expect. I wondered why Alex's solutions always tended to be more complicated than the problem. Simon voiced the same thought, but with a sharper insight: it was that sort of thinking that had created the situation in the first place, he said.

If she had examined his statement she would have found it was a lifeline. She glanced at it and discarded it as irrelevant. Soon afterwards she went out again, this time to see a solicitor in town. The purpose of the visit was not clear: it was just Alex going out again.

One afternoon when we had hardly communicated for days she came up to me in the vegetable garden and said she wanted to talk to me. I stopped what I was doing and waited, but she would only talk in a place away from the house, so we went and sat under the chestnut tree.

She started to talk about our relationship. She talked urgently for half an hour, and made no sense. I kept trying to tell her that our relationship was not important, that what was important was the dislocation of her relationship with the group and whatever lay behind it, and that that was what she should look at. Focusing on our relationship was an evasion, I said, and she was in danger of taking herself in. I was by now very worried. Even her insistence on talking away from the house seemed sinister, as if she was set on placing as many barriers between herself and the group as possible. I asked her what she was protecting, but she wouldn't listen. She said, over and over again, that we had to let each other be free.

'Of course,' I said. 'I know that. If there is no freedom there is no relationship. But to have a clear relationship you must be clear in yourself: and *you* are evading something.'

In the end we both gave up. I was left confused, but with a strong feeling that she had wanted to confuse me. There was something I must not be allowed to see. I knew that whatever it was she only dimly sensed it herself. I also knew that she was desperate.

That evening as I was cleaning out the car, preparatory to its being 'done up', I heard the dogs bark and saw that we had visitors. Walking up the drive were a couple we knew in the town; they had probably come to find the reason for our prolonged absence from the pub. No sooner had I registered this than there was a flurry of feet and Alex thrust me aside and jumped into the car. I was in the middle of washing the windows.

'Where are you going?' I said, stupid with surprise.

'To get some watercress,' said Alex, as if it was obvious.

'But – I'm in the middle of cleaning the car,' I said.

'Well, that's your look-out,' said Alex. 'You know I go out in the evenings to get watercress.'

She released the handbrake, spun the wheel, and roared down the drive past the astonished faces of our visitors.

I looked at Simon, who was sitting on the patio and had witnessed this scene. He looked at me gravely. It was either the behaviour of someone who did not know what she was doing, or a declaration of war.

I had a busy morning at the office next day, and by half-past twelve I was hungry. Usually I brought sandwiches, but this morning there had not been enough bread. The idea of a roll from the shop, lifeless white bread stuffed with rubbery cheese and a limp lettuce leaf, did not appeal. An old desire began to gnaw at me. I struggled with it, but in a few minutes it had won. After all, what did it matter? I slipped across the road and bought myself a Scotch egg from the bakery.

I bit into the spicy, fragrant sausage-meat and was suffused with ecstasy and guilt. It was freshly-made and delicious. The egg-yolk was golden and creamy. I wolfed it. I was about to take the last mouthful when Alex walked through the door.

She took one look at the morsel in my hand and burst out

laughing. I felt myself blush crimson. Then I started to laugh too.

'Well, well,' said Alex. 'So this is what you get up to.'

'I don't!' I protested. 'This is the first time – '

'Oh, don't tell me,' she said. 'I don't care what you eat. It's your problem.'

We went out and had a cup of coffee together. There was a barely-concealed grin on her face. I couldn't blame her: I must have looked ridiculous sitting there with a piece of sausage-meat frozen halfway to my lips. I tried to recover my poise, but without much success. I told myself it was unimportant, but somehow it was not. A few months earlier it would have drawn us together in a shared joke; instead, it had added another layer to the thickening wall of glass that stood between us.

By evening I had almost forgotten it. After supper we gathered in the parlour and talked. It was like the early days of the group. With no Sessions there seemed to be much more time. We talked in a relaxed way about how the work was proceeding. The repair of the red barn had distracted us temporarily from the west wing, and there had been several days of intermittent rain which made slating impossible. We discussed what work could be done inside, and in particular what we were going to do about the floor.

The upper storey of the west wing had originally consisted of two rooms separated by a raised landing to which a couple of steps descended from the main part of the house. It was an odd arrangement and looked even odder when the walls of the rooms were knocked down to create what Alex had intended as a single large studio, for in the middle of this area there now stood a little island about six feet wide raised a foot above the rest. Part of the floor was rotten and had been taken out, but the island, being sound, had been left intact. The question now was what to do about it.

It had never occurred to me to doubt that a floor should if

148

possible be level. Simon however looked at it with different eyes.

'Why should a floor be all on the same level?' he asked. 'It might be nice to have a small platform in the middle of the floor. People might like to sit on it to eat their muesli.'

Everyone smiled. I pursed my lips. In the East people sat on the floor to eat; in the West they did not. I found the idea of an eating-platform in a Cornish farmhouse ridiculous and rather repugnant.

'Kay does not want to sit on the floor to eat her muesli,' said Simon.

'No,' I said. 'I regard sitting on the floor to eat as being probably unhygienic and certainly bad for the digestion.'

Dao's eyes were dancing with laughter. 'In my village . . .' she began.

Alex cut in. 'You're so middle-class, Kay,' she said.

It was openly contemptuous. There was a moment's stillness in the room. Simon attempted to repair the damage.

'You could try looking at it another way,' he said to me. 'People are sitting on one piece of wood rather than another, that's all.'

As usual, I found his mixture of humour and analysis irresistible, and laughed. It was a cultural block, I said, and I would try to eliminate it. Simon would have let it go at that, but Alex couldn't.

'When are you going to start?' she said.

I caught mockery in her eyes. It was obvious that she was thinking of the Scotch egg and implying that if I couldn't wean myself away from meat and eggs there wasn't much chance that I could wean myself away from a cultural prejudice against sitting on the floor. Then I glanced at Simon, who was regarding me with gentle amusement, and felt certain that she had told him. Embarrassed and humiliated, I had little spirit to parry the ensuing thrusts which Alex playfully delivered during the remainder of the evening.

In the bedroom I reproached her for mocking me in public,

149

but she denied it hotly. She seemed astonished that I should think her capable of mentioning the Scotch egg to Simon. She intimated that my imagination was getting the better of me. I went to sleep feeling wretched and confused.

Next day things seemed to have returned to normal, but again Alex surprised me.

'What's the programme today?' enquired Pete as we washed up our bowls after breakfast.

Simon smiled, and said, in joking reference to the discussion of the evening before, 'I think we should demolish the west wing.' It had been decided not to leave the raised platform after all, but to take out the entire floor.

Pete went off to get his tools, and I was vaguely aware of Alex slipping out of the door behind him. I did not see her again before I left for work.

She was not in evidence when I came home in the evening. There was an air of disquiet in the kitchen. Almost the first thing Dao said to me was, 'Kay, please, what is the meaning of "demolition"?' Dao frequently asked me the meaning of words. She was a keen student of language, and liked to compare my definitions with Simon's. Fortunately they usually agreed.

'Demolition?' I said. 'Destruction. Breaking something up.'

'To demolish means to break up?'

'Yes,' I said.

She nodded with satisfaction, and returned to her cooking pots.

Simon and Pete came in a few minutes later.

'Have you seen Alex?' I asked.

They looked serious. Alex had hardly been seen all day. She had announced abruptly that she was going to see Mr Pascoe, one of the neighbouring farmers, about harvesting the oats, and disappeared. When asked whether she was going to help with the west wing she had replied that if they wanted to pull the house down they would have to go ahead without her.

Light dawned. 'God!' I said in exasperation. 'What's the matter with her?'

'We were hoping,' said Simon, 'that you could tell us.'

I understood with relief that I was not struggling alone to make sense of Alex's behaviour.

'I don't know,' I said. 'But it seemed to me that there was something odd going on last night in the parlour. As a matter of fact I thought she was mocking me, although afterwards she said she wasn't.'

'She was,' said Simon and Pete together, with a certainty that drove all doubt from my mind.

'It was very strong,' said Pete. 'It really wasn't nice at all.'

'Well, she did have a reason,' I started to say, but Simon interrupted.

'There was no reason for what I saw last night,' he said. 'It was cruel. And you are making excuses for her.'

I stopped in my tracks. Cruel. Alex had mocked me for years, for being unadventurous, resistant to new ideas, careful with money, respectful of the written word . . . all the things suggested by the epithet she had flung at me last night – 'middle-class'. She had mocked me for being everything she was not for so long that I took it as an inevitable part of life. It was time I looked again at this habit and called it by its proper name. Mockery hurt: it was intended to hurt. There was a word for that.

'Yes,' I said softly, 'I suppose it is cruel.'

I looked up and was enfolded in the kindly warmth of their smiles.

At first I was not sure whether Alex had changed or whether my view of her had changed. Then I realised that something simpler and more dramatic than either was happening: Alex, under pressure, was revealing herself.

The ponies got out again, as they were bound to. Once they had got out they went on getting out until they were bored with it. This time they had broken through the hedge bordering

151

the stream and gone on to Mr Webb's land. It would be difficult to get them back. Alex got up early, fetched two bridles from the barn and asked me to come with her.

It was a superb morning, and I just had breath as we climbed the steep hill on the far side of the stream to admire it. There was a heavy dew. A few white puffs of cumulus floated in a blue sky. Alex was silent and self-absorbed.

Suddenly she said, 'I hope I can count on your support.'

I stared at her, appalled.

'Support in what?' I said.

She walked on in silence. The unhappiness surrounding her was almost tangible.

'Support in what?' I repeated. 'What are you going to do?'

'I'm not going to do anything,' she said.

'Then what are you talking about?' I asked.

She didn't answer for a while. Then she said roughly, 'Oh, forget it.'

I tried to get out of her what she meant, but she refused to say any more. Without speaking we went on and collected the ponies, and brought them home.

I went to work with a dull feeling of dread in my stomach. Alex was going to do something terrible. She was going to break up the group.

That day or the next she came to the office again in my lunch-hour and asked for the keys of the car. She was very tense. I went out to the car park with her so that we could talk. I asked where she was going. When the answer came I could hardly believe my ears.

'I'm going away for a few days,' she said.

It was some moments before I could find words.

'But . . . what for?' I finally managed.

'Because I have to,' she snapped.

'You don't *have* to do anything,' I snapped back. 'You're going because you want to. Why do you want to?'

'To think things over.'

152

'What things, for God's sake? What can you think about there that you can't think about here?'

'It's none of your business.'

'It *is* my business. It's the group's business. You think you can come and go as you like and never mind what effect it has on other people.'

'Don't I have a right to come and go in my own house?'

'It isn't like that, Alex, you know it isn't. We're a unit. You're destroying the unit.'

We were shouting at each other, both desperate. Alex got into the car, slammed the door, and began to reverse out of the car park. I followed her, banging my hand on the bonnet and still shouting, conscious of nothing but the need to prevent this disaster.

She drove into the street and stopped. I put my hand on the door and said furiously, 'What the hell is the matter with you?' and the scene started all over again. Then suddenly it stopped, and we stared at each other, badly shaken.

'All right,' said Alex. 'I'll put the car away and we'll talk about it.'

We went to the lounge bar of a hotel we used to drink in. It was spacious and private. Alex had a glass of water. I had a half-pint of lager. It tasted synthetic and bitter.

We talked. Both of us were trying hard, but we did not manage to communicate. I knew that if Alex went away there would be no hope for her. She would have surrendered her chances of spiritual life to the Alex who went away whenever things got difficult, and she would have surrendered them finally. I pointed out that she was running away, and that it was vital she should find out what she was running away from.

'The answer is *here*,' I said. 'It's inside your head.'

What Alex was trying to tell me I was not at all sure, but it appeared to be a paranoid fantasy about Simon. He had, she insisted, been deliberately spiteful about the house; he had spoken of 'demolishing' the west wing.

'Oh don't be ridiculous,' I said. 'He was referring to taking the floor out.'

'He said, "Let's demolish the west wing".'

'For heaven's sake, you don't imagine he wanted to raze it to the ground, do you?'

'No. He wanted to hurt me.'

'Alex.' I held my head in despair. 'Simon doesn't want to hurt anyone. He isn't capable of spite. You know that. You've known him for five years and in that time he's never said a spiteful word. Why are you telling yourself that he wants to hurt you?'

'I don't know why he does, but he does. I think he thinks that I wanted to take over his position as leader of the group. Simon is a bit paranoid, you know.'

My head spun. It was as much as I could do to keep pace with Alex when she deviated this far from rationality, but I clung to my perception that behind the mental contortions was a need to evade a truth, probably a simple truth.

'Why are you twisting everything?' I said. 'You *must* find out *why*.'

But she could not move outside the small, mad cage she had made for herself. We achieved this much, that she said she would not go away. Exhausted, I returned to my office.

Alex did not go away, but she did the next best thing. She retired to her room.

I went in to see her several times, to try and get her to talk or coax her downstairs. She refused, and all but dismissed me. I usually found her sitting at the bureau. She seemed to be spending most of her time writing in a big old-fashioned exercise book. I knew what that meant. In times of stress, especially when confronted with an emotional problem, Alex would attempt to sort it out on paper. It was exactly the wrong strategy to adopt, because Alex was a talker, not a writer, and as soon as her pen touched paper she lost herself in labyrinthine sentences and quagmires of abstract nouns. In spite of this she maintained that writing helped her to organise her thoughts.

She sat now at the big oak bureau that, together with the double bed, took up nearly all the bedroom, and tried to organise her thoughts about what was happening. It was poignant, because I knew that not only was it a hopeless task but the very fact that she was attempting to deal with the situation in this way meant that she had no understanding of what was happening. If there was one thing utterly contrary to the group's philosophy it was sitting down alone at a desk and writing about one's state of mind; and the very reason why Alex found it necessary to do this was that she had temporarily lost touch with the group's philosophy. To break the vicious circle all she had to do was get up, go downstairs and say 'Hello'. I told her this. She stared at me as if I were speaking Chinese.

I was full of pity for Alex in her isolation. I took her cups of tea or fruit juice when we had a drink; I took her some lunch. She thanked me curtly. She did not appear at supper, so afterwards I took her a bowl of soup. She had gone to bed, and said in a cold, peremptory tone, 'Put it on the chair.' I felt her ingratitude, but told myself that she was disturbed and I should not expect anything.

When I returned to the kitchen I found Simon's eyes on me.

'Where have you been?' he asked conversationally.

'I took some soup up to Alex,' I said.

'Is she ill?' asked Simon.

I hesitated. 'No,' I said.

'Then why can't she come down and get it herself?'

There was no answer. I sat down on the one stool in the room and studied the patterns in the rough slate shelf.

Simon said, 'Why is she making you take food to her?'

I was startled. 'She isn't,' I said. 'She hasn't asked me to.'

Simon said, 'She is sitting up there in that room silently demanding that you take food to her.'

I reflected. Certainly she hadn't asked me not to. Certainly her attitude to me was more that of the hotel guest to the waiter than that of friend to friend. As I thought about it I realised that in fact it was a monstrous impertinence.

Simon said, 'Why do you let her get away with it?'

'She has to eat,' I said. 'She won't come down for it.'

'If you didn't take it to her she'd have to come down for it. She would be so hungry she would simply come down. By taking it to her you're keeping her up there.'

Of course I was. Why hadn't I seen it? I realised the reason why I hadn't seen it was that I wanted to serve her. I had wanted to preserve our relationship, make her feel I hadn't abandoned her.

'You are doing her a disservice,' said Simon.

There was a long pause.

'Yes,' I said.

'So,' said Simon. He crossed his legs on the wooden chest and tucked them under him. It meant he was preparing for a serious talk.

'Why do you let her get away with it?' he said.

'She's . . . well, she's very disturbed,' I said.

'Is she ill?' repeated Simon.

'No,' I said. 'She's . . .' I buried my face in my hands. I didn't even know what I meant myself.

Simon said, 'She's manipulating you.'

'No,' I protested.

'Yes she is,' said Simon. His voice was steel. 'She goes to her room and snaps her fingers and you jump to attention. What a way for one human being to treat another. She's pushed you around for years.'

I felt as if I had plunged off a cliff edge.

Simon said, 'She has so little respect for you that she will actually drive off in the car when you're in the middle of cleaning it. I've never seen anything like it. Why do you let her treat you like that?'

I became aware that our voices had risen and were probably audible to Alex in the bedroom above. There was a gap in the floorboards which we had never got round to filling. Instinctively I raised a finger to my lips.

He gazed at me incredulously. 'You're afraid of her,' he said.

There was nothing I could say. Behind my gesture lay years of compromise, renunciation and dishonesty, all dedicated to the cause of keeping Alex happy. I never got what I wanted because Alex always wanted the opposite. Alex always got what she wanted because there was hell to pay if she didn't. I gave in, always. I was afraid of what would happen if I refused.

I sat quite still and absorbed it. I would never be afraid of Alex again. I saw how utterly powerless she was to hurt me. And I saw something else: I saw why it had been so difficult for me to grasp the very simple nature of my subservience.

'I've always thought,' I said slowly, 'that Alex had a special quality which I lacked. A sort of spiritual compass. I knew she was capable of behaving badly; but ultimately, where moral questions were concerned, I always trusted her judgement. I thought she knew better than me. And now, when something happens which throws doubt on that belief, it is very difficult for me to adjust.'

Simon said, 'I know exactly what you mean. People have felt much the same way about institutions such as the Church.'

His words released such a burst of clarity in my mind that for a few minutes I said nothing, but sat bathed in its radiance.

Simon smiled affectionately at me. He knew I had made a great breakthrough.

I did not take any more food to Alex, and the following day she came down in mid-afternoon to get herself some bread and apples. To my delight, as I passed through the kitchen, I saw her in conversation with Simon.

It could not have been the conversation I hoped, however, because when I went in there again about quarter of an hour later they were sitting in silence, Alex staring moodily at the

157

floor. I interpreted the tableau without difficulty. Simon had asked Alex a question which she was not prepared to answer. As I stood there looking for the string I had come in for Alex got up and went back upstairs.

Then suddenly it seemed to be all right again. Alex was downstairs, once more smiling. She came in for supper. In the evening we all sat in the parlour and talked. Alex said she planned to go to London soon to collect the car from Harry, and we agreed.

Alex and Simon stayed talking in the parlour as the rest of us went off to bed or to finish various jobs. The parlour door was ajar as I passed it on the way to my study. They seemed to be talking about the evening when Alex had accused me of being middle-class.

Alex was saying, 'I didn't mean it to sound like that. If I was at fault, it was just insensitivity. I was feeling so high I didn't stop to think.'

And I heard Simon reply cheerfully. 'Yes, I can understand that. It's simply high spirits, as you say. One imagines everyone else is feeling the same.'

My heart froze. Had he been wrong, then, about Alex's behaviour? Had she persuaded him he had been wrong? If Alex could pull the wool over Simon's eyes when he had already perceived the truth, what hope was there for her or any of us?

Alex's talk with Simon went on until late. I went to bed, confused and unhappy. Eventually Alex came to bed, and she too seemed disturbed. We lay in silence, not together yet not apart, like uncertain children. I heard Simon come up the stairs and go to his bedroom. About an hour must have passed. The house was full of something threatening. It was like a bomb ticking.

Then I heard a door open and Simon's feet on the landing again. He stopped outside our bedroom door and said, without bothering to lower his voice, 'Since no one can sleep we might as well continue our talk, Alex.'

Alex started to get out of bed. It was like a repeat of the night when the ponies got out. I began to feel I was having a nightmare.

'What the hell's going on?' I said.

'I've got to,' said Alex with extraordinary vehemence. She went downstairs.

I lay and waited. Sleep was out of the question. I listened to the sound of voices from below.

It must have been well over an hour before I heard the parlour door open and footsteps go along the hall and into the kitchen. The outer kitchen door opened and someone went outside.

Then someone else came out of the parlour and up the stairs. The bedroom door opened. It was Alex, in a terrible state of agitation. She pulled her clothes off and climbed into bed, shivering and muttering. Utterly bewildered, I did not know what to do.

Finally she said bitterly, 'Keeping me up until three o'clock in the morning, when I have to go to London tomorrow.'

'*What*?' I said.

'I'm going to London tomorrow. Oh, don't you start, Kay. I've had enough for one night. Just go to sleep.'

I did eventually manage to get a little sleep. In the morning before anyone was up I drove Alex to the station to catch the early train. She seemed calm.

8

ALEX

It rained hard the morning I took Alex to the station: fat, heavy summer raindrops. I welcomed it as it streamed down my face and neck and soaked my shirt. The goats hated it, and I took them hay in their stalls. I was collecting a last armful of hay when Simon ducked under the doorway into the barn.

I did not want to talk to him. I wanted to be alone. My feelings about Alex had turned another somersault in the past few hours. She had been very gentle when she said goodbye to me at the station, almost as if she were concerned about me, when I had far more reason to be concerned about her. Her composure seemed unnatural and I was afraid to conjecture what lay behind it.

'Where is Alex?' asked Simon.

'She's gone to London,' I said. 'I drove her to the station.'

'She has gone to London?' he repeated incredulously.

I had assumed that he'd known she was leaving in the morning. I now realised that she had decided on this abrupt departure not in spite of her conversation with him but because of it. It was flight.

I met his eyes, and saw in them such distress that I was shocked.

'It's terrible,' he said. 'It's terrible.'

I leant against the wall of the barn and watched the rain. The world was dissolving, I thought.

Simon said, 'Can we talk?'

My brain computed automatically. It was half-past eight. I had to be at the office at nine. No, we could not talk.

'I have to go to work,' I said.

'This is important,' said Simon.

'So is my going to work.'

'More important than what is happening now?'

'I can't do anything about what is happening now,' I said, 'I can go to work, and I have an obligation to.'

'And you think that's more important?'

I closed my eyes. I felt very tired. Ahead of me I saw an emotional ordeal I did not think I had the strength to face. I wished it could all be over, without knowing what I wished for. I clung to the familiar.

'I'm sorry, Simon, but I'm going to work,' I said. I pushed past him with my armful of hay into the yard, where the rain had slowed to a patter of drops, conscious as I walked towards the goat-shed of his sad eyes pressing on me.

If I had not been so preoccupied I would have known that Myrtle would kid that day. She was due, and a goat due to kid will nearly always, in a dry spell, wait until the first damp day. When I came home from work the kid, pure white and a billy, was lying neatly folded in a corner, while Myrtle stood above him munching hay. Her udder was tight and distended. I waited until everyone else was out of the way, then took her into the stall to milk her. I did not want anyone to witness this scene.

It was essential to take off the milk, because the kid had already drunk its fill and Myrtle was producing enough for the normal complement of two. She was already uncomfort-

161

able: if not milked, in twenty-four hours she would have mastitis. Nevertheless she would do her utmost to prevent me milking her; she would want to keep every drop for the kid. I had dealt with Myrtle before: it would be a question of whose will broke first.

I tied her by her collar to the hook in the wall, gripped the collar in my left hand, pressed my left leg against her flank and, making noises as soothing as possible in the circumstances, reached for the swollen teat with my right hand. She leapt in the air, bucked violently, and threw me against the opposite wall.

I picked myself up and tried a different position, holding her against the wall with my thigh while with my left hand I gripped her left hind leg to stop it kicking. She lashed out with a kick like the recoil of a cannon and I found myself five feet away in the water bucket. After half a dozen further attempts we both had a rest. My elbow was bleeding. I had squeezed about an ounce of milk out of the teat.

I talked to her, explaining why I had to do it. She flicked her ears and bleated piteously. I fed her some bread from my pocket and tried again, cursing Alex who always went away when she was needed.

After half an hour I was exhausted, but so was Myrtle, and I had drawn off about two pints of milk. It had gone on to the floor, the walls, my jeans and boots. I hadn't bothered to bring a saucepan – it would just have been an additional hazard. I untied her, patted her, and with a grim sense of achievement walked outside into Simon's ice-cold gaze.

'What are you doing to that goat?' he said.

It was a disastrous moment to be pert, but I couldn't stop myself.

'It's more a question of what she's been doing to me,' I said.

'You tie her up, force her to be milked, and then make jokes about it?'

'Look,' I said, and all my strength drained away in utter

162

weariness, 'I had to milk her. She has too much milk. She'll get mastitis.'

'She was terrified.'

'I can't help it. I had to do it.'

'Hitler said he had to kill the Jews.'

'She would get ill, Simon. Goats can die from mastitis.'

He must have seen something in my face that convinced him. He opened the gate of the goat-pen to let me through. I went back to the house. He walked away without another word.

About an hour later I heard a tremendous clatter from the goat-pen followed by an agonised bleat. I rushed out in time to see Myrtle pinning one of the other goats, Janice, against the fence and butting her viciously. Janice had obviously gone too near the kid.

To prevent further violence I shut Myrtle and the kid away in their own part of the shed. Then I went down to the cottage, sat on a log and thought. In the space of a few hours the goats had become an enormous problem.

The previous evening, before Alex left, the goat question had been given a thorough airing. They were still being tethered. On a few occasions we had let them free, and as a result the apple trees in the orchard had suffered severely and a shrub on the lawn had been reduced to a mangled wraith. But I was conscious each time I led them out and snapped the chains on to their collars that I was doing something which ran directly counter to the aims of the group, and which escaped condemnation only because the other members of the group had nothing directly to do with the goats.

That Sunday, however, Pete had watched me as I moved their stakes and took them out to browse along a new section of hedge. He brought up the subject as we sat talking in the parlour. 'The goats are still being tethered,' he said.

We went through it all again, the necessity of preserving vegetables, the difficulty of fencing, the pointlessness of giving the animals away. I, as always, felt defensive about my role

163

as goat-keeper, which was silly because no one was attacking me. I also felt irritated. It was all very well for them to take this high tone about the subjugation of animals, I thought, but they were glad enough to have the milk in their muesli and their evening cocoa. So when Pete said, 'Why do people keep goats, anyway?' I said they did it for the same reason as we did: they liked the milk.

There was a silence, and then Coral said brightly, 'Well, let's stop drinking the milk. We'll have cows' milk instead.'

I mustered my patience and explained to her for the third time that while cows were not actually tethered they were subjected to treatment far crueller, being the raw material of an industry that systematically killed, castrated, and separated young animals from their mothers in the name of profit.

'Nearly half the beef in this country comes from the dairy sector,' I said. 'In every bottle of cows' milk there's a dead calf.'

The silence that followed this statement was even more thoughtful. Simon broke it by saying, 'Perhaps we should stop drinking milk.'

Of course we should. I did not want to, but was ashamed to say so. Everyone else was in agreement. Dao, asked whether the children could do without it, said that Thai children had never tasted milk until the Americans introduced it into the schools as a propaganda stunt. Alex reminded us that it was possible to buy a milk-like substance made from plants; it was used by vegans.

The upshot of the discussion was, firstly, that we should stop drinking milk, and secondly, that we should begin immediately on fencing off a whole field for the goats. Until it was ready we would keep them in their enclosure where, although they did not have much freedom, they were at least not tethered. They would still, for a time, have to be milked, but I would take a little less each day until eventually the yield dried up. The question of cheese and butter did not arise, since

164

we hardly ever ate cheese and used soft margarine on our bread.

It all seemed very simple, until Myrtle had her kid. Now I could not leave them all in the enclosure together because Myrtle would savage the other two intermittently all day. In the ensuing panic the kid might even be trodden on. I could not let them out, because they would eat the vegetables. There was no other enclosure into which I could put them. There was only one thing I could do. I would have to leave Myrtle and the kid in the pen, and tether the other two.

I knew that I should say something about it instead of simply getting on with it, but I had never shaken off the idea that the goats were my responsibility. I also knew that to raise the subject at breakfast time would invite another lengthy discussion which would make me late for work. So in the morning I slipped out and led the two goats down to the field. The sun was already hot, and I had trouble finding a patch for them that was both shady and good pasture. They made things difficult for me as only goats can, giving a tremendous tug on the chain when my grip was most relaxed, then suddenly careering in a circle and wrapping the chain round my legs.

With mounting irritation I hammered in the stakes in what I knew was not the best position, and started walking back towards the house. I continued walking for about twenty yards after I heard Janice bleating, but when the bleating rose to a pitch of frenzy I had to turn back. I had committed an elementary mistake: the curve of the hedge partially hid one goat's grazing circle from the other, and when her companion was grazing close to the hedge Janice could not see her. Goats hate being alone.

I went back and moved Janice's stake. Then, hot, tired and depressed, I walked slowly back up the drive. At the top, under the laurel tree, stood Simon, pale with disbelief.

'Why have you done that?' he demanded.

'I had to,' I said, 'because of the kid.'

'Two days ago the group agreed to stop milking the goats.

165

Last night you milked a goat which was so unhappy to be milked that you had to use force. Two days ago the group agreed not to tether the goats. You have just tethered them.'

'I have to tether them,' I said. I tried to sound calm. 'Myrtle is attacking the other two because of the kid.'

He jerked out his arm and pointed down the field. 'It bleated after you,' he said, with such emotion in his voice that it was as if I had chained him to a stake.

'No it didn't,' I said.

'It bleated after you and you moved it a few yards and left it there.'

'It bleated after the other goat because it couldn't see it,' I said. 'That's why I moved the stake.' I was no longer trying to keep the exasperation out of my voice.

The anguish in Simon's eyes darkened into anger. He towered above me.

'You knew it was wrong,' he said. 'You walked up that drive with your shoulders slumped and your feet dragging. You are suffering.'

'I'm tired, and it's hot, and I have a lot of things to do before I go to work.'

'To work?' He forced the word out as if he could not believe I had said it. 'You are going to work when *this* has happened?'

I had a suffocating sense that we would go on playing this scene until I capitulated. I did not want to listen to any more.

'Yes, I'm going to work,' I said. 'I'm late and I don't even have time for breakfast.'

I walked past him into the house. When I came out ten minutes later he was still standing under the tree.

'Goodbye, Kay,' he said.

I looked him in the eyes. Blue, fathomless eyes. I did not care.

'Goodbye, Simon,' I said, and slammed the car door shut.

I got through my day's work mechanically, my thoughts circling round what had happened. I felt emotionally drained. It seemed suddenly a great strain to go on living in the rarefied atmosphere of the group. I longed for ordinary things: pub conversation, rough laughter, the tolerance and humour of the world. I yearned for the company of people who accepted the necessity of milking and tethering goats, people who did not require of me a remorseless and unremitting self-scrutiny. But even as my mind formed these images I saw behind them the unconscious cruelty, the moral sleep of the animal soul I had rejected. I belonged to neither world: I was condemned to myself.

I thought about Simon. He seemed to be two people. The second, the Simon whose granite silences and unexplained withdrawals frightened and baffled me, appeared only rarely, but when it did it was as if I had found myself alone on an alien planet. The first Simon was capable of infinite understanding, wisdom and love. I did not know what the second Simon was capable of, and the doubt terrified me. It terrified me not because I was afraid of being hurt by him, but because I had placed my soul in his hands and I might have been wrong. If the second Simon could strike such fear into me, I thought, what might he have done to Alex, whose tough exterior concealed such vulnerability, such frail balance? Her mental distress when last I had seen her might, for all I knew, have become something I could not even think about.

Yet, I remembered, Alex was always strong when I was weak, and only weak when I was strong. I needed to talk to her. On my way home from the office I telephoned Harry's number in London. She was out. I was on my own.

I did not go in to supper. I milked Myrtle again: she made an initial demonstration, but soon quietened. I took her some sycamore branches and stood stroking her as she ate, and she pressed against me affectionately.

I busied myself in the barns, avoiding Simon. Later I brought the other two goats in and milked them. I took the same amount of milk as usual. I left it in the kitchen without bottling it. Dao could decide what she wanted to do with it.

Simon was sitting in a chair on the patio as I went out.

'Hello, Kay,' he said.

'Hello, Simon,' I said.

His humorous half-smile swept through my defences as if they had not been there.

'Is there something you would like to talk to me about?' he said.

I brought out another chair and sat down.

I hoped he would begin, but of course he did not. I waited for the disquiet in my mind to crystallise.

I said, 'I have been avoiding you.'

'Why have you been avoiding me?'

I said carefully, 'I see two people in you. One is kind, humorous, and motivated by love. The other is harsh, and motivated by something which I don't understand. Sometimes I think you're cruel.'

He seemed surprised. I thought he was surprised, not that this should be said to him, but that I should say it.

'Cruel?' he repeated.

'Not unwilling to hurt people.'

'Do you think I like hurting people?'

'No. But you're ready to do it.'

He said, 'I don't hurt people. I try to help them.'

'Kindness might do as well,' I said.

He did not reply. His eyes scanned the valley and focused on something far beyond it. The silence deepened and became more than silence. My heart began to labour painfully, filling the silence that went on and on.

'Why can't you love anyone?' he said.

There are things that can only be said to a person once in a lifetime, because after they have been said the person is not the same. In the moment when the words are spoken, something happens which is a kind of death. Simon's question struck the flesh from my bones.

I found myself in a strange country. It was wasteland as far as the eye could see. Nothing grew there. I wandered in it. It was my life. Bare rocks, dusty plains, paths that led back on

168

themselves. I seemed to recognise a few landmarks, but as I approached them they dissolved: mirages. I read a milestone. It was a gravestone.

I wandered there a long time. I felt no emotion. I had no emotions. I was a ghost. This was my country.

At some time I came back to where I sat, in a chair, overlooking a green valley. I remembered that I had been asked a question, and that I had a voice.

With my voice I said, 'I am afraid of love.'

I heard him speaking, and knew there was nothing he could tell me that I had not seen. In the wasteland there were no excuses, and even fear was an excuse. There were no causes: what did it matter why I had been afraid? There was no past, there was no future, there was no cover for nakedness. The wasteland was all there was.

He began to lead me out of it. At first I resisted, preferring despair to such gigantic effort.

'In the Middle Ages there was a word for the state of mind you are experiencing,' he said, and I remembered it. The old theological term for the deadly torpor of the soul.

'Accidie,' I said.

'It was recognised as one of the gravest sins.'

How well he knew me. I smiled, and followed him.

'There is always something that can be done,' he said. 'Usually it is very clear. It is simply the next thing. If for instance you have taken something from someone, the next thing is to give it back. After that, the next step will in turn become clear. But it all rests on seeing in the first place what it is you've done. That is the most difficult part, because the mind obscures from itself the knowledge that it has done something bad.'

He was talking quietly. It was the Simon I knew. I rested, and let him take me home.

'Truth is straight,' he said. 'If you put something straight beside something crooked, you see the crookedness. When a crooked person perceives his crookedness, there is pain. When he feels that pain, he is starting to get better.'

He paused.

'If you put a straight thing beside another straight thing, nothing happens. If you tell the truth to a straight person, there is no pain. If there is pain, it is because the person is crooked. If he is crooked, it is not kindness to tell him he is straight. Thereby one takes from him a great opportunity. It may be the only opportunity he ever has.'

I nodded. I knew.

'Do you still think I'm cruel?'

'No,' I said.

I fell into thought. Every painful word of truth he had told me had given me life. For his truthfulness I owed him a debt that could not be measured. Yet, suppose he had told me these things and I had not understood? Suppose I had seen only the knife, not the cancer at which it was directed? Would that experience not have maimed me for ever? Were there not some people who could not survive this terrible surgery?

'What is troubling you?' asked Simon.

'Perhaps some people can't survive the truth,' I said.

'Why should they not be able to?'

'Some people are mentally more vulnerable than others.'

'Vulnerable?'

'No. Unstable.'

'Who are you thinking of?'

'Alex,' I said.

'Why do you defend her?'

It always came back to that question. We had touched on it many times. We had never got to the root of it.

'I suppose I feel that she needs defending,' I said.

'Why?'

'I know her. And although you see things which I don't, I know things about Alex which you don't know. I know where she's most fragile.'

'So why do you defend her?'

'I don't want you to hit her on that spot.'

'But why do *you* defend her?' he said.

170

I started impatiently to reply, then stopped. His meaning gripped me and swung me round to face, once again, myself.

'I'm afraid,' I said.

'Of what?'

'What will happen if you do.'

'And what do you think will happen?'

I did not want to say it, but there was no way back.

I said, 'I think she might break up.'

It was said, and I could think about it. Alex's mother had, during Alex's childhood, been subjects to fits of insanity. I had sometimes seen Alex in states of paranoia that were only a hair's-breadth from madness. Throughout our relationship I had shielded her from truths that might arouse that slumbering demon.

'There is something in Alex which I don't understand and it frightens me,' I said. 'It's a kind of darkness. If it is released . . .'

'Yes?'

The fear caught me, so strongly that I could no longer deceive myself about whom I was protecting.

'It threatens me,' I said.

There was a pause. He smiled, as if fitting together an unusual puzzle.

'So, you want to defend Alex against me because something in her threatens you.'

It wasn't nice, but it was neat. 'Yes,' I said.

'So, *why do you defend her?*'

It was too much. Was no answer, no soul-baring, sufficient for the man?

'Because I love her,' I said angrily. It was the first thing that came into my head.

'You love her?' It was an unbelieving, lethal whisper. I sat motionless while he annihilated me.

'All your life you have loved no one. You have just admitted it. You have taken from people and given nothing.'

171

'I have tried to help people,' I said weakly. There were a few.

'You have never helped anyone. You hinder people. You kill them.'

'I *kill* them?'

'You help them to kill themselves. It is the same thing. There they are, trapped in their prisons, and you come along and say, "Here's another brick. I'll even help you cement it in." That isn't help. That's murder.'

I thought of the caravan girl. 'No,' I said.

'Yes,' said Simon. 'You will keep Alex in her prison because you're afraid of what will happen to *you* if she gets out.'

A long time passed. I was conscious of very little, except the dreadful emptiness in my brain.

'Isn't it true?' said Simon.

'Yes.'

'So,' he said. He crossed his legs and tucked them up under him. He was smiling.

'In this case, what is the next thing to do?'

It was alarmingly clear. It was the clearest thing I had ever seen.

'I'd better help Alex pull her prison down,' I said.

'And how will you do that?'

I said, 'I guess I start by not defending her.'

My decision not to defend Alex had opened a door which could not be closed.

Perhaps to test my resolution, Simon took an early opportunity of talking to me about her. He wanted to know what had been behind her precipitate departure to London. I could not help him: I knew less than he did, because I did not know what had passed between them the night they talked in the parlour. I tried to analyse my own perceptions of that evening, but could not get beyond the feeling of a threat, of something frightening in the house. I said that somehow it had been similar to the night the ponies got into the top field, when I had felt, to a lesser degree, the same unnameable disturbance. I asked him what had really happened that night.

'She left the gate open,' he said simply.

'Are you sure?' I asked.

'Yes,' said Simon.

It seemed unlikely. But as I thought about it it began to seem all too probable. Alex was careless. She often did not bother to take precautions which I would have taken as a matter of course, because she thought them unnecessary. She might well have left the gate open temporarily when the ponies were not about, intending to go back later and shut it, and then forgotten. Alex was forgetful.

'Oh, well,' I said with resignation.

'Oh, well?' said Simon. 'You and I had to get up the middle of the night. The whole house was disturbed. The crops might have been destroyed.'

'But they weren't,' I said.

'They might have been.'

'Yes.'

'Because of her. And she is the farmer. In this group we have a farmer who actually leaves gates open.'

I grimaced.

'We have a farmer who leaves the tools lying out in the fields all night. Nearly every evening Pete and I have had to bring in tools which Alex has left out.'

So had I, for seven years.

'We have a farmer who doesn't even see to it that there is a barn to put the hay in.'

True. It was I who had pointed out the necessity of clearing the barns before the hay was cut, and had done most of the clearing. Alex had not seemed to regard it as important. I recollected that this, too, had occurred regularly for years. I cleared barns, Alex filled them up again with junk, and every year I cleared them again just in time for the hay harvest. Alex was not interested in unglamorous jobs.

'In short,' said Simon, 'we have a farmer who does none of the work of a farmer.'

'She did arrange for the hay to be cut,' I said.

'Yes,' said Simon. 'She gets people to do things for her. And what other work has she done?'

'I don't really know,' I said. 'I'm at the office a lot of the time. I don't know what she does.'

'She goes out,' said Simon.

I searched for something to say that would not be an excuse, and found nothing.

'She chose the job,' pursued Simon. 'She didn't have to be the farmer. I made a list of jobs, and when I came to Farmer she jumped at it like a dog at a bone. But she doesn't do it. Why doesn't she do it? All the rest of you do your jobs. You look after the money, and every Thursday you tell us how much we've got and how much we've spent. Dao cooks: every day there is food on the table. Coral does the housekeeping: the house is clean. Except that the bathroom never seems to be particularly clean.'

Alex was responsible for cleaning the bathroom.

'And Pete does the repairs and fixes herb-racks and slates the roof. And she doesn't even seem to like the way he slates the roof.'

'She doesn't think he's doing it the right way,' I said miserably.

'But she doesn't do it herself. She goes out instead.'

'I know,' I said.

Simon leant forward. 'Why does she do it?'

'I don't know. She's always been like that. I've got used to it,' I said.

Through the open kitchen door came the sounds of cooking: Dao was preparing supper. Intermittent hammering from the other side of the house signified that Pete, undeterred, was still slating the roof. Fifty feet away outside the french windows sat Coral, feeding the baby. Sarah and Lily sat on the kitchen step, playing with an old tennis ball and talking in Thai.

174

'A lot of people could live in this place,' said Simon. 'There are hungry people out there. There is not much time. And we cannot progress, because of Alex.'

'She doesn't understand,' I said. 'I used to think she understood better than I did what the group was about. But now I wonder if she's ever understood at all.'

'She has never understood,' said Simon. 'But she is very good at pretending to understand things which she doesn't.'

It took me a while to absorb the full impact of his words. He had provided me with a key, a very simple key, to a number of incidents which I had long found disturbing.

I turned the key.

Harry. Tessa. A mousey girl from the village in the throes of a wretched divorce. Three of the people Alex had talked to over the years, trying to help them with their different problems by telling them the things she had learned from Simon. Always, as I listened on these occasions, I had heard a false note. Once or twice, feeling she had distorted a crucial idea, I had intervened, to Alex's irritation and the benefit of nobody. The rest of the time I had listened, puzzled. Alex's voice but Simon's words. Simon's words almost exactly. She could not match his eloquence, of course, or his inspired logic, but these were Simon's words. They had been right when he spoke them, so they must be right now. So what was wrong?

Alex, sensing my discomfort, had asked me why I didn't like her 'talking'. I had been unable to reply. She asked me if I thought she had misinterpreted Simon's meaning. No, I didn't quite think that. All I knew was that I felt embarrassed. I agreed and yet somehow did not agree with what she was saying. I wished she would let me do the talking instead. Ego? No, it was not. What then? I did not know.

My ears had picked up what my brain refused to consider. Alex did not understand a word she was saying.

How often had she not understood when I assumed that she had? I recalled our angry arguments about history, evolution and philosophy. Arguments which had left me bruised and perplexed because I could not see why subjects neither of us cared deeply about should generate so much feeling. Arguments in which I had felt like one of those mythical heroes grappling with an adversary who continually changed shape, becoming a lion or a tree or a pool of water. Arguments in which every weapon of logic I produced was shattered against an invisible wall. I had thought it to be a wall of obstinacy, and puzzled over the fact that time did not erode it, for Alex was usually susceptible to reason on issues which did not involve her emotions. But if obstinacy was only the protective covering for a huge deception in which incomprehension masqueraded as understanding, ignorance as wisdom . . . then no wonder my logic was rendered impotent, no wonder I was filled with an anger I could not explain. And no wonder Alex's defences were unbreachable. They had to be: there was everything at stake.

How had it started, I wondered. As a self-defence when she found herself among people with no greater native wit than she had but an immeasurably better education? Or much earlier, in the shadows of a childhood dominated by a terrifying mother whose fits of unreason had forced the child into a compensating wisdom too large for her years? And to what extent was it conscious? Surely one *knew* whether one understood a thing or not? And if one didn't, what purpose was served by pretending that one did?

I had almost forgotten Simon's presence.

'Well?' he enquired.

'You've explained a lot of things for me,' I said. 'But I don't understand what she can gain from it.'

'Respect.'

I pondered. No, it wasn't quite fair.

'I think there's more to it than that,' I said. 'And I think she does believe she understands, when she doesn't.'

'She's convinced herself.'

'No, listen,' I said. 'After Alex met you she used to talk to people, people we knew who were in trouble. She would talk

176

about your ideas, repeat the things you said. I admit there always seemed to be something slightly wrong with it – '

'She didn't understand what she was talking about.'

'Right. But the point is that she wanted to help them. And some of those people were helped.'

'Were they?' said Simon.

'Yes.'

'Whom has Alex helped?'

I scanned my mental list. Harry. Harry loved Alex, had done for years, with a devotion I had seen falter only once. That was the night she had 'talked' to him. She had tried to tell him that the trap in which he found himself, compounded of tax debts, a second mortgage, a house he needed to sell and couldn't sell until he had finished the renovations he lacked the money to complete, and work which he despised and which took all his time – that this closing trap, from which he escaped every night into a sea of beer, was an illusion and could simply be 'dropped'. He was so angry, this man whom I had never heard raise his voice, that at two o'clock in the morning he embarked on an investigation of a malfunctioning water heater with a noise that woke the entire house and probably half the street. Harry was still in debt and still drinking a gallon of beer a night.

Tessa? No, Tessa had learned nothing from Alex except a few useful attitudes with which to adorn her deviousness. However, leopards don't change their spots.

The girl from the village? I did not need to ask. If Alex had done anything there, it was harm. Alex had filled her head with fine phrases and lofty ideas, and the girl, emotionally disturbed and probably a little retarded into the bargain, had to my intense irritation fallen headlong in love with her.

'No, she didn't help them. But she tried to,' I said.

'She doesn't want to help people. She wants them to love her,' he said.

Oh, that was cruel. I started to protest, and stopped. It was uncannily close to my own thoughts.

177

'She offers them help, but she gives them nothing. She pretends to help them, just as she pretends to understand. It's all an act, a superb act. They're taken in by it: it even took me in. Behind it there's nothing. Alex is a sham.'

I stared numbly at the ground. A few feet away the paving petered out in a little wilderness of weeds and bare cement. Was that why she never finished anything?

'What does she do to people?' exclaimed Simon. 'It's terrible.'

I tried to say something but could not find my voice. What was the point of trying to hold back this tidal wave of awful truth, which my instinct had known for years?

'Look what she's done to Charles,' said Simon in a voice so low I could barely catch it. 'That really is terrible, Kay.'

Charles? What did Charles matter among so many? They surged into my mind, all the forgotten people who had loved Alex. Writers, painters, lawyers, thieves, professional men and con-men, economists and forgers . . . She had had affairs with all of them, asexual affairs, affairs of the mind, affairs which never lose their power to obsess because the obsession is never gratified. Some of them still struggled to maintain their side of the friendship in spite of the wrath of their wives, for behind nearly every man who loved Alex there stood a woman half out of her mind with jealousy over a relationship she could neither compete with nor understand.

Then there were the waifs who had drifted into her net, the drug-addicts and the sexual misfits and the simple-minded. She had been kind to them and then, tiring of them, thrown them back into the sea where they no longer had the will to swim. Maurice was one of these. Alex had discovered him, fêted him, dazzled him, and abandoned him, leaving me to stitch up the wound by writing his book. He could not understand how he had offended.

Help? Had she ever 'helped' anyone who had not ended up devoted to her? Even Tessa, I now remembered. There had been a time when Tessa pursued Alex with a persistence that

178

became socially embarrassing. She had only set her cap at Alex's brother when it had been made clear to her that she could not have Alex.

'It isn't even just people,' said Simon. 'Look what she does to animals. Look what she did to Esther. That was the most horrible thing I have ever seen.'

Esther in Alex's arms, a centre of elaborate attention, when it was too late. Esther in the vet's surgery waiting for the knife, waiting for Alex, who had gone to London.

I felt sick. I had opened a door, and through it was blowing a wind, a gale, a hurricane.

We had spent just under £19, and there was £43 in the kitty. I switched on the calculator to check that I had divided the expenditure correctly.

Simon said, 'Are you dividing it by three or four?'

'Three,' I said. 'Alex isn't here and she won't have any money anyway.'

'In nine weeks,' said Simon, 'Alex has paid her share three times.'

I switched off the calculator.

'I know,' I said. 'But if she doesn't have any money she doesn't have any money. I can divide it by four if you like, but all that will happen is that I shall end up paying half the total instead of a third. Which presumably isn't what you have in mind.'

'We don't want you to pay for Alex,' said Simon. 'We want Alex to pay for herself. For once.'

At the beginning, when it was agreed to split the expenditure four ways, I had felt the arrangement was unfair. I was still not entirely happy about it, but this was not the point. Alex had undertaken to pay a quarter of the expenses whenever she could. That had turned out to be hardly ever.

'How can she pay?' I said.

'She could sell some furniture,' said Simon. 'Some of the furniture in this house would fetch a lot of money.' He indi-

179

cated the carved oak sideboard behind him. 'I saw a sideboard like that priced at four hundred pounds.'

I wrestled with a moment of anger. That the sideboard was not worth anything like that sum, that it had been in Alex's family for many years, and that it was exactly right for the wide alcove in which it stood, were all alike irrelevant. Furniture did not matter.

'I'd be surprised if it was worth that much,' I said. 'And in any case, Simon, antique furniture takes time to sell. You can't just pop into town with it when you want some money.'

'She could advertise it nevertheless.'

His eyes travelled over the room. To most people it would have appeared very sparsely furnished.

'There are lots of small things that could be sold. Pictures. That mirror.'

A rather pretty oval Victorian mirror which we had bought for a pound at an auction.

'Oh, the mirror's nice, Simon,' said Coral. 'And it's useful.'

'Okay, not the mirror, since someone likes it. Pictures. There must be dozens of pictures in this house.'

Indeed there were. Most of them were in my study stacked against a wall, affording a haven to spiders. They were a residue of Alex's foray into picture-dealing.

'They aren't worth anything,' I said. 'Except for one or two which might fetch a bit if she restored them.'

'Then why doesn't she restore them?'

His eyes continued their journey, and came back to the sideboard. On it were a few modest ornaments, none of which would have attracted a second glance in a junk shop.

'Well, it's clear there are a number of things which could be sold to raise money,' he said. 'There is no reason why Alex should not pay her share. However, for this week I suppose we could make an exception. If Pete agrees.'

Pete, who had appeared sunk in thought since the start of the meeting, roused himself, smiled, and said 'Yes.'

I divided the expenditure by three.

When we had disposed of the financial business, Simon said, 'When are the oats going to be harvested?'

Alex had arranged for Mr. Pascoe to bring his combine harvester down to our field as soon as he had finished getting in his own crop.

'Probably on Saturday,' I said.

'And when will Alex be back?'

'She said she'd be back today, but that doesn't mean she will,' I said. 'She often doesn't come back the day she says she will.'

'I see,' said Simon. He thought for a while. Then he said, 'Until the problem that is facing the group is solved, there is no point in trying to deal with anything else. In the circumstances I don't think we can possibly have the oats harvested.'

I sat back in the chair and cleared my mind. There was no room for emotions. This was going to be a long evening.

Simon said, 'Is there anyone here who doesn't know what the problem is?'

No one spoke.

Simon said, 'There is a member of the group who does not want the group to work.'

He began to talk about Alex's behaviour. After a few sentences Dao interrupted.

'It seems to me it is not right,' she said, 'to criticise one who is not present.'

'This is not criticism,' said Simon. 'The intention is to help Alex. If the intent is right, no harm is done.'

The discussion continued. Alex was a farmer who did not farm, a builder who would not build, a businesswoman who could not be businesslike. She played at everything she did. She could not even handle the responsibility of having tenants. Everything she undertook ended in chaos; every job she started had to be finished by someone else, who would probably be told they had done it wrong. She was lazy: she got people to do things for her. She was mean: she liked to get things done on the cheap or if possible for nothing. She was good at this, because she charmed people. However, her relationship with the people who did things for her always broke down because she continually changed her mind about what she wanted. She would then shift the blame for the failure on to them. She was never grateful for help. She behaved like a *grande dame*: when she had tired of charming people, she treated them like serfs.

She confused everyone with whom she had dealings because she changed her mind, went back on her word and broke promises. She could not be relied on to do anything she said she would do, or even to remember tomorrow what she had said today. She would change her version of the past to suit her present requirements. She did not pay her debts. She caused immeasurable trouble to countless people and appeared to think that none of it mattered in the slightest. She had managed to live in this way for thirty-eight years and would doubtless continue to do so for the rest of her days as long as the people around her made allowance for her eccentricities and went on carrying her as a passenger.

'We cannot have passengers in this group,' said Simon. 'There is too much to be done, and not much time. There is a world out there hungry for a new way of life, and we are waiting for Alex.'

He paused. 'If I am wrong,' he said, 'someone will correct me.'

Pete, Dao and Coral glanced at me. I said nothing. What could I say? He had presented me with a picture of Alex more coherent than any I had possessed. It was exact in detail, and contained intuitions which my own knowledge confirmed. The most striking was his phrase '*grande dame*': he did not know that Alex, brought up in the woods, kept a picture postcard of her ancestral home in an upstairs pigeon-hole.

I had listened with all my mind for a small mistake in the damning litany: there was none. There was not the slightest chink into which I could insert a denial and try to prise apart this monstrous edifice. I gazed at the dark Alex who was taking

182

shape before my eyes, and knew that for seven years I had been the victim of a conjuring trick. The lights shone on an empty stage: what I had taken for a shadow was the only flesh.

I woke up feeling wretched. I had pledged myself not to stand between Alex and the truth. Where then did I stand? 'You must hate the offence but love the offender,' Simon was apt to say. I wondered if I was yet capable of such a mature discrimination.

The rest of the group seemed happy and treated me with more than usual gentleness. There was an air of waiting for something. Alex had telephoned late the previous evening to say she would be back on Saturday night. I could not remember what I had said to her.

I was ill at ease, and went into town to do some shopping. I bought groceries, a pair of scissors for Coral, and some small brass screws with which to fit clothes-hooks on to the bedroom doors. There were no wardrobes at Bethany because Alex always threw them away.

On the way back I drove up the hill towards the lane that led to Mr. Pascoe's farm, and found myself driving past it and on towards the lay-by at the top in which there was a telephone kiosk. I stopped there and sat behind the steering-wheel, considering. It was as sensible to telephone as go there. All I had to do was deliver a simple message, which could be entrusted to anyone in the house: we did not want the oats combined tomorrow. I would have to give a reason, of course.

I said to Mrs. Pascoe, 'Could you tell your husband that we're not quite ready to get the oats in, and if he could put it off for a few days it would be a help. I'll ring again.'

She said yes, that was all right, their own oats weren't quite ready anyway. I put the phone down with relief, and went home.

As the day wore on I forgot my unease. I had no time to think about it in any case: I had to finish clearing out the red barn to make room for the oats. The straw alone would take up a third of the space.

I finished just as Coral made the afternoon drink. I had been working hard, and I lingered over my peppermint tea.

'Did you tell Mr. Pascoe about the oats?' asked Pete as he stood up.

'Yes,' I said. Pete nodded and walked away.

'What did you say?' asked Simon casually.

As casually, I answered, 'I said we weren't quite ready and could he leave it a few days.'

There was a pause before Simon said, 'That is not the message you were given.'

I had been asked to tell Mr. Pascoe simply that we did not want him to combine the oats on Saturday.

'Why didn't you pass on the message you were given?' asked Simon.

I gazed stupidly at the ground.

'I don't know,' I said.

He was smiling. For a moment I thought he would let it go: he often did, if it was a small point and he had drawn one's attention to it. But something had alerted him. The smile vanished.

'You did not deliver the group's message,' said Simon. 'You substituted one of your own. Why?'

I said nothing.

'To anyone outside,' said Simon, 'it would not appear to matter. People do this all the time. They are entrusted with a communication and they change it. The world as a consequence is full of untrue statements. People accept these statements and act on them and the result is chaos. It seems to me to matter a great deal.

'It is so simple,' he said. 'One is given a message and one delivers that message. Why should one wish to change it?'

He looked hard at me. 'The motive for altering information is that one wishes to influence people or to control events. But it doesn't work. The opposite happens. When one delivers a message exactly as one has received it, one discharges one's responsibility totally and nothing is left behind. One is free of that situation. If one changes the message, one is left with something: a responsibility which one cannot be free of. One has chained oneself to the series of events which will result from that false message. And instead of influencing those events, one will be influenced by them.'

It was a nice paradox. I regarded it without much pleasure. 'Yes,' I said.

'So why did you change the group's message?'

'I . . . well, I thought he wouldn't understand if I just said we didn't want the oats combined. He would expect some sort of reason. So I gave him one.'

'But the group did not authorise you to give him one.'

'No.'

'You decided to act on your own initiative.'

Simon gazed piercingly in front of him, brows puckered.

'It's very serious,' he said.

I knew it was: it was even more serious than he had realised. I prayed that he would follow the track he was on and not scent that there was another.

He followed it.

'If you act apart from the group, you act against the group. After all these weeks, you are still acting against the group.'

He talked for a long time, about the desire to assert one's individuality, and the misunderstanding on which it rested, and the unhappiness that was caused by it. After a while, seeing my dejection and that I was not resisting him, he softened and said it was not easy to break the habit of a lifetime and a conditioning which valued the illusory and destructive thing called personality, but one must try.

'One must be constantly on one's guard,' he said, 'so that one sees when it starts to happen. See it, and you can stop it. In fact when you see it, it stops itself.'

He smiled at me, got up and went into the kitchen. I sat for about five minutes, watching the slow purposeful movement of the cows in the field beyond the stream. Whether he had known or not, he had left me to contemplate, in the light of his words, the true depth of my betrayal of the group.

I had changed the group's message to one that would be acceptable to Mr. Pascoe because if the group broke up I would still have Mr. Pascoe as a neighbour. For the same reason, I still had not given up my job. It did not require Simon to tell me that by insuring myself against the group's failure I was even now contributing to it.

That evening we did a communication exercise. Simon gave us all a piece of paper and a pencil.

'Draw a vertical straight line in the centre of the paper, extending from one-third of the way down the paper to the bottom of the paper,' he said.

'I can't draw straight lines,' I protested. I couldn't draw anything.

'Draw a straight line,' said Simon patiently, and repeated his instruction.

I drew one.

'At right-angles to that line, and starting at the top of it, draw a straight line from left to right extending to the edge of the paper.'

I drew one. The instructions continued, until the diagram was quite complex. I sneaked a look at Pete's, and was glad to see that his looked more or less like mine.

'Don't concern yourself with anyone else's drawing,' Simon reproved.

I grinned. It was like a maths lesson where for once you understood what you were supposed to be doing. It was fun. It was rather an odd occupation for five adults, but it was fun.

Simon finished and said, 'Now, everyone should have a drawing that looks something like this.'

He showed his own. We showed ours. They were all the same. We smiled at each other.

'Communication is a matter of seeing the same thing,' said Simon.

Before going to bed we talked again about Alex. Dao, who had had a great affection for her, was sad. She had believed Alex to be a rare person, with a generous heart and what she called 'a man's spirit in a woman's body', but she had been mistaken. These qualities were not there, she said.

Simon nodded.

Each member of the group had been struck by a different aspect of Alex's behaviour. To Dao the most upsetting thing was that she broke promises. For weeks she had been promising to label the herb jars: she still had not done it, and Dao had a kitchen full of anonymous herbs, none of which she dared use in case she poisoned us all.

Coral complained of her laziness and untidiness. The bathroom was never really clean, she said; there was dust under the bath and behind the washstand, and the floor was hardly ever washed. I pointed out that the bathroom floor, consisting of bare floorboards which did not quite meet, was difficult to clean properly, but Simon said, 'The hall also consists of bare floorboards, but you manage to wash it regularly,' to which I could find no reply. There was no reply either to Coral's complaint that no sooner had she tidied the kitchen than Alex would come in with an armful of something, dump it in a corner, and leave it there all day.

Small things. Inconsiderate, selfish things. Symptoms.

Pete was concerned with something deeper: the bullying ego he had glimpsed on several occasions when Alex had felt threatened or had been indulging her wit at my expense.

'It's surprising,' he said simply. 'For a long time you don't realise it's there, then suddenly it comes up.' He made a movement with his hands to suggest something breaking surface. 'And when you see it, it's so big.'

Simon said, 'The purpose of this conversation is to find a

187

way of helping Alex and solving the problem which confronts the group. Has anyone any suggestions?'

'If we could just *explain* to her,' said Coral.

'It has been explained to her,' said Pete.

'Pete is right,' said Simon. 'She has been given every chance. People have been very patient with Alex. She has abused their patience. She has such a distorted idea of her importance that she expects to receive special treatment, and such is the force of her personality that she does receive it. She has always been allowed to get away with things.'

He looked round the room. 'This is a person who does not want to hear what is said to her. This is a person who twists what people say into something they have not said. This is a person who cannot do anything straight. Whatever we say to Alex, it has to be so carefully worded, so clear, that she cannot possibly interpret it in any other way.'

It was obvious that he was the only person who could find such a formulation. We saw that he had found it already.

'There is a single element which complicates the problem,' he said. 'Normally it would not be difficult to deal with behaviour such as Alex's. A member who disrupted the group would be asked either to change his or her behaviour, or to leave the group. What makes it difficult in this case is that Alex is not in the same position as an ordinary member of the group. Alex is the owner of the house.'

I began to listen intently.

'This makes it impossible to deal with her in the obvious way,' said Simon. 'One cannot say to the owner of a house, "Change your behaviour or leave." So the situation can only be dealt with as it should be dealt with if Alex ceases to be the owner of the house.'

Something had hit me very hard between the eyes. I stared at this man whose logic flinched from nothing.

'The situation could have been avoided if the original intention, that the house should belong to the group, had been carried through. But it was not carried through. At the partnership meeting I saw that the owner of the house did not want to give the house to the partnership, and since I do not wish to take something from someone who does not want to give it, I withdrew. There is no point in forming a partnership when one of the members does not want it to work.'

I blinked with astonishment, convicted him of injustice, and immediately realised he was right. Alex could work near-miracles when she wanted to, but there was no evidence that she had even tried to give the house to the group.

'I therefore propose,' continued Simon, 'to put three alternatives to Alex when she returns. I have looked for further alternatives, but I can find only three. These are the alternatives. One, that she sells the house to someone else in the group, and remains here. I will offer to buy the house from her. Two, that she leaves. Three, that she gets what she wants.'

There was utter silence.

Pete said, 'I don't understand the third alternative.'

Simon said, 'We will give her exactly what she wants.'

It was too simple for us to grasp immediately. Then we saw. If she rejected the first two alternatives she was rejecting the discipline of the group and at the same time the life which that discipline offered. She would be rejecting them in favour of whatever *she* wanted. What that turned out to be did not matter.

'If she leaves,' said Coral, 'does she have to leave for good?'

'No,' said Simon. 'If after a while she wanted to come back, the group would consider her request in exactly the same way as it would consider a request from anyone else to come and live here.'

Dao said, 'But you have not given her the choice that she changes herself.'

'That is not a possibility,' said Simon. 'She has refused to change and one supposes that she can't. And as long as she continues to own the house no measures can be taken to induce her to change. The choice you're asking for is included in alternative one.'

189

We sat and thought. To every question Simon had an answer, and every answer brought us back to one of the three alternatives. The longer we looked at them the more inevitable they became. It was the economy of genius. However, it flashed into my mind that if Simon was the most brilliant human being I had ever met he was also the blindest, because surely Alex would not accept these alternatives. I was on the point of saying something, but stopped. I must not pre-judge. Certainly I must not predict another's actions, and thereby attempt to limit their freedom. In any case, if Alex did not accept the alternatives she would have condemned herself to a region beyond reason, because the alternatives were the only alternatives there were.

It was agreed to put the alternatives to Alex when she returned. If that was late on Saturday night, we would do it on Sunday.

Simon looked round the room with a smile. 'Good,' he said.

'I've been reading a good book,' said Simon next morning.

I had been surprised to see him reading. I thought he had given it up. He had once said to me that people wrote books in order to understand the thing they were writing about, which was why no book ever contained the knowledge promised in its title. I could see no reason why a man who knew that should ever read another book in his life.

It was a book Alex had borrowed from a friend and left in the parlour. No one had bothered to look at it until now. It was by the founder of the organisation with whose psychological techniques we had experimented in Sessions. It contained, said Simon, a development of his ideas. We sat round in the kitchen and Simon told us about them.

It was a formulation of behaviour, attitudes and life-orientation in terms of what the author called 'tone'. There was a tone scale ranging from 0 to 4, with a dividing point at 2. At 4 the individual was functioning perfectly in all respects: at 0 he was dead. From 4 downwards his general level of being

190

deteriorated through lesser states of happiness to boredom, then to irritability, anger, sadness and finally to apathy. The individual's tone fluctuated as he was affected by other people's behaviour and external events, but for everyone it was possible to plot a normal level.

What gave this rather unattractive scheme its value was the author's insight that above level 2 the individual's goals lay in an upward direction, but below 2 they lay downward. A person at 2 or below strove, consciously or unconsciously, in everything he did, to bring about failure, destruction and death.

Below 2 was the area of the criminal, the psychopath, the drunkard and the suicide. It was also the area of millions of apparently normal people who quietly made life difficult for everyone around them. People who criticised or slandered others, people to whom lying had become a habit, people who enjoyed other people's discomfiture, people who made promises and didn't keep them and took on obligations and didn't honour them, people who received friendly overtures with suspicion – they were all, in their daily lives, sowing and nurturing little seeds of destruction.

Every enterprise undertaken by a person below 2 on the tone scale would end in confusion and disaster. Every communication made to a person below 2 on the tone scale would be distorted by the recipient. Every relationship between that person and a person above 2 on the scale would drag the latter down to a lower level. And every group containing a person below 2 on the scale would be in danger of fragmenting in disorder, without anyone understanding why.

The tone level of such people could, except in the most desperate cases, be raised, said Simon, but this had to be done gradually and required understanding and patience. An immediate substantial improvement was not possible. Great care must be exercised, and great love.

When Simon finished talking it was as if Alex stood physically before us.

He put down the book thoughtfully. 'Communication is

191

sharing the same reality,' he said. 'Alex's reality is very low on the scale. In bringing her up to the reality of the group, we must be very gentle.'

I was completely happy. A barrier which I had until the very last preserved between myself and the group had crumbled. I felt I belonged to a family. I had never felt that before. It was a joyful feeling.

I polished the brass stair-rods and all the brass door-handles until they gleamed. Then I polished the brass coat-hooks which had been taken years ago off an Edwardian hallstand disintegrating in the barn, and fixed one on the back of each bedroom door and a couple in the hall, using the little brass screws I had bought the previous day. Simon inspected the work approvingly.

'You like to do things well,' he said. 'That's good. Pete and I would have banged them on with a few nails. It looks very nice.'

It was too wet to work outside so I busied myself indoors all day, cleaning my study with a thoroughness it had never known and ruthlessly emptying drawers of accumulated papers. I was conscious that I was preparing myself for a new start. I did not know what it would be and I did not think about it. I had no idea what would happen when Alex came home. I had no idea what I was going to say or do. When it happened, I would know what to do.

I saw that only when one is in such a state of emptiness, of not having thought about the future, can one act rightly. I saw that all my troubles with Alex in the past had arisen from the fact that each time I tried to deal with a situation I was thinking about the future. Thus not only had I been unable to deal with the situation properly, but in perpetually sacrificing the present to the future I had lost both, for the future is never what one calculates.

All my life, I realised, I had made decisions in the light of their probable effects, not their innate rightness. If I had

192

thought about their moral content I had included it among the factors to be weighed. I had not seen that only by considering that factor to the exclusion of all others could I possibly make the right decision. And the right decision was always so simple. If one cleared one's mind of the effects, it would present itself.

Do the right thing, and let the consequences be what they may. For the first time I saw the daring, and the beauty, of that act. I was going to do it.

We sat in the parlour that evening and talked as we had done at the beginning, before the clouds gathered. We talked quietly of many things. The room was still and full of light. A thin curl of smoke rose from the joss-stick on the black slate mantelpiece.

Simon made some reference to Blake, whom I had read years ago at university and never understood, and never known that I did not understand. I started to say that if Blake were to be understood in his profundity by the professors who lectured on him and the students who read him, the educational system into which he had been incorporated would collapse.

I stopped in mid-sentence. They looked at me in surprise. It was several seconds before the dogs started barking, but my nerves had heard it. A car was turning into the drive.

Alex.

9

TRUTH

Knowledge is power. It cannot be otherwise. One cannot disclaim that power.

I must be so careful.

He told me repeatedly I must be careful, but he did not tell me how.

If one has lost one's innocence, what can be done about it? Perhaps in that case it is better not to go on a journey where there are dragons. But there is only the journey. If I do not continue on this journey I might as well be dead.

In all religions, mystical knowledge is pursued under strict controls. One has a spiritual counsellor, whose job it is to see that one does not stray into the territory where one will be tested beyond one's strength. There is wisdom in this, but not the greatest wisdom, because it leads only to a partial truth. It must, for the vision is controlled. In the end, it does nothing but reinforce the religious system from which it sprang, and all religious systems offer no more than a keyhole-glimpse of the truth. They themselves have put up the door which shuts out the truth.

I want to go through that door.

All desire is bad, the Buddhists say. All desire leads to suffering. Does even the desire for truth lead to suffering?

Yes, for desire comes between the soul and enlightenment. Desire is itself the lack of innocence.

So one must go on the journey without wanting.

It is the same thing as being without motive, or as being motivated only by love, the one motivation which does not harm. Thus motivated, one cannot be harmed oneself. I have arrived by a different route at something I knew already.

In fact I have come back in a circle to the point at which I always stop, aware that there is a chasm at my feet. The chasm is this: how does one rid oneself of wanting, without wanting to do so? How, without motivation, can one purify one's motives?

I know the answer: Simon has explained it, seeing in his compassion that I would spend the rest of my life trying to untie this Gordian knot if he did not cut it for me.

The answer is that one lets everything go: all the ideas, all the desires. One's being, free of restraints, then does the thing which is natural to it and moves towards its happiness, which is enlightenment.

I objected that there was a motivation involved in letting everything go, but he said no. It was as if a child on a warm night were to throw off a blanket in its sleep.

Why do I have such difficulty with this answer, which I know must be right? Why is it that every time I approach it my intellect trips me up and imprisons me in an endless series of Chinese boxes? Why can I not banish the spectre of a selfish motive?

It is so simple. The pure motivation is love.

I was once afraid of love.

She comes out from the kitchen carrying two mugs. It is kind of her to bring me a drink. I must be watchful.

'I want to talk to you,' she says, sitting on the grass.

'Okay.'

'I want to ask you a question.'

'Yes?'

'When Simon said he wanted to resign as Organiser of the group, did you take that to mean that the partnership was dissolved?'

My head spins slightly, as it always does when she plays this trick. Does she really understand so little of what happened, or is this a device to fool me into thinking that what happened was something different altogether? But of course between the blindness of the first and the corruption of the second there is almost nothing to choose. Any blindness of that order must be a willed blindness.

'The question is pointless,' I say. 'The partnership and Simon's resignation have nothing to do with what happened on Sunday.'

'And suppose I tell you that Simon's resignation was absolutely crucial? It dissolved the partnership, and I was the only one who realised that. You all thought the partnership was still in existence, and that's why my behaviour seemed so black to you.'

Oh, poor Alex. But I know that the only way I can show my pity is to stamp on this lie, as I have stamped on all of them and will continue to stamp until the thing that is producing them is finally dead.

'You are evading the truth,' I say. 'Everything you say is an evasion.'

She turns on me, of course.

'Kay, I have been over everything that happened, everything that Simon said. For the past three days I have done nothing but think about it. There is no other explanation.'

'There is another explanation,' I say, 'but you will not find it by thinking. Thinking will only lead you away from it. That, in fact, is why you are thinking. You should look in your heart instead.'

There is a pause. The birds sing from the trees.

Alex gets up.

'Look in your own heart,' she says. 'Look in your own treacherous heart. If you can bear to.'

Treacherous. Yes, of course she would say that. She has to say it although she cannot believe it, for even to an understanding as depraved as Alex's my motives must have been perfectly clear. She cannot resist a weapon so obvious that it clamours to be used.

What cynicism. That is the real betrayal, Alex.

I have no need to examine my heart. I know what I have done, and I know what the world calls it. I have no need to go through it again.

Perhaps, even so, I should go through it again. I owe it to her. There may be something I missed.

I missed nothing. She wants to confuse me.

But I cannot be confused unless I am trying to avoid something.

Very well.

The morning after her return, since we had agreed to say nothing that night, Dao rang the bell for a meeting. (Curious, that it should have been Dao both on this occasion and the earlier one, when it was I who had offended. Curious, too, that the two stages were repeated: the evening and the morning. But I acknowledged my fault. Alex could not acknowledge hers. The gulf between right and wrong is as small as that: a word: a hairline: and it cannot be crossed.)

We sat again in the parlour. Alex sat on the floor. She was wearing a bright new shirt. Battle colours.

Simon began to talk. I was taken completely by surprise by his opening remark.

He said, 'It is as if the Humber belonged to Coral.'

Yes, that was how it started.

From the beginning, then.

'It is as if the Humber belonged to Coral.'

I glance at him, puzzled. I cannot see the relevance.

'One sees that sooner or later a situation will arise that cannot be dealt with adequately by the person who is required to deal with it.'

Oh, he's clever. The Humber is twenty years old and needs skilled maintenance. It belongs, naturally, to Pete.

'Or it is as if,' pursues Simon, 'the house belonged to Sarah.'

I wince. Sarah, five, looks up, sees that some adult game is afoot, and goes back to her toy. Alex does not move.

'If the house belonged to Sarah, one could expect certain things to happen. Decisions that ought to be taken would not be taken, or they would be taken on a basis which was not rational, or they would be taken one day and rescinded the next. Responsibilities which normally accompany the ownership of a house would not be accepted by the person who was the owner. People who were obliged to have dealings with the owner would find themselves confused. But nobody would be surprised by these things, because the house belonged to a little girl.'

He pauses.

'But this house belongs to a woman of thirty-eight. And yet the effect is as if it belonged to a little girl.'

Alex, cross-legged on the floor, gazes at the carpet. She looks tiny. My palms are sweating. This has to be done.

There is a lot of pain in that scene.

It is true that suffering purifies. But this is not because there is any virtue in pain: there is none. It is simply that the process of purification is itself painful, very painful. As the roots of the bad thing are pulled, loosened and drawn out there is a moment of pain so intense one thinks one cannot bear it. Then it is all over. The healing is instant.

198

Why does no one tell us these things? We are told only lies. Who benefits from the vast conspiracy to accept suffering as something ennobling? Oh, we are our own demons: we punish ourselves endlessly for the things we have made ourselves do. Why do we make ourselves do them?

I am sure it all rests on a misunderstanding. Evil is simply a misunderstanding. It must be, for egotism is a misunderstanding. It is a taking of the dream for reality and the reality for a dream. The ego is the dream of the soul.

But why should the soul, being truth, dream this lie?

This is the question at the centre of the universe. There is not the remotest possibility that I shall be able to answer it.

On the other hand, perhaps we are all capable of answering it. If this question is at the centre of life, it is also at the centre of each living creature. We all contain, locked up in us, the answer. Perhaps the seeking for the answer is the motive-force of the universe.

Of course it is.

The seeking for the answer, that is life.

Life is the product of truth's seeking for itself.

How beautiful, the dance. The eternal movement towards the always elusive goal, the lover circling the beloved.

So that is what we are doing.

And Alex too is part of this dance.

And I dare not tell her so, for she will use the knowledge to escape from her necessary pain, her necessary purification, not seeing that her soul has dreamed a nightmare in which it will suffocate if it is not cut free.

I must remember why I am here.

The scene must be run until it is complete.

Simon talks about the house. He says that Alex's ownership of the house puts her in a special position in the group. He says that this would not matter if the responsibilities of that position were faithfully discharged, but they are not. It is as if the house belonged to a child.

He talks about Alex's behaviour in the group. It is disruptive, he says. She undertakes to do things and does not do them. She starts things and does not finish them. This confuses people. She is always going away. This weakens the unity of the group. It is as if she does not want the group to succeed. If Alex were any other member of the group it would not be difficult to deal with this. But in Alex's case it is more complicated. Because Alex is the owner of the house.

I admire, yet again, the sure sweep of his approach, the inevitability of his logic, the elegant shape of his argument. Twin propositions, mutually dependent, equally unassailable.

He is saying that the group will offer Alex three alternatives. We discussed them, he says, while Alex was in London, and no one could think of a fourth alternative. This is true. What I did not say then, and do not say now, is that it won't work. Alex will not play ball.

Alex does not understand these civilised games of 'Either . . . or'. She was brought up in the woods and she has the instincts of a wild animal. If you try to drive her into a corner she will make a break for the open, and she will always get there. She has to.

Why do I not say this? Because one must never speak for others, never interpret, particularly before the event. And because I realise that I am still making allowances. For Alex is not a wild animal, she is a human being. She is not a child, she is a woman of thirty-eight. If she has not learnt the rules of civilisation, it is time she did. For her own sake as well as for that of the society in which she lives, Alex must stop expecting, and getting, special treatment.

Simon lists the alternatives. 'The first alternative is that you remain here but not as the owner of the house. I will offer to buy it from you. The second alternative is that you leave. The third is that you be allowed to have exactly what you want.'

The third alternative probably means that the group will break up. With it will go Alex's last chance.

'Do you understand the alternatives?'

'Yes,' says Alex. She looks at the floor. 'If I choose the second alternative, how soon must I leave?'

'At once.'

Harsh. Logical: what point in her staying once she decides to go? But it will not come to that. His resolution will break, he will find a way out.

Alex says, 'I choose a fourth alternative.'

The group stirs. Simon's eyes darken.

'There is no fourth alternative. The group has been unable to find a fourth alternative.'

'I do not accept the group's alternatives.'

So might Lucifer have said before the throne of light, 'I do not accept your decision.' Until that moment there had been no alternative. Evil is a misunderstanding of the nature of the rules.

And I see that the misunderstanding is deliberate.

'The alternatives the group is offering this member cover all possibilities,' says Simon. 'She can choose to go away from the group. If at some time in the future she undergoes a change of heart, she may ask to be re-admitted to the group. Meanwhile she can go wherever she likes. She might like to go abroad.'

Alex probably does not have the price of a gallon of petrol in her pocket. And why, when the other day we were discussing Alex in terms of a being lost almost beyond the point of recovery, is he now talking like a college principal giving a student permission for a Sabbatical?

'Or,' continues Simon, 'she can sell the house to me and continue living in it. I have no desire to own this or any other house, but I am willing to buy it if that will help.'

This alternative has surprised me. I thought he had no money. Perhaps Gordon will lend it to him.

'Or,' he says, 'if she will not accept either of these alternatives, there remains the third alternative, which is to let her have what she wants.'

At the spiritual level to which Alex has sunk, a being has stronger orientation towards death than towards life. They will leave her to complete her self-destruction.

And I, what shall I do?

Alex says, 'If I go away, I would like a little time to put things in order.'

'How long a time?'

'Three days.'

Simon's eyes scan the group, and see on every face the same thought: that this distressing situation cannot possibly be allowed to prolong itself another three days.

'Your request is not granted,' he says. 'If you go you must go at once.'

I can see that even as Alex appears to be thinking she has made up her mind.

'I choose a fourth alternative,' she says.

It is confirmation, if any were needed, of her utter perversity. Alex cannot and never could do anything straight. Presented with three simple, inevitable alternatives, what would she do but reject them and prefer a fourth of her own?

Simon says there can be no fourth alternative: all logical possibilities have been covered in the three offered. Nevertheless the group will listen to Alex's idea of a fourth alternative.

'My alternative is to stay here for a short time, and to leave when I am ready,' she says.

It is a compromise between going and not going. It is, like everything Alex does, messy, inefficient, selfish and dishonest.

Simon does not look at her as he gives his judgement.

'You are beyond help,' he says.

No, Alex could never submit to a set of rules, even when she had formulated them herself. I have seen her refuse to do a thing for no other reason that that she had previously decided to do it.

She thinks freedom is a matter of not being bound by rules;

and she does not see that the thing she is protecting from the supposed chafing of these rules is the monstrous, tender abscess of her ego.

And so, because she did not like the rules, she scuppered the Ark. Never mind who else was on board at the time. Never mind who might have needed to come on board later. None of these things mattered in face of Alex's need to be free. And so Alex's ego is free and Alex's soul, smaller and paler, is back in its cage.

It is no use being angry. The damage she does to other people is as nothing to the damage she does to herself. They can find their way out of what she has done to them: she cannot.

I must help her find her way out. That is why I am still here. It is my responsibility. How odd, and how fitting, that at the end of the long quest which I began with that word, I should find myself faced with the most awesome responsibility a human being can be asked to bear.

Yet, what has she done?

It is as if a child had been murdered by its mother. For it was Alex who brought the group to birth. It could not have happened in the city: this was the place. Why did she do it? I remember the evening when she asked them to come here, how hesitant she was, as if half-frightened by what she was saying. Was she aware then of some deep duplicity in her motive?

Simon believes so. In his final despair he called her corrupt.

'I choose a fourth alternative,' says Alex.

Her perversity is endless. So is her blindness. She rejects truth itself.

Simon looks drawn. Life has been taken out of him.

'You are totally corrupt,' he says. 'There is no hope for you.'

Alex sits silent. There is a wall around her. Thus the dark thing protects itself.

With a movement of his arm Simon beckons all of us to look at Alex. Alex cross-legged on the floor.

'Look at her,' he says. 'Look, and remember. This is how a being looks when it is totally corrupt.'

We look.

If there had been any doubt in my mind, it would have been extinguished by what I saw then.

The wall around Alex is impregnable. She appears to feel nothing, sitting cross-legged on the floor. Her features are composed, her hands still. It is a total, silent defiance, mocking even in its serenity. There is something blasphemous about it.

Simon feels it: it has goaded him to a display of emotion I have never seen.

'Corrupt!' he says, pointing his finger at her, inviting us to share his perception of her evil so that we may learn, and remember. There is no need: we see it clearly, the dark wall that grows out of her.

Simon is on his feet, pacing the room, his beautiful lean body angular with pain, the blaze in his eyes dulled by misery.

'I loved you!' he exclaims.

Oh yes, he did: he loves her still, I can see him fight to rid himself of his love.

Many people have loved Alex. It has not helped her.

What I saw then was a ring of darkness so concentrated that no communication could pierce it. What I saw was a withdrawal from communication of such intensity that it had become a psychic force. Until that moment I had not fully understood that love and communication are identical; that withdrawal of love and withdrawal of communication are identical; and that withdrawal of love is evil.

I saw Alex protected by a wall of evil. I was awed by it.

Simon was torn apart by it.

Simon, on his feet, catalogues Alex's crimes. But not in his normal way, measured and lucid. Distress makes his speech disjointed, almost violent, although he has barely raised his voice.

'Deceiver. Confuser. Manipulator. Schemer.'

The words spill out of him.

'She says she will do things, and she doesn't do them. People are confused, they are hurt. What does she care? She's off doing something else. She won't finish that either. She'll leave it for someone else to finish. This is a human being who gets other human beings to do things for her.'

He paces the room. The children are fretful. Alex is still.

'She charms people. That is why they do things for her. What is charm? – it's making people think you love them. She doesn't love them. It's a lie. Everything she does is a lie.'

My mind races through seven years' memories. I can find no defence. Alex charms. Alex manipulates. Alex lies. It is all true.

'She pretends to help people. She has never helped anyone in her life. It's a confidence trick. She doesn't help because she can't help. She has nothing to give. But she goes through the motions of helping, and people believe it. They're grateful. They respect her.'

True. Wretchedly true. All those people who came to Alex hungry went away hungry, but never knew it. A plate had been put before them: in their desperation they didn't see there was nothing on it.

'All those people,' says Simon. There are tears in his voice, whether for them, or for himself, or for Alex, I cannot tell. 'All those beings who have trusted her, and have been lied to and betrayed and abandoned. People, animals. Hurt and betrayed. What a trail of destruction. How terrible.'

His voice breaks. A sigh, almost inaudible, goes up from the group. Alex bows her head. Will she speak?

Simon wheels round on her. 'It's true,' he says. 'Every word is true. If it were not true there is someone here who would defend you.'

But there is no defence.

Very well, it is treachery. The very thing Alex has always feared people would do to her; the very thing I have fallen over backwards for seven years not to do.

What does she think, for seven years, I have been doing? Killing her slowly, letting her soul suffocate in lies. What does she think loyalty is, but a refusal to face the truth which has been cynically elevated to the status of a virtue?

Can't she see that this is the greatest act of love, perhaps the only act of love, I have ever performed for her?

If I had defended her, knowing the truth of Simon's accusations, it would have been the cruellest treachery of which any human being is capable. It was not enough that she should hear the truth from Simon's mouth: she could too easily have dismissed it. She had to see that I, who know her and have always defended her, shared his perception.

And even that proved not enough. Driven to accept that something really was terribly wrong, her mind has resorted to spinning fantasies which can explain the event in terms of a trivial misunderstanding. Simon's resignation from the partnership: utterly irrelevant. Completely mad. I do fear for Alex's sanity. But I must not follow that line of thought because it will lead me into compromise, and that is exactly where she wants to lead me. Simon has opened my eyes to the fact that what I always took to be a mental instability in Alex is a moral one: the demon is not madness, it is badness. And it is very clever.

She will try to destroy me. Spiritually. She will try to drag me down. They always do. And she can do it. If I let her confuse me, even for an instant, I shall lose my clarity, and that will be the end of me.

I have so much to understand, so far to go. The journey is endless, and I have barely started. I cannot let her stop me.

No, I don't mean that. I hope I don't mean it.

'Be careful,' he said. Be careful.

If I put my own enlightenment before Alex's needs, it will not be forgiven me.

And if I prize clarity above compassion I shall lose my clarity.

And if that is the best reason I can find for feeling compassion I have no clarity.

Simon, I need you.

This is what he would call non-productive thought.

Should I run that scene again? No, the pain is discharged from it. There is nothing more there.

And afterwards?

Very little happened. Simon had no more to say, so Pete, Dao and Coral tried to reason with her. She smiled, and answered politely, and denied every word they said.

Dao accused her of possessiveness, of refusing to relinquish her ownership of the house in spite of her statement that houses should belong to the people who lived in them. Alex replied that she did not think of herself as the owner of the house and couldn't understand why they were making such an issue of it.

She was then asked why, in that case, she refused to sell the house to Simon and solve her financial problems. She shook her head, and stared at the carpet.

She did not seem to grasp what was happening at all. She said that, whatever the difficulties, the group should carry on until the end of the five-month trial period – as if she had not made its continuation impossible.

It seemed to go on for hours. At last Alex got up and left the room.

As the door closes it is as if the current has been switched off: we sag.

I am exhausted. I stretch my head backwards and turn it slowly, trying to ease the tension in the neck-muscles.

Simon glances round at us, a tired, wry glance.

'I am still waiting for a miracle,' he says. 'I shall wait another hour, and then, if there is no change of heart, I shall gather together what possessions I have and leave this house. You must make your own decisions independently of me. If anyone wishes to come with me, they will be welcome.'

'The children and I will come with you,' says Dao.

How delightful she is, expressing in her smile a gentle humour at Simon's solemnity, at the very idea of his wife and children making a decision independent of him. I wonder whether Simon really knows Dao, then realise how ridiculous the thought is.

'I will come with you,' says Pete. Of course. Where Simon goes, he goes.

'And me,' says Coral. 'And baby boy.' She bounces the baby on her knee.

They look at me. There is no question where I belong.

'I think my place is here,' I say.

They understand, but are concerned. I explain that I have no fears for myself.

I say, 'I may be able to help Alex.'

They are leaving. Simon may have few possessions, but as a group they have a great many. The truck is piled high with clothes and mattresses.

I help them bring things down from the bedrooms. I give them all sorts of things – food, a sleeping bag, odd things they may find useful. Tokens of love, tokens of gratitude.

Alex has disappeared. When they have gone, what on earth, across this impassable gulf, will we find to say to each other?

In fact I was surprised by her restraint. I expected her to tell me to go. That she didn't indicates presumably that she is willing to listen to me. If I can find a way of getting through the wall.

I must have hurt her dreadfully. She is brave, Alex.

There was a moment when I thought Simon had gone too far.

'Keep away from that child!'

Alex has put out a hand to prevent one of the children from falling. Simon snatches the child away.

'You're corrupt. Don't you dare to go near a child.'

I feel a surge of protest.

Alex accepts it in silence.

She has not said a word for about an hour, while Simon has moved gradually from exposition to anger. He has called her a deceiver, a manipulator, a schemer. I have not defended her because it is all true.

But she would never hurt children. With children she does not lie, or scheme, or charm. I know. She loves children.

I feel slightly nauseated.

I should like to get out of this room, but I cannot leave. Cannot leave until this dreadful meeting is over.

I will go and talk to her. After all, she came to me.

'Alex.'

She is sitting at the bureau, writing in an exercise book. Oh dear.

'I understand it now,' she says.

I lean in the doorway, waiting.

'It was all a terrible misunderstanding,' she says. 'A series of misunderstandings, none of which was ever cleared up.'

I wait.

'Do you know why Simon resigned from the partnership?'

'Yes,' I say. 'He resigned because he felt there was someone who didn't want the partnership to work. That being so, there was no point in forming it.'

'He wrote "Communication break" in the diary.'

'Yes.'

'Whose communication break was it?'

'Yours.'

'It was *his*.'

I close my eyes for a moment. I initiated this conversation: I must see it through.

'He couldn't cope with the responsibility. Imagine: taking over a twenty-two-thousand-pound house with another four thousand pounds' worth of assets – for him and his friends! He suddenly saw what it looked like, and he couldn't do it. He got cold feet.'

I stare at her. It's wickedly ingenious.

'He didn't realise that I knew all that, and that it didn't matter, and that I was going to give them the house anyway.'

'What d'you mean, you were going to give them the house anyway?'

'That's why I went to see the solicitor a few days later. I wanted to know if I could make the house over to them. The solicitor said I could only make a gift to specified people, but I said that wasn't any good because other people might come to live in the house, and I wanted to give it to whoever was living in it. He said I couldn't.'

Is she lying? No, I think she's telling the truth. In that case Simon was wrong about what happened at the partnership meeting. He imagined a communication break. Well, it's unfortunate but it's not important. The business of the house has never really been important in spite of what was said on the last morning. It obscures the real issue, which is Alex's character.

'All right,' I say. 'I accept that. But it's unimportant.'

'It is *not* unimportant. It was part of the evidence against me, and it was based on a misunderstanding. All these things mounted up until in the end I was made to appear like a monster.'

'All right. One part of the evidence against you may be discounted. What else?'

'When Simon resigned the partnership was dissolved, but you all went on thinking it was still in existence. So you expected things of me which I didn't realise were expected of me. Quite naturally, when I didn't behave as you expected, you thought I was acting against the partnership. But it didn't exist.'

All anyone has ever expected of Alex is truthfulness and love.

'The others may have thought the partnership was still in force. I certainly didn't. But it makes no difference. What concerned the group was your behaviour in the group.'

'Do you admit there may have been a misunderstanding?'

'Yes, it is possible that there was a misunderstanding.'

'Thank you.' She consults the page of writing in front of her. She has been working very hard.

'The day my brother came here,' she says.

She never refers to Philip by name.

'Yes?'

'Dao thought I'd said something unpleasant about Simon to him.'

'Yes, but you told her you hadn't, and that cleared it up.'

'But it didn't. She didn't believe me. Simon didn't believe me. He couldn't have done, or he wouldn't have accused me of telling lies. What other lies could he possibly have been referring to? I haven't told any lies.'

She believes it. I wonder if she knows what a lie is.

'I think you're mistaken,' I say. 'If Simon had meant that, he would have said so.'

'No, he wouldn't. He's never specific. It's part of his cleverness. He lets people condemn themselves.'

'You should pursue the implications of that remark.'

'Kay, can you be absolutely sure that that wasn't what he had in mind?'

I hesitate fractionally. Whatever the risk of her misusing the truth, not the slightest deviation from the truth is permitted.

'No.'

'Right. Now we come to the most crucial misunderstanding of all. Do you remember the night before I went to London, when Simon and I talked in the parlour?'

211

'I don't think I shall ever forget it.'

She darts me a look which I can't interpret.

'He thought I walked out on him,' she says.

'What?'

'We weren't getting anywhere. He suddenly got up and left. I thought he'd gone to bed. I thought it was one of his dramatic departures. So I went to bed. But he hadn't gone to bed, he'd gone outside – for a pee, I suppose. I heard him come up the stairs later.'

She watches intently for my reaction.

She is telling the truth, and I can see how it would have upset him. He would interpret it as the most extreme form of communication break short of violence. But something is missing from the data.

'Okay. But if you knew that, why did you go to London instead of staying here to sort it out with him? You must have wanted not to continue the conversation.'

She is silent. I pursue it.

'You must have been talking about something pretty important.'

She doesn't want to answer. She doesn't have to tell me what it was: but she must confront it.

'*He* talked. I wouldn't answer him.'

'Why not?'

Alex makes a gesture of hopelessness.

'All right. I didn't want to tell you. Simon loved me.'

This is a depth-charge compared with which the other evasions are little squibs. My head rocks with it. Doesn't she care what she does to people's minds?

'Of course he did,' I reply. 'He said so.'

'Yes, and he couldn't handle it. He kissed me once, you know.'

'So what?'

'Properly. On the mouth.'

If she carries on like this I'm afraid she may begin to con-

212

fuse me. I feel anger and pity. I repress the first and keep the second on a short leash.

'Are you suggesting that his feelings for you were so strong that they threatened his relationship with Dao and the survival of the group?'

'No,' says Alex. 'I think he could have handled it if it hadn't been for my own feelings. If I'd just done what he wanted, the way all the rest of you did what he wanted, it would have been all right. He's used to being surrounded by adoring women. But I can't play that game. I've never submitted emotionally to a man in my life.'

'What are you saying, exactly?'

'I was in love with Simon. That's why I had to fight him. That's why I had to go away. *That's* what upset him.'

I lean against the door-frame and breathe slowly. There it is, unveiled. The final, enormous, pitiable evasion. And clever. Let me not underestimate its cleverness. If I were just a shade less clear in my mind I should have been thrown by it, by its plausibility, its emotional weight.

'I tried to tell you,' says Alex. 'That day we sat and talked under the chestnut tree. But it was no good because I was in such a turmoil I wasn't coherent, and all you could say was that I was evading something. Which I was, I suppose: I didn't really want to tell you.'

'You are still evading something now.'

She looks at me, startled.

'I was in love with Simon for a time,' I say.

'I know you were.'

'Everybody who meets Simon is in love with him for a time. They don't use it as an excuse for everything unacceptable they do.'

'You're still in love with him,' says Alex. 'You've become Simon. You talk like him, you stand like him, you walk like him. He's taken you over.'

'I expect I do talk like him. I say what I perceive to be true, and the same truth is likely to be put into the same words. Does it matter who uses the words first?'

'You see what I mean,' says Alex.

I shrug.

'All the time I'm talking to you,' says Alex, 'I sense that you aren't listening.'

'I am listening more carefully than I have ever listened to you in my life.'

'But you're listening *for* something.'

This sets me back a little. Yes, I am listening for the lie. How else, in the circumstances, should I listen?

'Yes,' I admit, 'I am testing the truth of what you say as you say it.'

'It's more than that. You're screening it for bad motives. For weeks, everything I've said and done has been screened for negative content.'

'Nonsense. One simply sees things. You know that. You've experienced that clear perception. One sees.'

'One sees what one looks for.'

I gaze at her blankly.

'There's good and bad in everyone,' she says.

'Oh for heaven's sake, spare me the platitudes.'

'But it's *true*, Kay. I understand your perception – for God's sake, if I didn't I'd have kicked you out as soon as they left. The bad you see in me is there. But there's bad in everyone. There's bad in you: Simon found it.'

'Yes, and I acknowledged it.'

'And I didn't acknowledge mine because I will not be bullied and shouted at.'

'He didn't shout at you.'

'He did. Just before they left, he lost his self-control completely, and he raved at me.'

'You're lying.'

'I am not lying. For days every time I've opened my mouth you've told me I was lying.'

'So you were.'

214

'I have to see what you see, don't I? You won't let me see what I see.'

'What you see is a distortion.'

'It's my reality.'

'That's your trouble. You won't share anyone else's reality. Then you wonder why you can't communicate with them.'

'What I see is true for *me*. We're all right in our own way.'

'Including Hitler, I suppose.'

'Yes, including Hitler. Even he had a little bit of truth. We've all got our own kind of truth.'

I am about to hurl myself with all my weight against this lie, when something holds me back. A tiny thing, a flicker in the mind. A flicker of infinity. In an instant it has sapped my strength.

'That is sophistry,' I say. 'You are using a small truth to evade a larger one. That's a very dangerous game.'

She turns on me and hurls four words.

'Don't change my data.'

I walk quickly away from the suddenly dark room, down the stairs and out into the garden.

How beautiful the roses are. Delicate, thin-veined. The bees investigate them, as bees have always done.

I sit on the grass. The sun is hot.

I should like to sleep now.

In front of me is a door. If I do not open it I am dead. If I open it I may find my death inside.

Open it, then.

Oh God, the height, the terror. The unimaginable dance.

Rest. Breathe. Rest.

I cannot face it.

It must be faced.

Consider it as a philosophical problem. Is there one truth, or are there many? Are there degrees of truth? Is truth absolute or relative?

It is absolute. I know it is. I have seen truth.

215

And a moment ago, what did you see?

The sky turned over and I saw its back.

What did you see?

I saw infinity, and everything in it was true.

Very well. If everything is true . . .

No. With all my being, No.

I saw the truth of Alex. I saw her darkness. That truth excluded what she calls her truth. I saw that her truth was a lie.

I cannot have been mistaken. I cannot have been mistaken.

Who is right?

My truth condemns her. Hers condemns me.

If we are both right, then she is right and I am wrong.

If I am right, she is wrong.

But I must not change her data.

This is not a philosophical problem. This is a question on which hangs the meaning of my life. And if of my life, then of Alex's life and of life itself. If I do not find the right answer, I shall have destroyed myself. If the answer I find tells me I was wrong, I shall have destroyed myself. If I do not find an answer, I cannot go on living because I shall not know in what way to live. I am required to decide, now in this garden, what is the truth of the universe.

And where do I begin, when I do not know with what eyes to look?

I cannot solve this problem with my reason. It will work only from the premises supplied to it, and I do not know what premises to supply. I do not have a starting-point. My reason will not find its own starting-point.

What will supply me with a starting-point? Not any recollection from the past, because my understanding of the past depends on my understanding of the present, and it is the present I am seeking to understand.

Should I then trust my intuition? It arises in a region beyond consciousness and I cannot search its motives: it will

216

supply me with the starting-point I need to prove that I am right, and in doing so it will destroy me.

I cannot look outside me for the answer. No other human being can answer this question for me. I can trust no one and nothing, least of all myself.

Dear God, help me.

It is a kind of crucifixion. We are all Christ.

I must put down this burden, and I cannot. I carry the universe on my back. I am Christ, I am Atlas. I cannot lay it down without destroying the world.

On the past depends the present.

On the present depends the past.

If I look at the past with the eyes of the past I see Alex enclosed in a wall of darkness.

If I look at the past with the eyes of the present I see nothing at all.

I see something.

It is the same scene, but there is a difference.

It is a different scene.

It is the same scene.

We are all assembled in the parlour. Dao has summoned a meeting. The group is serious and silent. Simon sits waiting in his chair. He is waiting for the obstructive member of the group to see her error. She will not see it. She refuses to accept that anything that has been said to her has any connection with her. She does not seem to understand what is happening. There is a wall. On one side of it is darkness. She cannot see what is happening on the far side of the wall, and no one can tell her. I cannot understand a word they are saying to me.

Alex. Me.

Me. Alex.

On what happened then depends what is happening now.

On what is happening now depends what happened then.

If I was right, Alex was right.

If Alex was wrong, I was wrong.

But I admitted that I was wrong.

And I did not believe it. To my dying day I shall believe that Simon was wrong and I was right.

Why then did I submit to him, that afternoon on the landing?

Because I could not bear to leave this house.

It is very cold out here.

Follow it, follow the path. There is nothing left now, except the path. Follow it to the end.

'We have thought of three alternatives,' says Simon. 'Between them they cover all the possibilities. Alex will choose the one that suits her best.'

He speaks cheerfully, almost affectionately, like a kind schoolmaster propounding a simple choice.

I am struck suddenly by the depth of his ignorance about Alex. He does not understand her at all: he never has. What I thought was understanding was merely his brilliant grasp of the general principles of human psychology, which fitted her as well, and as roughly, as they do anyone. By the accidental closeness of the fit here and there one is misled into thinking that the whole suit is tailor-made.

So Simon, assuming that Alex is like most people in a respect in which she is unlike most people, puts to her three alternatives. To him, to most people, they are three discrete ideas; three diverging roads; three apples on a table. But Alex, brought up in the wild, does not see three separate things. She sees a net.

She sees a net and before it can close over her she darts under it and away.

'I do not accept the group's alternatives.'

Of course she doesn't. She doesn't understand that she has

to accept them: that this is her test. Simon doesn't understand that she can't accept them: that this is his test.

Only I understand.

Only I understand that they are both doing the only thing they can.

Only I can see what is happening, and I say nothing. Why do I say nothing?

Because one must not interpret. Never interpret another's words or actions.

But they need an interpreter. They cannot hear each other. Why do I say nothing?

Because Alex is not a wild animal but a human being.

But they are hunting her like an animal. *We* are hunting her.

Why do I say nothing?

Because . . . because Alex must learn the rules.

But people learn from kindness. This is cruelty.

Why am I allowing it? Why do I not defend her?

Why do I let him drive his cruel words into her, blow after unanswered blow, if not because I know that only by unleashing its destructiveness can this group be destroyed; that to soften the injustice of Alex's hell would be to prolong my purgatory for ever.

So they are leaving. I bring them gifts. I give them food, sleeping bags, vegetables from the garden.

I will give them anything. Anything, as long as they go.

No sacrifice is too great. None.

What have I done?